Library of Congress Control Number: 2024907853

STAY INFORMED

I'd love to stay in touch! You can email me at kathleen@kathleentroy.com

For updates about new releases, as well as exclusive promotions, visit my website and sign up for the VIP mailing list. Head there now to receive a free story

www.kathleentroy.com

Enjoying the series? Help others discover the *Never Believe Series* by sharing with a friend.

NEVER BELIEVE A CON ARTIST TWICE

KATHLEEN TROY

DYLAN AND FRIENDS PUBLISHING COMPANY

To Dylan,
You inspire me.

Nothing like a little payola to guarantee instant friendship.
-Sage Christopher

CHAPTER ONE

It was a toss-up: Keep my mouth shut or get my Uncle Clive convicted of murder. Either way, this would be a Christmas my grandparents would never forget. Geez. Sometimes I was such an idiot. If only I'd stayed at the party instead of going to Uncle Clive's mansion, I wouldn't be in this mess.

The dull gray metal bars on the courthouse window were as thick as a man's thumb and looked like they could keep an elephant in. I used both hands to get a good grip and yanked anyway.

Nope. The bars were here to stay and so was I.

Bam! Bam!

I jumped at the sound and clapped a hand over my heart. When Officer Jacobs nudged the door open with his foot and entered with two cups of steaming hot coffee, I relaxed against the window—a little. After all, I wasn't the one on trial.

He nodded at my grandparents before setting the coffee on the table. "Jack. Frances."

"Where's mine?" It was a whopping six degrees outside. Inside the courthouse, it wasn't much warmer. I pulled my heavy coat around me. Evansville, Connecticut, had to be the coldest place on earth.

"You're thirteen," Gram said, reaching for her cup. "You can have coffee when you're older."

Officer Jacobs cleared his throat. "Sage needs to come with me."

Gram's reach stopped halfway. "Where?"

Pops stood up. "Now? My brother's trial is about to start."

Officer Jacobs kept his face neutral. "The prisoner requested a meeting with Sage."

I barked out a laugh.

"Sage!" Gram gave me The Look. "This is serious."

Sure, I knew that. But only Uncle Clive and I knew my testimony was the single thing standing between him and freedom. For Gram's sake, I mumbled, "Sorry."

Pops frowned. "Isn't this unusual?"

Uncle Clive may be on trial for murdering his wife Olivia, but he still owned *The Evansville News* and was the richest man in Evansville. It wasn't hard to imagine him getting a favor. Besides, nobody had liked Olivia.

On the other hand, Uncle Clive was a likable guy. Right now, everyone thought he'd shot Olivia in self-defense and felt sorry for him. I was betting all that would change when they found out he'd killed her in cold blood. And for her money.

People tend to draw the line at greed.

"This won't take long. Sage will be brought to the courtroom." Officer Jacobs eyed the wall clock. "Officer Okada will be here shortly to escort you." He motioned me to the door and gave my grandparents another nod. "Enjoy your coffee."

The Evansville Courthouse was a big building. I

followed Officer Jacobs down a hallway painted the color of a baked potato and wondered what it would be like to work here. Must be a lot like being in prison. No windows. No sunshine. On the plus side, it might be fun to carry a gun and boss people around.

Officer Jacobs' shiny black police shoes didn't make a sound on the tile floor. He looked left and right as he walked, one hand staying on his gun belt. "You and your Uncle Clive must be pretty close." His tone was casual.

"Not really." I kept my eyes glued on the endless hallway, but I'd noticed Officer Jacobs had slid a look my way. Nice touch, I thought. Two minutes ago, he'd called Uncle Clive the prisoner. Now he was saying Uncle Clive. I'd watched enough cop shows to know this was Officer Jacobs' way of buttering me up, getting me to say something I shouldn't.

"This must be hard on your grandparents," he continued.

Not as hard as it's going to be. "Uncle Clive is Pops' only brother."

"Yeah," Officer Jacobs agreed. "I got a younger brother. He's grown now, but I still worry about him."

All cops were the same. They pretended to be your friend. When he stood aside to let me in the tiny room, I spotted the mirror on the wall. Since Uncle Clive's arrest, I'd been to the police station a lot. Their rooms had two-way mirrors, too.

Someone was always watching and listening on the other side.

When Uncle Clive saw me, he shifted in his seat behind the battered metal table bolted to the floor. For the trial, he'd traded in his orange jail jumpsuit for a soft gray wool suit with matching silk tie. Starched white cuffs with monogrammed cufflinks winked out from under the sleeves. His hair was freshly cut. He looked like a powerful businessman and not the murderer he was. "Hello, Sage." His smile was cold. "Sit down."

"You got five minutes." Officer Jacobs moved to the corner of the room. Both hands stayed on his gun belt.

I took my time pulling out the metal chair, letting it scrape along the tile floor. I dropped into it and stretched out my long legs under the table. On the beige cinderblock wall behind Uncle Clive were nine words in big black stenciled letters: No Cell Phones. No Spitting. No Weapons. No Smoking.

I'd given up smoking when I started living with my grandparents, but I missed it sometimes. It's true what they say. Old habits die hard.

Uncle Clive leaned close, and his handcuffs rattled softly. He kept his voice low. "My trial is about to start."

I glanced at the watch I wasn't wearing. "The clock is ticking. What do you want?"

"To walk out of here a free man."

That cracked me up. "Not going to happen."

He raised both hands palms up in a what can you do gesture. "The way I see it, this is all your fault."

Some of it was. I could feel the room getting warmer and unbuttoned my coat. "What's your point?"

"You shouldn't have been snooping around my home."

"Snooping?" I shot back, a little offended. Someday I'd be an investigative journalist. The way I saw it I had jump-started my career. I huffed out, "I was investigating."

"You should've minded your own business," Uncle Clive insisted. "Then you wouldn't have seen Olivia and me fighting."

"You were playing around with her medication, making

her act crazy." I laughed in his face. "You wanted her locked up in a looney bin so you'd get all her money."

His eyes flicked away from me. How about that? I was right.

Uncle Clive managed to point to his left shoulder. "She shot me!"

"Good shot," I said, and meant it. Unless she'd been aiming for his heart.

"You," he growled and pounded his fist on the tabletop, "are going to tell the jury I tried to get the gun away from Olivia. Say we struggled and the gun went off." Two shoulders in an expensive gray suit shrugged. "Say it was self-defense. The jury will believe you. Tell them that's what you remember."

I remembered everything just fine. They'd been fighting over the gun, yelling, and crashing into furniture. When Olivia shot him, I thought it was all over. Then I saw him grab the gun away from her, aim steady, pull the trigger, and blow her away. She was dead before she hit the ground. "That would be lying."

Now Uncle Clive tossed back his head and laughed. "You lie all the time."

Okay, that was true. I stood up and pushed my shaking hands into my pockets. "This has been fun."

Uncle Clive hissed, "If I get convicted, I swear I'll get even. I'll see to it Jack loses his job at the plant. And that's just the beginning."

Fear rolled around in my belly like loaded dice. By now I knew what Uncle Clive was capable of, but I kept my voice cool. "Enjoy your six by eight-foot cell."

"You're a real smart ass."

I smirked. "You got a murder trial coming up."

"Jack is my big brother. If you send me to prison," Uncle

Clive relaxed in his chair and let out a long, almost believable sigh, "it'll kill him."

He was right. Pops loved him but I would never understand why.

"Time's up," Officer Jacobs announced.

"You're going to help me," Uncle Clive said matter-of-factly. "You'll do it. You'll say it was self-defense," he narrowed his eyes, "or else."

Uncle Clive was calling my bluff and I knew it. I'd been lying all my life so what was one more lie? I got up and walked out without looking back.

Officer Jacobs joined me in the hall. "Everything all right?"

I shrugged. "Uncle Clive wanted to talk about Pops." That was sort of true.

We walked past one closed door after another. I wondered which one led out of the courthouse and to the parking lot. Nobody locked houses or cars in Evansville. There had to be a car I could hotwire fast and get out of here. Without my testimony the District Attorney couldn't prove Uncle Clive killed Olivia. I didn't care about him. I cared about Pops.

I thought about how my grandparents took me in after my low-life con artist father Marty died. They were the only decent people I'd ever known. My heart grew heavier with each step. I didn't need a crystal ball to know how this would go.

Lying was the only way out.

We stopped at a wooden door like all the rest. Officer Jacobs pushed it open. "This is the judge's entrance."

I brushed past him. The courtroom stretched out in front of me, and two cops stood guard at the front doors. Every seat in the courtroom was filled. People were bundled in wool coats, snow boots and hats. The air smelled like winter and wet dog.

Attached to the judge's bench was the clerk's corral. Officer Jacobs stopped to lean over its low wall and whisper to a young guy. "Cliff, tell Judge Messina that Sage Christopher is in the courtroom."

Cliff reached for the phone on his desk. He pressed a button, gave the message, and hung up.

Twelve men and women wearing their Sunday best sat in the jury box, talking quietly to each other. When they noticed me, they stopped and stared. The bailiff sitting at a desk near the jury box looked up from the travel magazine he'd been reading. The court reporter shifted in her seat and pursed her lips. I ignored them.

It was all I could do to walk across the open space between the judge's bench and the counsel table. The lawyers sat at the long wooden table behind nameplates and piles of papers. Her name plate said Jessica Winslotten, District Attorney. His said Brad Knight, Defense. Both stopped reading the papers they were holding and studied me. The courtroom was so quiet I could almost hear people breathing.

Like the good cop he was, Jacobs delivered me to Gram and Pops in the front row. I gave the officers guarding the front doors one last look and sat down. I couldn't help it. I wanted to scream. A heavy sigh escaped instead.

"Sage," Gram leaned close, "are you okay?"

No. "I'm fine."

"What did Clive want?" Pops asked.

Everything. "Not much."

"I'm sorry you have to go through this." Gram patted my arm. "Don't be nervous. Just tell the truth."

I can't.

"When you testify the court will understand Olivia's death was a terrible accident." Pops' breath hitched. "I can't imagine what Clive is feeling. It will be a relief when this is over."

That's what you think.

"All rise," instructed the bailiff. "Court is in session. The Honorable Judge Messina presiding. No talking in the courtroom."

A tall woman with dark brown hair lifted her judge's robes a little as she climbed the three steps to the bench. She sat and nodded at the bailiff.

It was showtime.

"You may be seated," the bailiff said.

We sat.

Cliff picked up the telephone on his desk. The door behind him opened and a police officer entered with Uncle Clive. Voices exploded and fingers pointed.

Crack! Crack! Crack! Judge Messina's gavel sounded like rapid gunshot, and she gave her courtroom an even stare. "This is your first and final warning. Be silent or you'll be removed from the courtroom immediately."

The bailiff tossed the travel magazine aside and was on his feet. He searched the audience eagerly for troublemakers.

Brad Knight looked up at Uncle Clive and arched an eyebrow. Uncle Clive waited until the officer had removed his handcuffs before glancing at me. Then he gave Mr. Knight a slight nod, sat and folded his hands on the table.

Judge Messina picked up the papers in front of her. She scanned them quickly and then angled the microphone to speak. "In the matter of *State of Connecticut v. Clive Callen Christopher*, we're ready to begin." She put the papers aside.

"Ms. Winslotten, are you prepared to give your opening statement?"

"Yes, Judge." The District Attorney stood. "May I approach the jury?"

"You may."

A guy in the row behind us snickered. "When Winslotten ran for District Attorney, her campaign slogan was, 'Wins a lot, loses not.'"

Pops stiffened and I saw Gram cover his hand with hers. I wanted to turn around and punch the guy's lights out.

Ms. Winslotten walked confidently to the jury box and gave the jurors a pleasant smile. "Good morning. Thank you for being here today."

All twelve jurors were glued to Ms. Winslotten. Uncle Clive's trial was the biggest thing to happen in Evansville and they were a part of it.

"The case before you is a simple one," she began. "Clive Callen Christopher killed his wife Oliva Christopher, and we can prove it."

Shock flashed across every juror's face. Pandemonium broke out. Spectators started talking over each other. Judge Messina's gavel pounded.

"Clear the courtroom," Judge Messina ordered. "Now!"

Okay. I got up and stepped quickly into the aisle.

Gram was quicker and grabbed the back of my coat. "Not you," she said. "Sit down."

I did and slumped in my chair.

Ms. Winslotten waited until the bailiff had removed the grumbling onlookers.

"Continue," Judge Messina instructed.

"That is all." Ms. Winslotten smiled again at the jury and returned to her seat.

This was weird. On TV all lawyers talked nonstop. I

looked at Judge Messina. If she was surprised, she didn't let it show.

"Mr. Knight," Judge Messina began, "do you wish to make an opening statement?"

Brad Knight stood. He was easily six foot five and had a voice to match. "We reserve the right to make an opening statement at a later time, Your Honor."

"Very well." Judge Messina exchanged one stack of papers for another. "Ms. Winslotten, call your first witness."

Ms. Winslotten faced the courtroom. "The People call Sage Christopher to the stand."

"Now?" I looked at Gram.

"Go on." Gram urged. The court reporter was standing next to the witness stand, waiting.

I took my time walking to her, hoping the floor would open up and I would disappear. No such luck.

"Raise your right hand."

I did.

"Do you swear to tell the truth, the whole truth and nothing but the truth?"

I looked to Judge Messina. "Is this multiple choice?"

The jury laughed.

Judge Messina didn't. She leveled them with one look. "Answer yes or no, Sage."

"Yeah." Then I heard Gram clear her throat. "Uh, yes."

"You may be seated." The court reporter took her place behind her machine and waited.

Ms. Winslotten came forward. "State your name for the record, please."

"Sage Christopher." Up close Ms. Winslotten looked like a teacher I'd had when I was a kid. She'd been nice.

She leaned against the wooden railing in front of me.

"Sage, did you see Clive Callen Christopher shoot Olivia Christopher in cold blood?"

Twelve jurors gasped.

"Objection!" Brad Knight was on his feet. "Objection, Your Honor! Motion to Strike!"

Crack! No one had said a word, but Judge Messina's gavel spoke one more time. *Crack!* "Order in the courtroom!"

Ms. Winslotten addressed the judge. "May I remind Mr. Knight that the defendant is on trial for the murder of his wife. The question is relevant."

"Overruled." Judge Messina scribbled something on the legal pad in front of her.

My heart was a hard fist banging against my ribs. I looked past Ms. Winslotten. Pops had his arm around Gram, and she'd moved to the edge of her seat. I had Uncle Clive's complete attention.

Judge Messina spoke into her microphone. "Sage, you will answer the question."

I took in a breath and went back to Pops. He was looking straight at me and there were tears in his eyes. He'd guessed the truth.

My hands clenched and unclenched. I ran my tongue over my lips. They were hot and dry. I saw Pops close his eyes and hang his head. "Yes. He wanted her money."

"Thank you," Ms. Winslotten said. "That is all."

"Very well." Judge Messina kept her face blank. "Mr. Knight?"

Mr. Knight rose. "The defense requests an adjournment until tomorrow morning, Your Honor."

Judge Messina nodded. "Ladies and Gentlemen of the jury. You're excused for today. Please return at eight o'clock tomorrow morning. Sage, you're excused until then." She motioned to a police officer. "Escort the defendant out." She banged her gavel once. "Court is adjourned."

"All rise," the bailiff boomed.

We did.

Judge Messina left the bench and the no talking rule went with her. Jurors' voices scrabbled over each other as they jumped to their feet and yanked on coats. They hurried from the courtroom, pulling out cell phones and punching in numbers as they went. Poor Clive Christopher the recent widower was forgotten. He was now a murderer, and the news was too good to keep to themselves.

The officer pulled out his handcuffs and quickly stepped to Uncle Clive. "Turn around." When he snapped them on, Uncle Clive sent me an icy look. The officer took Uncle Clive by the elbow, leading him out of the court-room. Uncle Clive went quietly but I knew this wasn't over.

I watched District Attorney Winslotten carefully put papers into her briefcase and slip out. I thought about making a break for it, but I'd never get past Gram and Pops. Instead, I sucked it up and went over. "Sorry."

"You told the truth. I'm proud of you," Pops said. He pulled me into a hug and his big shoulders shook with sobs. "You did the right thing."

Maybe.

I followed Gram and Pops out of the courthouse. Pops held the passenger door of the Mustang open for Gram and I piled into the back seat. Night was creeping in, and Christmas carols jingled softly from somewhere. Shoppers with rosy cheeks hustled along the sidewalks carrying bags.

We rode home in silence. I'd said enough for today.

CHAPTER TWO

"Sage," Gram called. "Dinner is ready."

I was stretched out on my bed, playing a solo game of catch, but I sat up and tossed my glove and ball aside. The game had gone well. I hadn't hit the ceiling once with the ball.

"Coming." Good dinner smells filled our apartment, and I pictured Uncle Clive in a cramped cell, gnawing on stale bread for dinner. If I were a better kid, I would've been racked with guilt about that and not be able to eat for a week. Instead, I toed around for my sneakers and jammed my feet into them. I was starving.

Pops was already seated at the dining room table. His eyes met mine and I noticed he looked older than he had this morning. That hurt more than any punch to the gut. I slid into my seat and avoided any small talk by taking a long time to unfold my napkin before putting it on my lap.

Gram carried in a carved pot roast surrounded by vegetables on a platter. She set it in the middle of the table next to the mashed potatoes and gravy. "Today was diffi-cult," Gram began and untied her apron, "but we'll get through this. We're a family." She squared her tiny shoulders and sent us a small smile. "No talk of unhappiness tonight. We're going to have a nice dinner." Her smile slipped a little. "Because that's what a family does."

I'd been living with Gram and Pops for about three weeks, but I was pretty sure family didn't get each other arrested for murder. I kept quiet.

Gram put her napkin on her lap and said, "You two need to think about getting a Christmas tree."

The thought filled me with such glee I forgot all about Uncle Clive. A huge grin flashed across my face.

"We'll do it on Monday after school." Pops managed a smile. "Have you ever chopped down your own Christmas tree?"

"No." In Las Vegas we'd only had cacti.

Gram looked to me. "What do you like to do for Christmas?"

I'd never had a Christmas before. I shrugged.

"How did you and your dad celebrate Christmas?" Pops asked.

Was this a joke? On Christmas Marty always got roaring drunk and beat the daylights out of me. "The usual."

"What do you like best about the holidays?" Gram pressed.

Just before Thanksgiving, after a late-night poker game and a fifth of Seagram's, Marty had cashed in his chips for good when he'd run his car off the road playing chicken. A deputy had come to the motel to tell me the news. He'd stood in the doorway while I collected my stuff, and behind him the patrol car's lights had pulsed through the night. "I like the bright lights."

How these nice people ever had such a rotten kid like Marty was beyond me.

Ding-dong.

The doorbell interrupted our sentimental moment. Pops started to get up, but Gram beat him to it and waved him back into his seat. "Eat before it gets cold."

"Gotta be Sonny." I helped myself to pot roast and mashed potatoes while I had the chance. "It's six o'clock." The Bensons ate at five but that never stopped my best friend from showing up most nights in time to join us. He had the eating habits of a coyote and could gulp down food and help himself to seconds while we were still working on firsts. Using my spoon, I made a well in the center of the potatoes and poured in a big puddle of gravy. I was reaching for the rolls but forgot all about them because Chief Murphy was standing in the doorway of our dining room.

"Jack!" Gram brushed past Chief Murphy and went to Pops' chair. "It's about Clive."

"You need to come with me. Your brother has, uh," the Chief cleared his throat and looked at me, "made a statement."

"What does it say?" If Uncle Clive was trying to cut a deal, it seemed a little late. Besides, Connecticut didn't have the death penalty so life in prison wouldn't be too bad.

Chief Murphy's cop face didn't crack. "Can't say."

Pops put his napkin next to his plate. "I'll get my coat." He pushed away from the table.

"Me, too." I started to get up.

"No," chorused Chief Murphy and Pops.

"Stay here." Gram got up. "This may take a while."

Chief Murphy shifted his weight. "Time to go."

They left me sitting at a table loaded with food no one was going to eat. I didn't want Gram to come back to a mess, so I cleared the table and washed the dishes. Until I moved here, I'd never washed a dish before, but the funny thing was, I actually liked doing it. It gave me time to think.

My chest tightened. Fifteen minutes ago, I'd been happy about life in Evansville. Happy to be living with Gram and Pops. Happy to be looking forward to my first Christmas. But Uncle Clive had made a statement and that told me he was making good on his threat to ruin my grandparents.

In fifteen minutes, I'd lost it all. That's all it had taken. Fifteen lousy minutes.

"Geez," I muttered, drying the last plate and putting it inside the cabinet. "I sound like some drippy Hallmark card."

When I shut the cabinet door, my sentiment turned to resentment. I couldn't let it go. Fifteen minutes ago, we'd been talking about getting a Christmas tree. Life had been good. Then Chief Murphy had shown up, and all that had disappeared. Just because Uncle Clive had made a statement.

Closing my eyes, I saw Olivia dead on the floor, blood soaking through her nightgown. Uncle Clive was lying next to her and bleeding bad. There had been so much blood everywhere.

When the police had arrived, Uncle Clive had grabbed my hand and gasped, "Tell the police the gun went off. Tell them I didn't shoot Olivia."

I blew out a breath, scrubbing my hands over my face. If only Uncle Clive had died, too, the truth would've died with him.

Talk about rotten luck.

The wildest part was a lie would've been so easy. I'd been lying all my life and I was good at it. All I had to do was tell the police the gun had gone off. That was it. That Uncle Clive hadn't shot Olivia.

But he had.

I could've lied today at the trial, but I didn't. Now my testimony would convict him. And Uncle Clive would take his revenge out on my grandparents. They loved me, but Uncle Clive was Pops' brother. There was no way I could stay here. I turned out the kitchen light. Time to get what's mine and go. Florida was calling my name. I'd never been there but I knew it was warm, had beaches and was far away from here.

From the hall closet, I pulled out the blue suitcase and tossed it onto my bed. I put in jeans along with sweaters, flannel shirts, and woolen socks, clothes I'd never need in Florida. Lifting the mattress, I grabbed my lock picks and Marty's deck of lucky cards, always useful if I had to make some quick cash. On my bookshelf was my prize possession, a first edition of *Huckleberry Finn* that I'd won off a dumb rich kid in a game of blackjack. I put it on top of my sweaters, but it seemed kind of lonely just sitting there so I added my baseball and glove. I shook my head at the sorry sight. I had to be the only kid who could put his entire life in one suitcase.

My next job wasn't so easy. In my desk I found a pen and paper, but I couldn't find the right words to say. After tearing up a few tries, I settled on the obvious: I'm sorry. Not wanting to think about it, I started down the hall to Gram and Pops' bedroom.

When I lived with Marty in Las Vegas, I didn't have two cents to rub together. Coming to Evansville had changed all that. I'd solved a nineteen-year-old murder with a million-dollar reward. Now I was loaded.

Most folks would keep a million bucks in a bank, but

this was Evansville. Nobody siphoned gas from cars left on the street, sticky-fingered money from the church's collection plate, or swiped his neighbor's deliveries off his front steps. To prove this point, The Bank of Gram and Pops was a cedar chest at the end of their bed.

After a lot of arguing, I'd convinced Gram to cover the cedar chest with a quilt just in case a roving band of robbers made their way to Evansville. After all, the money inside was mine.

Pushing the quilt aside, I opened the lid and got out my old duffle. I unzipped it, and Ben Franklin smiled back at me in bundles of ten grand each. Taking out eight stacks, I arranged them in a neat square on their bed. That was a lot of dough, but I owed my grandparents a lot.

Uncle Clive was clever and mean. It would be easy for him to make trouble for my grandparents. In case Gram and Pops needed to hire a lawyer, I added two more bundles. Justice couldn't always win but it could always be bought.

After putting my note next to the cash, I grabbed Pops' keys to the Mustang from the nightstand where he always kept them and turned out the light without looking back. It was too late for regrets.

CHAPTER THREE

The night sky exploded behind me, filling my rearview mirror with blinding white light, making it easy to read the speedometer on Pops' Mustang.

Eighty-eight.

The cop car's siren bleeped once.

The road out of town stretched before me like black licorice.

"Pull the car over," a male cop's voice boomed through the night. "Now."

The Mustang had a full tank, and my foot gently pressed the gas pedal, but who was I kidding? Easing to the side of the road, I switched off the ignition. I wanted to bang my head against the steering wheel for being so dumb. Getting arrested now would ruin everything, and I scrambled to think of a plan.

For one wild moment, I thought about jumping out and shouting, "You'll never take me alive." Luckily, I wised up in time and stayed in the car. Shooting a bad guy dead wasn't much of a challenge to a cop with a gun. Even if the bad guy was just a kid like me on the run.

The cop tapped the glass on the driver's side with a flashlight the size of a baseball bat. "Lower your window."

I did and then said the stupidest words known to man, "What seems to be the trouble, Officer?"

"Drivers license and registration."

So much for friendly chatter. At five-foot-ten, I could easily pass for an adult. Except that I was thirteen and had a face covered in freckles. Good thing for me, I had a secret weapon. A while back, I'd gotten Bongo Feltzer, the school bully, expelled, and you'd think the guy would be sore at me. With his newfound freedom, Bongo went into the paper forging business. Turned out he had a real knack for it and was raking in dough faster than the ink could dry on the paper. Since I knew the importance of keeping my options open, I'd paid Bongo fifty bucks to put together a whole new identity for me. I was now twenty-one.

Since then, Bongo's ill-gotten gains had bankrolled a slick, new car that his dad chauffeured him around in so he could do business from the back seat. Bongo was even thinking about going into real estate so in some ways he owed me. We'd had our differences but seeing how we'd both become rich businessmen overnight, they'd been forgotten.

"No problem." I fished the registration out of the glove compartment and handed it over along with my newly acquired drivers license. To show I had nothing to worry about, I sat up straighter.

The cop took my license, aimed his flashlight on it, and then studied me. I kept my face blank, looking straight ahead like this was just another Friday night. He slowly shined the flashlight over my face. Dots danced in front of my eyes, but I refused to blink.

He went back to studying my license. His lips moved,

reading the information. Using his thumbnail, he scratched at the mustache on the picture, and then held it in front of me. "Want to explain this?"

I rubbed my hand over my baby-smooth face, hoping friction would promote hair growth. "I just shaved."

He studied me some more. I thought again about making a break for it, but he still had a gun. A trickle of sweat ran down my neck and into my collar.

"You're the famous Sage Christopher?"

"Well." In a small town, gossip raced faster than a greyhound.

He pointed to my birthdate. "This license says you're twenty-one."

In eight years. I'd told Bongo to round up, just like we'd been taught in school. "Yeah."

His thumbnail scratched the mustache on my fake license again. "You've been in Evansville about three weeks?"

I nodded.

"Yup. Quite the busy boy." He waved the license. "Just like your dad."

Uh-oh. Here it comes. "You knew Marty?'

"Arrested him a couple of times when he was a kid." He snorted. "Still, I was real surprised to hear he'd been black-mailing Olivia Evans all these years for killing her father."

"Really?" It hadn't surprised me.

"When Marty disappeared, I'd assumed he'd ended up doing a twenty-year-stretch in prison."

Well, since you put it that way.

"After your dad died you improved on his blackmail scheme, by going after the reward money instead?"

Well, yeah. "Absolutely not."

"Chief Murphy said you'd gotten the idea when you

found some old newspaper articles your dad had. The ones saying Evans had disappeared and they were offering a million-dollar reward." He hitched up his gun belt.

"Inspiration is funny, isn't it?" I laughed.

The cop frowned.

I got the hint and took the sincere approach. "It's simple. I'm going to be an investigative journalist someday." Lucky for me, my Uncle Clive had married Olivia and owned *The Evansville News*, so I'd been able to ask a lot of questions about Evans. I rambled on. "You know, like my Uncle Clive."

"How'd you figure out Olivia Evans killed old man Evans because he cut her out of his Will?"

I shrugged like I'd been doing this all my life. "Good journalism work."

Unfortunately for me, Olivia had caught me when I'd broken into their mansion, and she went crazy insane. I'd only wanted to get her talking about Evans because I didn't want her to shoot me dead. Instead, she'd spilled her guts.

The cop shook his head. "Others tried to solve the case without any luck."

I shrugged again. "Nothing to it."

"How was it your uncle happened along and wrestled the gun away from her?"

And shot her in cold blood. For her money. "Timing is everything."

"If it wasn't for him, you'd be dead, too."

Since I'd ratted Uncle Clive out for Olivia's murder today, I'm sure he regretted that now.

"Poor Clive Christopher."

I choked back a laugh and hoped it sounded like a sob.

"Just like that," the cop snapped his fingers, "his life changes. I guess being rich isn't everything."

Oh yeah, it is. Ask Uncle Clive.

"Still, his arrest was big news."

Even Uncle's Clive's own newspaper couldn't ignore the story and had run it on page one. Sales had exploded, and *The Evansville News* sold more papers than in the last presidential election, which only goes to show crime does pay.

"Jack Christopher," he read the name on the registration out loud. "Your grandfather?"

Cops were like lawyers. They never asked a question they didn't know the answer to. As for me, I never answered a question I didn't have to. So, I didn't.

"You've been a busy boy." He repeated, handing the registration back to me and gave a whistle only dogs could hear. "Pretty mean to steal a man's car."

"It's not like that," I said, thinking of the cash I'd left for Pops before I helped myself to the Mustang. Still, I felt bad.

"Must be fun sitting around your family's dinner table at night." He put my license in his shirt pocket and walked away from the Mustang. In my side mirror, I watched him click on his radio. After a few minutes, he clicked off and came back to me. "Get out of the car. We're going in."

"I can't leave it here." My Cannondale bike and suitcase were in the trunk.

"Lock it. I'll have it picked up and taken to the station."

I held out my hand. "Can I have my license back?" I could easily get another one from Bongo, but fifty bucks was fifty bucks.

"You're a real smart ass."

"I've been told that."

My duffle bag crammed full of Evans's reward money was on the seat beside me. I started finger walking my way over to it. This was America. Home of the brave and land of the bribe. Nothing like a little payola to guarantee instant friendship.

"I'm sure," my fingers closed over the handle, and I dragged the bag onto my lap, "we can come to a little understanding." I gave him an easy smile just to show there were no hard feelings.

The cop had a droopy face, droopy eyes, and a droopy mustache. His nametag read Huckleberry. His hat looked like the kind the Canadian Mounties wear and made me wish I had one. His hand dropped to his gun. "Don't even think about it. I'm having a hard enough time keeping track of your misdemeanors and felonies as it is."

"You've got this all wrong."

"Not likely. Besides, I'm in a hurry."

I looked at the empty road. The night was so quiet even the stars couldn't be bothered to be out. "For what?"

"To collect my bet." His droopy mustache twitched. "After what happened today in court, the Chief bet you'd wait a week before skipping out of town. Me," he tapped his badge, "I said you'd hightail it out in less than seventy-two hours."

"You've been waiting for me?"

"Yup."

That was so low. "How much did you bet?"

A big grin spread across his face, and his mustache flattened out like a dead squirrel across his upper lip. "An Alexander Hamilton."

Geez. It was one thing to get caught, but to get caught for a measly twenty bucks was just wrong. Hefting my bag, I got out, slammed the door, and locked it.

Officer Huckleberry waited.

"What?"

He snapped his fingers twice.

I handed the keys over.

Huckleberry pocketed the keys but instead of slapping on the cuffs, he said, "Follow me."

Trudging behind him, I thought about running, but the night was pitch black with a cold bite. I thought about Florida where it was always warm. Where I'd have a boat. Where there would be girls on the beach in bikinis.

"Get in."

I climbed in, tossed the duffle on the floor, and slumped back against the seat. After Huckleberry hauled me in, he'd phone Gram and Pops. They'd discover I wasn't in bed asleep, and they'd find an empty garage where the Mustang used to be.

So much for making a clean getaway.

CHAPTER FOUR

"Hey!" My boot kicked the back of the front seat. "This isn't the way to the police station." Not that I was anxious to get arrested but maybe this cop was crooked and was only after my stash of cash. Anyone who would be happy about catching a kid for twenty bucks would be ecstatic over stealing a million. I pulled my bag onto my lap and hugged it to me in case I needed to move fast.

Huckleberry didn't answer but turned left at the traffic light.

I gave the seat two more kicks in case he was hard of hearing. "You're going the wrong way." I tried the door handle. Locked.

A few minutes later Huckleberry pulled the cruiser into the Evansville Community Hospital parking lot and picked up his radio. "We're here, Chief."

I groaned. Chief. As in Police Chief Murphy. This night was rapidly going from bad to worse. When I saw the local news vans in the lot and an ambulance parked by the emergency room entrance, my gut clenched. Nothing good ever happened at night.

"What's going on?" I tried to keep my panic down, but my heart was hammering.

Because I was at the hospital instead of sitting in a jail cell, something bad must have happened to Gram or Pops.

Garble came back from Huckleberry's radio, and he switched off. "Grab your stuff."

I sucked in my breath. "Why?"

Huckleberry got out and started walking toward the emergency room entrance like he was already late.

"Huckleberry!"

He didn't turn around or even slow down. I took this as a bad sign and sprinted after him.

"Hey, I'm talking to you," I said to his back. This guy was really getting on my nerves. "Don't you know it's rude not to answer when someone's talking to you?"

Huckleberry skirted around the parked ambulance and stopped so quick I nearly ran into him.

Flash! Flash! Cameras lit the night sky and a dozen microphones were shoved into our faces.

"Over here," voices shouted.

Flash! "Sage, how does it feel to turn against your family?"

Flash! Flash! "Sage, it's true? Mr. Christopher had a heart attack?"

Pops! Heart attack? I squinted through the white blur, trying to find the voice. It came from a short, squatty reporter clutching a cigarette between his teeth. He blew smoke out of the corner of his mouth, letting it trail off into the dark night like a lazy, gray eel.

"You," I pointed at him, "what are you saying?"

He dropped his cigarette and ground it out with his shoe. "He's on life support."

I rounded on Huckleberry. "Why didn't you tell me?"

"Let's go." Huckleberry started walking again.

This time I barreled ahead of him to the emergency room entrance. Three weeks of Catholic school hadn't given me a conscience, but the nuns were always chanting some prayer. I started mumbling Hail Mary, the only one I knew, over and over. I had to get to Pops.

Pushing open the doors, I looked around for my grandparents. The waiting room had watery blue walls, watery blue linoleum floors, and algae green, plastic furniture. I'd read somewhere that blues and greens were supposed to be soothing, but this was like being inside a dirty aquarium.

The room was deserted except for a doctor with a mom and a boy about six.

The kid was grinning at the bright, white cast on his arm, waving it in the air and making airplane noises. His mom looked ready to collapse.

"Pay attention, Theo," she sighed.

The airplane cast zoomed around once in the air before the mother caught it and yanked it down to his side.

"Ow!" Kid Pilot immediately had the plaster plane up and flying again.

The doctor interrupted the flight, holding the boy's arm at his side. "You have to understand you can't fly."

I looked around for Gram and Pops like I could've missed them in this small room. Fear gripped me and the lights seemed to dim. Maybe I was having a stroke. They had to be here. I couldn't be too late.

Huckleberry strode past me and disappeared through the exit door on the other side of the room. I hustled forward and caught the door before it slammed shut.

In the hall, wheelchairs and gurneys were lined up like waiting limos outside of a hotel. The place was quiet. Too quiet.

"Hi Officer Huckleberry," cooed a pretty nurse from the nurse's station. She was wearing a very perky smile and very snug purple scrubs.

"Elizabeth." Huckleberry nodded to her but kept walking.

My stomach was flopping around like a fish on a pier. Instead of following Huckleberry, I raced over and put both palms on the counter. "We're here for Mr. Christopher."

Two pink Raggedy Ann patches appeared on Elizabeth's cheeks. Her eyes darted from me to Huckleberry. "Um."

Huckleberry double backed and snagged my elbow.

"Hey!"

He marched me down the long corridor, past hospital rooms, our shoes squeaking on the shiny, linoleum tiles. When we entered the Intensive Care Unit, a tinny sound began in my ears and my vision blurred.

Outside Room 318, a young cop snapped to attention. "Sir."

Huckleberry nodded. "I'll take over, Caletti."

My lungs were refusing to breathe. "What's he doing here?"

"His job." Huckleberry stood aside to let me pass. "You can go in."

I left Huckleberry outside and nudged the door open, letting a runway of soft light spill into the room. My heart hiccupped. Machines surrounded a hospital bed way too small for the man who filled it. I've never cried before but when I rubbed my face, snot was running from my nose.

Next to the bed, a boxy machine beeped noisily like a baby chick. Across its screen, a bright, green line zipped, spiked, and flattened out. Above the line, 120/80 popped up like Bingo balls. I had no idea what they meant but I hoped they were his lucky numbers.

"Pops," I whispered, dropping my duffle on the floor, "it's me. Sage."

There were no chairs in the room, so I slid onto the foot of the bed. I tried to think of more to say but gave up and hung my head. "I'm sorry."

My plan had been so simple. All I had to do was come to Evansville, prove Olivia had murdered her father nineteen years ago, collect a million-dollar reward from *The Evansville News*, and then hit the bricks and go to Florida.

Unfortunately, I hadn't planned on Olivia being insane.

But then I hadn't planned on her pulling a gun on me and Uncle Clive.

And I really hadn't planned on Uncle Clive grabbing the gun and shooting her.

So much for my great plan.

"Sorry, Pops." I said again, dropping my head into my hands. "Should I have lied? Told the police it was self-defense?" I looked up at Pops, but he wasn't giving any help.

Beep! The machine's green line flashed bright and briefly lit up the dim, hospital room. A thick, white bandage was wrapped around his head. In the middle of his forehead, blood had seeped through, making a perfect bull's eye. His pale face was bruised and swollen and the size of a dinner plate. A row of ugly stitches ran underneath his right eye.

"Why Pops?" It was hard to believe the thought of Uncle Clive going to jail could've caused a heart attack. Jail wasn't that bad. I've been there lots of times.

"This is my fault." Guilt bubbled up inside me for all the trouble I'd caused. Sure, my grandparents loved me, but even I knew I wasn't worth a heart attack. And I liked myself a lot.

I blinked a few times, getting used to the dim light. A tube traveled from Pops' body to a ventilator. More tubes traveled from his body to plastic bags on an IV pole that glinted like a tall, silver reed. Electrical wires ran from wall outlets and snaked around the floor to the machines. They were the only things connecting him to life. Two of the machines around him I recognized from watching doctors' shows on TV, but I had no idea what the others did.

Curiosity got the better of me, and I scooted off the bed to get a closer look at them. My size ten sneakers got tangled in the wires and I kissed the floor. Pain ricocheted from my mouth to my brain, and I ran my tongue over my front teeth. All was good.

Rolling to my side, I craned my neck to see if I'd unplugged anything, but all I saw were dust bunnies under the bed and nightstand. I kicked my feet free from the wires. Cripes, they were a death trap.

Exactly.

If I'd unplugged a machine, I could've killed Pops.

There was no point thinking about what could've been. I sat on the edge of the bed to think about what was. I'd never seen Pops like this. Quiet. Dependent. None of this was like him.

I went back to the man in the bed. The reporter had said Mr. Christopher. Hmm.

There was only one way to be sure.

This time, I stepped carefully over all the wires around the bed. When I got to the door, I flipped on the light switch. The fluorescent lights screamed bright white. Hustling back to the bed, I pushed aside the head bandage, stuck my face close, but immediately jerked back. "Uncle Clive?"

If I were a nicer kid, I would've been so glad this wasn't Pops. I would've forgotten about Uncle Clive being a rotten, lying guy. But I wasn't a nicer kid.

Instead, I threw off his blanket. A handcuff was wrapped around his wrist and attached by a short chain to the bed railing.

Excellent.

I grabbed Uncle Clive's cuffed hand and yanked so hard it flew out of mine. His knuckles slammed back against the bedrail. That must have hurt a lot, and it cheered me to no end. "Take that," I sneered. "Because of you, I'm getting cheated out of Christmas." I gave his hand one more yank.

Beep! Beep! The machine protested for Uncle Clive.

The racket was bound to bring Huckleberry charging into the room with his gun drawn, but I was too mad to care. "You lousy coward." I poked my finger hard into his cheek above the stitches. "You're not getting out of this so easy."

The gray machine went crazy. *Beep! Beep! Beep!*

White jagged lines like rows of shark's teeth shot again and again across the monitor's screen.

"If you come out of this alive," I leaned close to Uncle Clive's good ear, "I swear I'll get even."

Uncle Clive didn't move. My left leg dangled over the edge of the bed, my sneaker kicking at the wires on the ground. I'd never hated anybody. Not even Marty and he'd been mean. He'd knocked me around all my life, but I hadn't hated him.

But I really hated Uncle Clive.

The noisy machine calmed down, but my anger didn't. "You're lucky you're in a coma." The toe of my sneaker kicked at the wires, keeping time with the mechanical beats.

The wires.

The only things connecting Uncle Clive to life.

No sounds came from the hallway.

It would be so easy.

I slipped off the bed and went to the outlet where the wires were plugged in. It didn't matter which wire went to what machine. If I jerked them all out at once, his life would be over. My fingers grabbed a handful.

"Sage!"

"What!" I whirled around.

Gram raced toward me, her tiny feet completely missing the wires on the ground.

Pops followed behind her. His big arms reached out and pulled us into a group hug. "Thank God you're here."

I looked past them at Uncle Clive who lay still. "You're just in time."

Gram drew back. "Has Clive regained consciousness?"

"Not yet." Almost not ever.

"What do you mean?" asked Pops.

"You're in time in case he does."

That didn't make sense, but then grief has a way of numbing the senses. Gram and Pops hugged me again, and I hugged them back.

"The guards found Clive in his cell." Pops' voice broke. "I still can't believe it." He scrubbed his hands over his face. "He tried to commit suicide."

"In prison?" There had to be rules against that. "How?"

"Clive made a noose out of his shirt and tried to hang himself. The noose broke, and he hit his head." Pops' finger touched his forehead and then traced an invisible line under his eye. "When they found him, he was having a heart attack."

Amazing. When Aunt Olivia shot Uncle Clive, he

survived. Right after, he'd escaped from the hospital and tried to choke the life out of me. I'd decked him, but he survived. Now he tries to hang himself, and he still survives. I shook my head.

"I know," Gram sniffed. "It's a tragedy."

That some people just won't die.

"Now Clive's in a coma," Pops said, stating the obvious.

"Sorry." Even though Uncle Clive was a lousy brother, Pops couldn't help but love him.

"He's young." Gram blinked back tears. "That's good."

For Gram's sake, I gave her my best smile, but really, even a cat has only nine lives.

The machines erupted into harsh sounds.

"Clive!" Pops rushed over to the hospital bed, yelling for help. "Somebody! We need help!"

A nurse ran into the room, checked the machines, and shouted over her shoulder, "Get a crash cart, stat."

A doctor and two nurses appeared, pushing a rolling cart into the room. Huckleberry jogged in behind them, hand on his holster.

"Stand back," ordered the doctor.

Huckleberry must've decided Uncle Clive wasn't faking it because he didn't argue. We moved away from the bed so the crew could work on Uncle Clive. A nurse pulled down the front of his gown. Another nurse squirted something onto his chest, and the doctor grabbed two paddles. "Clear."

Uncle Clive's body jerked and collapsed.

"Clear."

His body jerked again and fell back.

"Doctor?" the nurse asked.

Everyone watched as the green line threaded straight across on the monitor.

The doctor shook his head. "He's gone."

Gram gave a small cry and turned to Pops.

Pops folded Gram into him, and his big shoulders began to shake. I should've gone to them, but I couldn't.

Clive Christopher was dead, and I was happy about it.

CHAPTER FIVE

Pops barreled into the dining room, waving his big hands in the air. "I don't want to talk about it," he said.

"Okay." I had no idea what he was talking about.

Gram's voice chased after him from the kitchen. "I can't believe you told Lincoln Mortuary we'd have a memorial service for Clive!"

"Whoa, Pops. I can't believe you decided something without asking The Boss." I laughed at my own joke.

Pops pulled out his chair and dropped into it. He cut his eyes to me. "Good morning."

I gave up on being funny when Gram came scurrying into the dining room, carrying a plate of homemade cinnamon buns and waving a spatula. "Jack Christopher, now you listen to me."

"Don't ask," Pops said out of the corner of his mouth.

I didn't know anything about Lincoln Mortuary, and I didn't know anything about women, but I knew when to shut up.

"Well?" Gram came to a stop between our chairs.

"It's not up to me." Pops reached for the coffee pot. "Clive made his funeral arrangements years ago."

Gram put two cinnamon buns on my plate.

I closed my eyes and inhaled the wondrous smells of vanilla and cinnamon.

"I said no." Gram waved the spatula at Pops before putting a cinnamon bun on his plate.

"Clive was my brother."

"He was a murderer."

"Not convicted." Pops poured coffee and added cream.

Gram and Pops both looked at me and I shrugged. Pops had a point but not a strong one.

Gram slid another cinnamon bun onto my plate and icing oozed onto the tablecloth. Running my finger around the edge of the plate, I got a huge glop of icing and licked it. Cream cheese, my favorite.

Pops slapped his big hand on the table, and his coffee cup jumped in its saucer. "We're having a memorial service for Clive at Lincoln Mortuary, Sunday evening at seven o'clock."

His jaw was set, and he was staring straight ahead. Gram still held the plate of buns, but she was glaring at him. It was kind of funny to see a guy the size of a mountain trying to ignore a hundred-pound woman armed only with a spatula and a ruffled apron.

"That's final." Pops picked up his cinnamon bun but put it back on its plate.

Gram started to put another cinnamon bun on my plate, but I waved her off. Gram baked when she was mad, sad, or glad. I was the luckier for it, but three cinnamon buns would put me in a diabetic coma.

"How do you want your eggs, Sage?"

I took a sip of fresh, squeezed orange juice and waited

for Gram to mention the rest of the breakfast menu. Usually, we had waffles or French toast. At the very least, oatmeal with homemade whipped cream and strawberries. Hopefully the call from the mortuary didn't mean a skimpy breakfast because I really needed to keep up my strength. "Uh, scrambled?"

"Fine."

"I like mine scrambled," Pops added.

Gram cracked him on the shoulder with the spatula. "I know what you like."

The kitchen telephone rang.

"Now what?" Gram put the plate of cinnamon buns on the table and wiped her hands on her apron. "That had better not be the mortuary again," she grumbled and left us.

"Saved by the bell," I chirped.

Pops ignored me and hunched over his plate.

It was sad to see him like this, but they would work it out. Besides, I was starving. Taking another bite of my cinnamon bun, the sugar rush went to my brain. Gram did breakfast better than anyone. There had to be bacon to go with the eggs.

I was halfway through my second bun when Gram appeared in the doorway. She was carrying an oval platter heaped with eggs and surrounded by bacon. My teeth were feeling a little numb from all the sugar, but my stomach was just fine.

"That was Clive's lawyer," she said.

Pops' head shot up. "Slimy?"

Chunks of cinnamon bun flew out of my mouth. "Uncle Clive's lawyer is named Slimy?" Shock.

Gram gave Pops The Look. "Sylvester Mee is a well-respected lawyer."

"His name is really Slimy?" This was too good to ignore.

"Sly," explained Pops, "is short for Sylvester." He shrugged. "Sly Mee."

Yeah, right. Nobody gets a nickname like Slimy on accident.

Gram pulled out her chair. "He wants us in his office after breakfast for a reading of Clive's Will."

Pops served himself but held onto the platter. "This seems really sudden."

Gram sat down and put her napkin on her lap. "He said there were important matters that couldn't wait."

I drank some orange juice and tuned them out. This was perfect. I could go over to Sonny's and get away from all this for a while. When I glanced up, Gram and Pops were looking at me. "What?"

"You're coming, too," said Gram.

"Why?"

Pops passed the platter to me. "You're family."

I stopped listening because I'd just noticed the hash browns next to the eggs on the platter. Life didn't get any better than this. After using the serving spoon to slide half the foodstuff onto my plate, I started to dig in. That's when I remembered everything went better with ketchup, so I squirted a huge mound on my hash browns.

"Both of you have to change, of course." Gram said.

"To what?" I ran my hand over my Chicago Cubs jersey, smearing a little cream cheese and ketchup along the way. My washed-out jeans had a hole in one knee, and I was wearing my favorite pair of wooly socks. I looked fine to me.

Gram arched her eyebrows. "Wear what you would wear to church."

"Why?"

"Because I have to." Pops gave me a gloomy, tight-lipped smile but suddenly he brightened. "I'm not if Sage isn't."

Pops hated to get dressed up. On Sundays, his suit was the last thing he put on in the morning and the first thing he took off when he got home. To make him wear a suit on Saturday was criminal. Pops was the best guy I knew. This was my chance to save him but in front of me was the best breakfast on earth. Lunch was four hours away, and I'd be dying of hunger by then. Besides, Sonny came over for lunch on Saturdays, and Gram always made us something special. Earlier, she'd hinted at French fries, corn on the cob, and barbecued chicken. I smiled at Gram. "Sure."

Pops narrowed his eyes and mouthed, "Traitor."

"That reminds me." Gram smiled back at me and got up.

When Gram returned with a bowl of strawberries topped with homemade whipped cream, I knew I'd made the right decision. The only breakfast sounds for the next fifteen minutes were me cleaning my plate.

"Go get dressed," Gram said to both of us. "I'll do the dishes."

Holding up my end of the bargain, I put on tan slacks, a clean white shirt, and a dark green pullover sweater. Even Gram wouldn't insist on me wearing a tie on a Saturday. I hoped.

When I arrived in the foyer a few minutes later, Pops was already there. He was in his best blue suit, and his thick fingers were fidgeting with his tie. I hurried into my coat before he got any ideas about making me wear a tie.

"We'll be done in no time," I said cheerfully, buttoning my coat. "What's the worst that can happen?"

When Gram came into the foyer Pops helped her into her coat and handed her a red and green plaid scarf. Without waiting for her to put it on, Pops reached around her and opened the door. "Ready?"

Outside, the day was as dingy as cement. The kind of day that made me want to hole up inside, watch mind-numbing reruns on TV, and eat junk food. Gram and I shivered on the sidewalk while Pops pulled the Mustang out of the garage. There were perks to living in a small town, and it'd been decent of Huckleberry to have the car delivered this morning. When a gleaming red fender emerged and then Pops' silhouette, a tiny sigh escaped me. It should have been me behind the wheel, with the top down, driving around the sunny beaches of Florida. The freezing, December wind whipped my hair across my eyes, and I glared at the gunmetal sky. I couldn't help it. This time I groaned.

"Are you all okay?"

Let's see. The temperature was in the single digits, my nose was running, my eyes were watering from the wind, and my chapped lips were peeling. "It's hard to believe." That anyone would live here on purpose, I wanted to add, but it was so cold my lips were sticking to my teeth.

"I know." Gram sniffled. "One moment Clive was clinging to life and the next, he's gone." She took a handkerchief from her purse and dabbed her eyes. "He probably lost the will to live."

I probably shouldn't have wished him dead.

Crack! A finger of lightning shot toward me, and I yelped. The wind howled like a wounded animal, and I took a step back.

"Sage?"

My fingers trembled as I adjusted my muffler. The nuns at school were always preaching the virtuous life and rattling on about karma. Until now, I'd thought it was just another Catholic scare tactic.

Sure, Uncle Clive had turned out to be a bad guy. Some

might even say he'd gotten what he deserved. Just because I'd wished him dead and he'd checked out, that didn't mean it was my fault, right?

In fact, he'd started it all by hanging himself. So, him dying like that had nothing to do with me. The wind caught the ends of my muffler, smacking me in the face. Around me lightning popped and fizzled, leaving tiny sparks of white light. I squinted into the wind and turned up my collar. Maybe the whole karma thing wasn't a bunch of hooey.

"Are you okay?" Gram asked for the second time.

I'd read somewhere that people lie about four times a day. That was a staggering one thousand, four hundred and sixty lies in a year. I gave her the most popular one, "I'm fine."

Pops tapped the horn. I'd been working on my manners since I'd moved here and opened Gram's door for her. After she got in, I closed it. Sonny's house was just down the street. In case he was looking out the window, I waved in his direction before sliding onto the backseat. "What's going to happen at the lawyer's office?"

"Slimy," Pops began.

"Mr. Mee," Gram corrected.

Pops met my look in the rearview mirror. "He'll read the Will and discuss any legal matters, like charitable gifts."

The idea that Uncle Clive had developed a conscience in the last forty-eight hours and given anything to charity was so crazy I laughed out loud.

"Sage!" Gram turned around in her seat. "This is a very important matter."

"Sorry." Nothing seemed important enough for church clothes on a Saturday, but now seemed like an important time to practice being an investigative journalist. "Pops, are you going to get everything?"

"I don't know."

"You should," Gram argued, "after all you did for him."

Gram must've forgotten about being broken up over Uncle Clive, but then I'd never seen her smack Pops with a spatula before. I liked the new Gram and leaned forward, hoping for a story. "Like what?"

"Leave it be, Frances." Pops squirmed in his seat. "The farm is old business."

"Not old enough." Gram turned around to face me.

I knew Uncle Clive had pulled a fast one and sold the family farm without giving Pops a cent. What I didn't know was how he'd done it.

"None of this matters, Frances."

Sure, it did. "Go on."

"Sean, that's their dad, had a stroke and was doing badly. Jack agreed to work the farm so Clive could go to college. Clive couldn't be bothered to visit."

"Frances, you're being unfair."

"Ha! Clive didn't come home until Sean was on morphine and barely able to talk."

The wonder of drugs. This was getting interesting. "Do tell."

"Suddenly Clive couldn't do enough for the old man."

"Frances."

She let out a long sigh. "There was Clive always fluffing pillows and fussing around Sean."

The punch line was coming.

"Then Sean died. Wouldn't you know it, Clive found Sean's Will, quite by accident, mind you, in the old man's desk." Gram narrowed her eyes. "Lo and behold, the farm had been left..."

Drum roll here.

"...to Clive."

I thought about Bongo's paper forging business. Bongo may be a high school dropout with a low IQ but his paper got high marks for the best I'd seen. Uncle Clive could easily have found someone like Bongo. "Uncle Clive came up with a new Will and forged your dad's signature on it?" I'd bet the farm on it. Literally.

"Uh."

"Yes," Gram cut Pops off.

What a sleaze. "Did a lawyer make the Will?"

"Slimy," Pops growled. "They've been together ever since."

The Mustang turned a corner, and a blast of sunlight shot through the windshield, making me blink. With it came a happy thought, and I tapped Pops on the shoulder. "If Uncle Clive leaves you everything, you'll be the richest man in Evansville."

"Sage!" Gram sounded shocked but she didn't look it.

"Seems fair," I argued, feeling a big grin take over my face. There really was such a thing as karma.

Gram turned back around in her seat, putting an end to my interview. For the rest of the ride, I tried spending Uncle Clive's money for Gram and Pops. Would they move? No. They'd lived in their apartment forever and knew everybody. A spending spree didn't seem likely. I couldn't see Gram grocery shopping in diamonds and designer clothes. Pops hated to get dressed up. Maybe they'd buy matching luggage and go on one of those cruises where people ate fancy food every two hours. That quickly got a no vote. Gram was the greatest cook on earth.

Pops could quit working at the Seamless Rubber Plant. I studied the back of his head. He had short, white hair and must be around sixty-five. He'd worked hard all his life and had to be tired. If he had money, he could relax and take up an old person hobby like gardening. I tried picturing Pops wearing overalls and fussing around a rose garden but couldn't make it work. Our apartment was on the second floor.

Pops parked in front of Evansville's version of the White House. In spite of the cold, a large, white sign advertising Sylvester Mee, Attorney and Counselor at Law, in charcoal letters sat on a lush, green lawn.

"Wow. Uncle Clive must've been paying him big bucks."

Pops pushed open his door. "Let's get this over with."

CHAPTER SIX

We followed the cobblestone walk to the front door. Pops immediately began squirming and running his index finger around the collar of his shirt. Gram stepped in front of him and pressed the doorbell.

Pops wiggled his tie loose. "Rotten nuisance."

Gram smacked his hand away. "Honestly, Jack. You'd think you were being tortured."

"I am."

The front door slowly opened to a man wearing cowboy boots, faded blue jeans, and a blue work shirt rolled up to the elbows. "Howdy," he drawled.

Pops frowned. "Slimy."

"Mr. Mee," Gram brought me closer, "this is our grandson, Sage."

I'd been picturing the lawyer as a round, hairless, oily little man with nails bitten to the quick after years of dealing with Uncle Clive. Slimy was as tall as Pops but bigger. Not fat, just sort of thick. His skin was tan like he'd spent a lot of time outdoors. He was easily seventy but had jet-black hair combed straight back from his forehead. He looked like he could be famous. Like someone I'd seen a lot on TV or in movies or in history books. President Ronald Reagan? I stared some more and smiled. Gumby.

Slimy smiled back at me, his crow's feet wrinkling around bright, blue eyes. "I've read about you, son. Evansville's newest millionaire."

"That's me," I agreed.

"You're a super sleuth. You figured out a mystery when no one else could."

Slimy had a folksy twang and looked more like a ranch hand than a lawyer. Definitely not a match for this house or for Uncle Clive's money. That made me wonder how he ended up in Evansville. He was smiling again, waiting for me to answer. So help me, I found myself kind of liking the guy.

"It wasn't hard," I offered lamely, "figuring out the mystery."

He raised his eyebrows. "Do you want to be a detective someday?"

That surprised me. "No."

"Sage wants to be an investigative journalist," Gram said proudly.

"Can't talk him out of it," Pops grumbled, yanking off his tie and stuffing it into his pocket.

Slimy stepped aside to let us in. "You shouldn't try." He motioned for us to follow him down the hall. "Seems to me," he said over his shoulder, "an investigative journalist and a detective are pretty much the same thing."

We trailed behind Slimy, down a long hallway lit by crystal chandeliers. The walls were covered with framed photographs of smiling people, shaking hands with him. There was one of Slimy with Mayor Lee. Slimy with Fire Chief Vigliotta. There was Slimy on the golf course with

Councilman Alda. Slimy on the deck of a yacht and clinking glasses with Senator Bixby. And Slimy and Uncle Clive with Congressman Bruno on a tennis court. No wonder the guy had a tan.

At the end of the hall, we went through an open door to a small reception room. More photographs of Slimy and smiling people were on the walls. This guy knew everybody.

A man sitting in an upholstered chair with a black canvas bag at his feet looked up from his magazine, but Slimy didn't introduce us. "This way."

Slimy opened a door to a large office with green, wall-to-wall carpeting plush enough to be a golf course. Three people sat in a semi-circle of six chairs. I knew two of them but couldn't figure out what they'd be doing here. Pellam, Uncle Clive's ancient butler, sat in the first chair. On his right was Charlie Weinstein, our neighborhood grocer. In the third chair was someone I'd never seen before. She was small like a girl, but a lot older. Maybe twenty-five. Her short, black spiky hair stood out from her face and would be a threat to balloons. She gave us one glance before going back to typing on her iPad. After a moment, she paused and blew an enormous bubble. A sniff told me it was grape.

Three empty chairs were on her right. Next to a huge antique floor safe, a mousey-faced court reporter with thick glasses and an incredibly tight ponytail sat staring straight ahead. Her hands were in her lap, and her steno machine was in front of her. She was ready to begin.

"This is quite the gathering," Pops said, stepping into the room. "What are you doing here, Charlie?"

Charlie looked at Mr. Mee. "I'm not sure."

"I don't understand," said Gram.

Slimy squeezed himself into a leather chair behind a

desk that a hundred-year-old sequoia tree had sacrificed its life for. "Please sit."

Gram took one of the vacant chairs. The leather sofa against the back wall looked comfy. I headed toward it.

"Come join us, son," Slimy said.

Pops stayed put. "These people shouldn't be here. Clive's Will is a private matter. I want them to leave."

Pellam and Spiky Hair Girl began making noises like threatened mink. Their voices rose, fell, and trampled each other. Questions about Uncle Clive being dead, questions about his money, and questions about what was going to happen now. This was more interesting than the couch, so I sat down in one of the chairs.

"Either they go, or we go." Gram got to her feet.

"Fine by me." Mr. Weinstein slapped his hat on his head and the other two started bickering again.

Slimy raised a hand like a traffic cop and put a pair of reading glasses on. "This concerns everyone." He peered over his glasses. When he had our attention, he picked up some notebook paper. His voice dropped an octave. "This is the Last Will and Testament of Clive Christopher."

"You're kidding." I looked around Slimy's office with its fine furniture paid for by many unfortunate clients. "His Will is on notebook paper?"

Slimy took off his glasses. "This," he gestured with the notebook paper, "is a holographic Will."

"A hollow what?"

"A holographic Will is a Will written entirely by Clive Christopher." Slimy bit his lip and laid a hand over his heart like he'd been stabbed. "He wrote this last night just before he took his life."

Gram, Pops, and I exchanged looks. Last night when

Chief Murphy had said Uncle Clive had made a statement, he must've meant the Will.

"Let's hear it," I said like I was in charge.

Slimy turned to the court reporter. "Patsy, we're on the record."

She nodded and Slimy began.

"I, Clive Christopher being of sound and disposing mind, do declare this to be my Last Will and Testament, written by me and on the date below. I am a resident of Evansville, Connecticut. This replaces my earlier Will made by Sylvester Mee.

ONE: I name Charlie Weinstein to be my Executor and to carry out my wishes.

TWO: I give my home and everything in it at One Evans Peak to my brother, Jack Christopher."

I sneaked a peek at Gram and Pops, but they sat quietly. Uncle Clive's mansion had fifteen bedrooms and a staff the size of a small city. Gram and Pops were about to move up in this world. I wondered which bedroom would be mine.

"THREE: I give three million dollars to my brother, Jack Christopher, and to his wife, Frances Christopher."

Awesome. They would be set for life.

"FOUR: I want Faith Mackie to stay with *The Evansville News,* run the newspaper, and make all business decisions. If she does, her salary will be increased by twenty-five percent. If she leaves then Charlie Weinstein is to find someone immediately."

Smack! The girl with the spiked hair expertly drew in a purple bubble and replaced it with an enormous grin. Obviously, she was Faith, and the twenty-five percent met with her approval.

"FIVE: I give five hundred thousand dollars to Ian Pellam for his years of service to my family."

Pellam had a face like a doorknob, so if he was surprised it didn't show. Still, he had to know he'd get something.

"SIX: I give what is left of my estate to my nephew, Sage Christopher."

"Holy, moly, joly!" I jumped to my feet and pumped my fists in the air. "I'm rich! I'm rich!"

The oxygen was sucked out of the room as five other people realized where all of Uncle Clive's money just went.

"Sage," Gram pulled hard on my sweater. "Please sit down."

"No way!" For about half a second, a little pang of guilt had me considering taking back the awful things I'd said about Uncle Clive. Forget that. "I'm rich!"

Slimy waited for the shock wave to die down. "As I was saying." He returned to the Will. "*The Evansville News* is to be held in trust until Sage turns twenty-one. Sage is to begin working part-time at the newspaper as Faith sees fit. When Sage turns twenty-one, he'll take over the newspaper."

"Cashing in on a little nepotism, are we?" Faith rolled her eyes. "Must be nice."

"You bet!" Dollar signs and zeroes were having a party in my head. Less than a month ago, I was in Las Vegas with Marty, eating cold stew from a can and drinking stale beer. Then I'd moved to Evansville. Gram and Pops' landlady, Lucy Riley, had died and left me all her property because she'd had a soft spot for Marty. Two days ago, I'd gotten a million bucks in reward money, and now this.

Money was flying in at me from all directions. Uncle Clive had to be worth a bundle, at least five or ten million. He'd been the richest man in town so in some ways, ten million seemed kind of puny. I thought about twenty million and decided I liked twenty much better. Such a nice, round number.

I sat back down. It would be summer soon and Connecticut had a lot of beaches. I rubbed my hands together and grinned like an idiot. I could buy a really big boat.

SEVEN: I forbid Sylvester Mee to be the attorney for my estate or to receive any money from my estate in any way. He made enough off me in my lifetime, and I refuse for him to make anymore."

"Wow, Slimy," I blurted out. "That's gotta sting."

"Sage! Mind your manners," Gram warned. Then she added under her breath, "Serves him right for cheating Jack out of the farm."

Faith perked up. "Perhaps we can have an interview sometime, Mrs. Christopher."

Pops pointed at Slimy. "There's a word for what goes around, comes around."

"Karma," I said. Not even the nuns would feel sorry for Slimy.

Slimy ignored us and turned to the court reporter. "Let the record show this Will was signed and dated last night by Clive Christopher."

Patsy nodded, tapped the keys a few times and then let her hands slide off her machine and back into her lap.

Pellam stood up and straightened his suit coat. "Mr. Mee," he ignored the rest of us, "I'll be going."

"Me, too," said Charlie, hefting himself out of his chair. "I've got a business to run."

"Before you mosey along," Slimy drawled, "there's one more little matter." He picked up a thick stack of papers and held them out to me. "For you, son."

This inheritance thing was easy. A few fancy words,

and Uncle Clive's stuff was all mine. I didn't bother to hide my greedy smile and snatched the papers from him. Thank you, Uncle Clive!

"Congrats, son," Slimy gave me a wink. "You've been served."

"What?" I tried shoving the papers back into his hands.

Slimy chuckled, letting the papers fall onto his desk. "You're being sued for three million dollars."

"I'm a kid!"

"Why?" demanded Pops.

Slimy handed Pops an equally impressive stack of papers. "As grandparents for Sage, this is your copy." He dropped back into his chair and gave me a smug grin. "I'm contesting Clive's Will on the grounds of undue influence."

"Undue what?" I whipped around to Pops. "What's he talking about?"

"It's simple," Slimy swiveled in his chair. "Clive's second Will should be declared invalid, and his first Will valid."

Faith was typing like crazy on her iPad and blowing a bubble the size of Manhattan.

"This is one more of your scheming tricks." Gram picked up her purse. "Like when you helped Clive forge his dad's Will and steal the farm away from Jack." She was on her feet and jabbing a finger in his face. "You were a sneak then and you're a sneak now."

Faith stopped blowing bubbles. "May I quote you?"

"Hold on." I jumped in. "What's undue influence?"

"Glad you asked, son." Slimy leaned back in his chair like he was settling in an easy chair to watch TV. He put his cowboy boots up on the corner of his desk and began ticking off on his fingers. "First, there's susceptibility to undue influence. Second, there's opportunity to influence. Third, disposition to influence." A big, ugly grin split his face. "And fourth, my personal favorite, coveted result."

"Speak English."

His boots slid off the desk, and he sat up straight, the leather chair protesting his bulk. "You took advantage of a weakened man, heartbroken over the recent death of his wife."

"He shot her to death!"

"We'll never know for sure, will we, son?" Slimy actually looked happy about that. "Pellam will testify you took advantage of his fragile mental condition."

No wonder the old geezer was in a hurry to get out of here. "What's he talking about, Pellam?"

Pellam didn't flinch. "You were always telling him you wanted to be an investigative journalist."

"So?"

Slimy steepled his fingers together. "The biggie is the coveted result. By buttering Clive up, you got his money, his property and what you wanted most, the newspaper."

What idiot wouldn't want all that? "Gram. Pops. Can he sue me?"

Pops' fists were clenched. "Anyone can sue anybody."

"We'll fight this," Gram and I said together.

Slimy laughed. "Nobody will take your case. I'm the lawyer for everyone in town." He waved to the photographs of smiling faces. "There isn't a single, important person or business I do not influence, including the bank." He shrugged. "Don't even think about it, son."

Did he really have the town in his back pocket? I snatched the papers off his desk and stood straight. There had to be a lawyer somewhere who wouldn't be afraid. "I'm young. I've got a lot of time and a lot of money. And I'll win."

"Can't win. You've got to be reasonable, son."

"You'll hear from my lawyer," I said like I had a whole law firm working for me.

"You'll come around, son," Slimy argued.

"Karma is what comes around, and you'll get yours." I started for the door but stopped halfway. "And quit calling me son."

CHAPTER SEVEN

"Go after him, you moron," Faith shrilled.

The man in the reception room grabbed a camera from his bag and jumped to his feet. He shoved past me, crouched low and began power walking backward, taking photographs like a maniac.

The flashes were blinding. And irritating. "Stop that." I put a hand up in front of my eyes.

"Hey." He went from snapping photos to snapping his fingers at me. "Look my way."

"Get out of my way," I warned. There was another flash and bright, white light hit me between the eyes. "Give me that!" Through the light show, I lunged for his camera.

He tried a dip and dodge maneuver but stumbled. Reflex made me try to catch him, but I missed, swiping empty air instead. He hit the ground, and his head slammed back hard against the floor.

"O-oh." He struggled to sit up but couldn't make it and patted his chest. "I'm h-having a h-heart attack." His head rolled to the side, and his eyes stared straight ahead.

Both legs were twitching so I was pretty sure he wasn't

dead. I gave the soles of his feet a couple of quick kicks anyway. "Knock it off."

"O-oh," he moaned. "My head. My back."

"Geez," I muttered, reaching down for him.

"Help! Help!" he squealed, squeezing his eyes shut and wiggling away. "Don't hit me in the face."

That was a good idea, but I had a better one. I grabbed him by the lapels, hauled him to his feet, and went for his camera again.

"You c-can't take my camera. The press has free speech." He clutched the camera to his chest the way a kid clutches a stuffed animal. "My camera is p-protected by the First Amendment."

He may have the First Amendment in his hands, but I had youth on my side. Besides, the United States Constitution said nothing about shaking him until he dropped the camera. "Give it." I grabbed for it again.

"I'm the press. I'm the press," he warbled.

"Cut it out." Faith dove between us, pushing us apart.

I shoved her aside. "You," I pointed to the man, "give me the camera."

The little man hugged the camera tighter to his chest. "No."

"Tell him," I said to Faith.

"Tell him what?" She squinted at me. "He's right."

"Tell him I own the paper. Tell him that means the camera is mine."

Faith blew a bubble and sighed. "You heard him, Whiny. Give him the camera."

He handed the camera over.

I took out the SIM card and gave the camera back. "Your name is Whiny?"

"It's really Willie," he mumbled.

"At the newspaper we call him Whiny," Faith arched her eyebrows, "because he's such a whiner."

This was a day for nicknames. "What do they call you?"

She blew a bubble and popped it. "Boss."

"I'm the boss."

"Not for eight years, son."

"Don't call me that."

"I like it." She gave me a wide grin, showing perfect, white teeth. The bubble gum must be sugar free. "Catchy."

I threw my hands up into the air and backed away. Today I inherited a fortune and got sued for a fortune. And it wasn't even noon. "Tell my grandparents I'm going to Sonny's." I didn't wait for her to answer, just started loping down the hallway.

"Wait. We need to talk."

"Later." I needed to think of a plan. I needed to talk to Sonny. I needed to find a lawyer. I made my way to the parking lot and yanked open the door to the Mustang.

Rats. I needed the car keys.

It occurred to me that since I was rich, I could buy a car when I turned sixteen. Trouble was I had no idea what I'd want. In the past I'd always driven what was easy to steal.

I could wait for my grandparents, but they'd be talking to Slimy for forever. Good thing for him, Gram wasn't packing her spatula. It was still bitter cold, and Sonny lived across town, but without the keys to the Mustang, all I had was my own two feet. I started in the direction of Sonny's house. Questions about today began flying around in my head, and soon my mind was going faster than my feet. I broke into a jog.

Pounding the pavement helped me think about what I knew and what I didn't. Slimy said he'd made an earlier Will for Uncle Clive but not what had been in it. Uncle

Clive's new Will made it clear Slimy wasn't going to get a dime. I'd assumed they'd been friends all these years but maybe not.

Once I'd thought Uncle Clive was a good guy. I'd even wanted to be like him someday. Too late I'd found out it was all a con. When I'd met Slimy this morning, he'd conned me with his slow drawl and cowboy boots. He'd suckered me right in with all that folksy stuff when he asked if I wanted to be a detective. What really ticked me off was in the last three weeks, I'd been duped twice. Maybe I was losing my touch. None of this would've happened to me in Las Vegas. This made me so mad I missed Nutmeg Street and had to double back.

So why was Slimy going to all this trouble to fight Uncle Clive's Will? I couldn't see Slimy as the Champion of Lost Causes. All that blather about poor Uncle Clive being rattled after Aunt Olivia's death was a crock. There was only one reason why Slimy would go to all this trouble.

Money.

The easy answer to so many hard questions.

Why he wanted the money didn't matter, but how he was going to get his hands on it did.

Evansville was waking up. I ran past Mrs. Shapiro sweeping the front steps in front of the library.

"Good morning, Sage," she called. "Sorry to hear about your uncle."

I waved and kept running.

Mr. Dinco appeared in the doorway of his dry cleaners. "Tell your grandfather we're praying for him."

"Sure."

In front of the post office, I made the mistake of slowing down, and Mrs. Salter hurried out. "Here." She put a change of address form in my hands. "Give this to your grandparents so I can forward their mail when they move to Evans Peak."

I checked the sky for smoke signals, but there was nothing coming from Slimy's office announcing a change in the Christopher family fortune. "Thanks."

Traffic slowed so I jaywalked across the street. In front of Pat's Diner, Mr. Patrizi flung open the front door and started trotting along beside me. He was wearing his white, cook's apron, and underneath, his enormous belly bounced up and down like a big snowball. "Your Uncle Clive was a wonderful man."

"Uh-huh." I gave him a quick smile and picked up my pace.

"He'll be missed. "

A vision of my inheritance and all those zeroes danced in my head. "I'll think of him every day."

"You're," he panted, red faced, "a good boy.

When I looked back over my shoulder, too many years of pounding down pastrami on rye had Mr. Patrizi bent over at the waist. He caught my eye and raised a beefy hand in surrender, waving me on.

In less than an hour, life had become very complicated. I had to put things in order, had to make sense of this. I definitely had to come up with a plan. My feet were frozen bricks, but I kept running.

In front of Weinstein's, Mrs. Joyce was struggling to put out the sandwich sign offering today's special. "Is it true?"

"Depends." We angled the sign toward the sidewalk. Today's special was rib eye.

"Mr. Mee is suing you?" Her red lips curved down in a serious frown. "He never loses."

"Then he'd better get used to it." I gave her thumbs up like I sued people every day. "Bye."

When I turned the corner at Watkins Place, I was struck with an idea so simple I screeched to a halt. Since the first Will had all the answers, all I needed to do was to get it. Slimy had to have a copy, but he also had an office safe the size of a bank vault. Unfortunately, I'd left Las Vegas before I'd learned to crack a safe. Dynamite would be quick and effective but also nowhere to be found in this little town.

When Slimy made the first Will, he must've given Uncle Clive the original. Since a Will was very important, it didn't seem likely Uncle Clive would have kept it at his office at the newspaper. I'd bet money, it was at his mansion.

That meant I needed to get into the mansion.

That meant I needed Sonny.

By the time I got to Sonny's house, my calves were burning, my butt was dragging, my frozen feet were threatening to break off, and snot was running down my face. I pounded on the door and did a foot stomping dance on the front step.

The door opened, and a blast of hot air rushed out. Sonny was still in his pajamas and holding a Superman comic book. He blinked at me from behind his glasses.

"Hi." I barreled in and Sonny had no choice but to move aside. "Want some hot chocolate?" This was Sonny's house, but he couldn't make hot chocolate on a bet.

"Whipped cream or marshmallows?"

"Whipped cream." My stomach growled. "Do you have cookies?"

"Probably." He trailed behind me. "Sorry about your uncle, I guess."

"Don't be." I jerked a thumb over my shoulder. "I was just at Slimy's for the reading of Uncle Clive's Will."

"I know."

"Did you see me leave this morning?"

"Nope. My mom talked to Mrs. Joyce when she was getting a rib eye roast from Weinstein's."

Secrets traveled faster than mercury in this town.

In the kitchen, I helped myself to the milk in the refrigerator. "Get a big saucepan and some chocolate."

Sonny tossed his comic book on top of a basket of fruit. He went to the cabinet, managed to find both, and put them on the counter. "I heard he left you almost everything."

"Including the newspaper." I sighed, trying to look sad about the guy who'd made me filthy rich. "Now my life is all messed up."

"The scumbag."

I stirred the chocolate into the milk and set the pan on the stove. "That's him."

"Why would he leave you everything? You're the one who ratted him out." Sonny adjusted his glasses. "It doesn't make sense."

Sonny was right. I hadn't thought about that. "Uncle Clive probably had a guilty conscience." Geez. Now I sounded like Sonny.

"Still, it was nice of him."

I snorted.

"Maybe you can just accept him for what he was and appreciate the gifts he gave you."

The hot chocolate was beginning to boil, and I turned it down. "Have you been watching those self-help talk shows with your mom again?"

"It beats cleaning my room. Since you moved here, I've been put on restriction until my next birthday." He folded his arms across his chest. "Why are you here?"

I stirred the chocolate some and tried to look as troubled as I should feel. "First, I need to tell you what happened at Slimy's."

"Okay."

I started with Slimy opening the front door and sucking me in and ended with being sued.

"Wow. He's never lost."

"Yet." I grabbed two mugs from the cupboard and poured the hot chocolate into them. "Give me the whipped cream."

Sonny got the whipped cream out of the fridge and handed it to me.

"What's this?" I held up the container.

"What's it look like?"

"Looks like something in a can." I shook it. "Gram makes everything from scratch."

"You're so lucky."

True. I took off the cap and shot a stream of whipped cream at him.

"Hey."

He lunged at me, but I shook the container again and squirted huge glops of cream on top of the chocolate. The cream ran down the mugs and onto the counter. "This is what we're going to do."

"We?"

I looked around the empty kitchen. "Of course, we. Who else?"

"Depends on what you have in mind."

I picked up my mug and started walking to the kitchen table, dribbling a little on the floor on the way. "Where are the cookies?'

"Hold on."

Sonny tore open a fresh packet of Oreo cookies with double stuffing and dropped it in the middle of the table. "Do you have a plan?"

Not yet. "Of course." Shoving a cookie into my mouth, I

gave it a quick chew. "The first Will is really important." I reached for another cookie, broke it apart, and licked the icing. "We need to get it."

"There you go with the we thing again."

I tried to look offended. "We're a team. Christopher and Benson."

"Benson and Christopher."

"Right." I needed his help. We could worry about billing later.

"Why do you want to find his Will so bad?"

Not sure. "Because Slimy wants it so bad."

"What's in it for me?"

Criminy. "We're a team," I repeated. "I couldn't have solved Evans's murder without you." Or gotten my fat reward that I didn't share with you. I moved on quickly in case he suddenly remembered that part. "You're my best friend."

"We're on another case?"

"You bet. It's," I thought fast, "*The Case of the Missing Fortune.*"

"Sweet. Like Jimmy Olsen and Clark Kent?"

The kid really needed to get new reading material. "Yeah."

"You know," Sonny took a sip of hot chocolate, "we're kinda like detectives."

"Yup." Slimy had said the same thing. He might be right. "After we get the Will, we'll need to show it to a lawyer." I was making this up as I went along.

"You'll never get a lawyer in this town. Mr. Mee owns everybody."

"Not me." I liked the sound of that and took a big swig of my hot chocolate, burning my tongue. "I'll get one."

Sonny slurped some more hot chocolate and wiped off a

whipped cream mustache with the back of his hand. "You still haven't said how we're going to do this."

I stared at him like he could've somehow missed the most important part. "We're going to break into Uncle Clive's mansion, of course."

"Are you nuts? The last time we did that your uncle shot your aunt dead." Sonny shuddered. "I still get nightmares."

Me, too. I gave him my best smile. "Look on the bright side. That can't happen again."

"What if the plan doesn't work?"

It has to. "Then we'll go with Plan B."

"Which is?"

No idea. "It's complicated," I lied. "Tell me what a memorial service is all about. Pops said Uncle Clive is having one."

"It's tomorrow night at Lincoln Mortuary at seven o'clock."

"How do you know?"

"Everybody knows." Sonny broke the cookie apart, dropped it in his hot chocolate, and swirled it around with his finger. "For someone who wants to be an investigative journalist, you really need to pay more attention."

Oh, I was paying attention all right. "Is it just for family?"

"Oh no." Sonny shook his head so hard he had to straighten his glasses. "Until your uncle got arrested, his life was perfect. Everybody liked him. Then he shoots Olivia dead, and no one knows why. Before the gossip can get started, he goes and hangs himself." He took a gulp of hot chocolate. "This is like something out of *The National Enquirer*. Everybody and his dog are going to be there."

Perfect. "That's when we'll do it."

"Do what?"

"Pay attention, Benson." I finished my hot chocolate. "Break into Uncle Clive's mansion."

"No."

I took a cookie out of the bag and handed it to Sonny. "Pellam will go to this service thing, right?"

"Right," he said, chewing slowly.

"No one will be at the mansion. All we have to do is wait for him to show up at the mortuary and then ride our bikes over there." I took a cookie from the bag and pointed it at Sonny. "We'll have lots of time. How long do they last?"

"A couple of hours."

"With all the people there, Pops and Gram won't notice we're gone."

Sonny took my cookie and popped it into his mouth. "That's the dumbest plan I've ever heard."

Maybe but I didn't have another one. "It's always the simplest plan that works the best. You'll see."

"I'm starving." Sonny rubbed his stomach. "What's your gram making for lunch?"

I glanced at the kitchen clock. Both hands were straight up. I didn't think I could eat for a week, but Sonny was better than a stray cat. Feed him and he was yours. "Let's go find out."

CHAPTER EIGHT

Sonny cocked his snout in the air as soon as I opened our front door. "We're having something barbecued." He inhaled deeply. "I bet chicken with French fries and corn on the cob."

"You're downright scary," I said but I was impressed. When I'd been looking for Evans's body, I'd thought about asking my grandparents for a bloodhound puppy. I should've put a collar on Sonny and gotten him to do the job. "How do you know that?"

"There's nothing like the smell of barbecue or French fries." He tossed his coat on top of the coat rack and kicked his muddy shoes off. They missed the entry rug and landed on the clean hardwood floor. "The chicken and corn on the cob were a hunch."

With hunches like that, I should teach Sonny to play the ponies.

"Boys?" Gram called. "Lunch is ready. Go wash your hands."

I hung up my coat. "Okay."

Sonny started for the dining room, but I grabbed his arm. "You heard her."

"I washed them this morning." Sonny showed me his grubby hands. "Might've been yesterday."

"Do you want to eat or not?"

"Your gram really has a thing about being clean," Sonny grumbled, but he headed for the guest bathroom.

When we got to the dining room, Pops' chair was empty. Gram was already seated but looked up from the notes she was making on a pad next to her plate. "I hope you're hungry."

A platter of barbecue chicken, a platter of corn on the cob, and a heaping bowl of French fries were on the table next to a pitcher of lemonade and a basket with three pieces of cornbread. Gram always made enough to feed ten men, and my stomach growled happily.

Sonny searched the table. "No dessert?"

"Over there." On the sideboard were four huge slices of chocolate cake with fudge frosting. "Where's Pops?"

"He and Charlie went to see Mr. Ashton, the lawyer."

Maybe this was good news. "Why?"

Gram motioned for us to eat.

"Thanks, Mrs. Christopher." Sonny was already digging in. "I couldn't last much longer."

"As you know, Clive named Charlie the Executor of his Will."

I reached for the basket of cornbread and helped myself. When I gave the basket to Sonny, he dropped a piece onto his plate and took a big bite out of another one before passing the empty basket to Gram. She sighed but put the basket on the table.

"What's that?" Sonny mumbled through a mouthful of cornbread.

"The Executor represents Clive's estate and carries out Clive's wishes under the Will," Gram explained, handing me the platter of corn on the cob.

"Huh?" Sonny took another bite of cornbread.

"He makes sure people get what Uncle Clive says they're to get," I said. For the last twenty-four hours, I'd been picturing myself running *The Evansville News* and getting my first Pulitzer before my twenty-second birthday.

Sonny snorted. "Gotta love Uncle Clive's money."

Oh, I do. Even if he was a murderer.

"Also," Gram sighed, taking a sip of lemonade, "Charlie needs a lawyer to do the legal work. It's a big job."

"Frances, I'm home," Pops called from the foyer.

Gram brightened. "Your grandfather can tell you all about it." She picked up the empty breadbasket and winked at me. "I'll get more."

Pops patted my shoulder on the way to his chair. "Did Sonny leave me anything to eat?"

"Barely." Sonny had two pieces of chicken on his plate and was taking a third. I slapped his hand away and gave the platter to Pops. "What did Mr. Ashton say?"

"Let's wait for your grandmother." Pops filled his plate and put his napkin on his lap.

I bit into my corn on the cob and began munching happily. Two weeks ago, Mr. Ashton had come over on a rainy night to tell us our landlady Lucy Riley had died. I should've been sad, but I was too surprised. Because Mrs. Riley had liked my dad-- nobody ever had, she'd left me everything.

Mr. Ashton had managed her money for years and must've been pretty slick because the biggest surprise was Mrs. Riley turned out to be loaded. She gave me everything and I got our apartment building, property in town, and enough dough to bankroll four years at Yale. Maybe even grad school. Bless her little heart.

Mr. Ashton was just the lawyer I needed on my side. He wouldn't be afraid to fight Slimy in the lawsuit. There was only one problem. Mr. Ashton had to be a thousand years old and could croak at any time.

Gram put the breadbasket next to Pops and sat down. "Well?"

Pops cleared his throat. "Mr. Ashton agreed to be the lawyer for the estate. He'll take care of filing Clive's Will with the court and making sure bills are paid." He picked up his knife and fork. "He'll do pretty much everything."

"Will he be my lawyer?"

"Can't." Pops cut into the chicken. "He can only represent the estate. Slimy's lawsuit is against you personally. That's a conflict of interest."

Well, that stinks. Given Slimy's reputation, the chances of me finding a rabid dog in a three-piece suit that would stand up to him in this he-haw town was dwindling to zilch. "No problem."

Gram and Pops exchanged looks.

"You're crazy." Sonny laughed out loud. "Slimy never loses. No one's going to help you."

Even if a lawyer didn't want to help me, he'd want my money. There may be no such thing as justice but that didn't mean it couldn't be bought. "I'll have one by Monday night." I stuck my chin out to show I meant it, but the thought was so depressing, I changed the subject. "Gram, what do you need to do for the memorial service?"

"A lot," Gram said, scanning the list.

"Like what?" I swirled a French fry in ketchup.

"Music, flowers, refreshments." She picked up her pen

and made check marks on the pad. "We're expecting the whole town."

"Charlie gave me the names of people who want to say a few words at the memorial service." Pops pulled a piece of paper out of his shirt pocket and handed it to Gram. "Father Flanders offered to do the eulogy at the funeral."

I hadn't realized that we'd actually have to bury Uncle Clive. "When's the funeral?"

"Tuesday." Gram patted Pops' hand and turned to me. "Clive will be buried in the Evans's family mausoleum. It'll be a quiet service. Only a few close friends."

"I know I should do the eulogy, but I can't." Pops reached for his handkerchief and blew his nose. "It's just too hard."

If I lived forever, I'd never understand why Pops loved Uncle Clive so much. All his life Uncle Clive had done Pops wrong, but here Pops was, practically in tears. There was no way I could help him out and do the eulogy for him. I may be a great liar, but I was no actor. A blind person could see how happy I was the guy was gone.

Gram smiled at Pops. "Let's focus on the memorial service."

Good idea. When Mrs. Riley died, she'd had a wake and the whole neighborhood had been invited. "Is a memorial service the same as a wake?"

"Wakes have booze and dancing," Sonny said through a mouthful of French fries. "They're fun. Memorial services are boring. You've got to get dressed up in church clothes. Everyone stands around crying, and there are only cookies to eat."

That sounded quick. Too quick. "How long will it last?"

"Two hours." Pops folded his handkerchief. "Frances and I will get there early to make sure everything is set up."

Good idea. That would leave me alone to work on my plan. "Do you need help?" Say no.

"I'll let you know if I do." Gram smiled.

"Sonny and I," I tried to look sincere, "have been trying to think of ways to help."

"We have?" Sonny's eyebrows shot up.

"Since you want to get there early, Sonny and I could ride our bikes over later. Before it starts." I gave Sonny a meaningful stare, hoping he'd get my message. "Then you wouldn't have to come back and get us." The plan was taking shape. We'd have our bikes, so slipping away from the crowd would be easy.

Sonny choked a little and reached for his lemonade. "Went down the wrong way," he squeaked.

I patted him on the back. "Anything we can do to help, right Sonny?"

Sonny's face was as red as his hair, but he nodded.

"Frances is right," Pops said. "There isn't anything for you to do."

"Don't worry." I bit my cheek to keep from smiling. "I'll find something."

After I polished off the chocolate cake, my brain was in high sugar gear, and I had the rest of my plan. Sort of.

"Gram," I said, pointing to her notepad, "your list looks pretty long. Sonny and I will do the dishes." I used my finger to scrape some fudge frosting I'd missed off my plate.

Sonny turned on me. "Say what?"

Gram pretended she hadn't heard him. "Thanks, boys. I really need to get the shopping done." She smiled at Sonny. "Then we can have more than cookies at the service."

Pops stood up. "I'll drive you. I have a few errands to do."

I dragged Sonny to his feet and started stacking plates.

Since he was about as graceful as a goat, I gave him the breadbasket. "Take only the unbreakable things."

"Is there any more cake, Mrs. Christopher?" He scooped up the silverware and dropped the pieces into the basket.

"In the kitchen." Gram pushed her chair back and picked up her notepad. "Help yourself when you're finished."

When they'd both left the room, I said, "I needed to get them out of the house."

"Why?"

"Because I need to get out of the house."

"Why?"

Criminy. I bet Clark Kent never had to explain the obvious to Jimmy Olsen. "Because they'd want me to go with them. We have things to do."

"Like what?"

I picked up the plates and he followed me into the kitchen. "We're going to the library."

"Unh-unh."

I ignored him and filled the sink with soapy water. "We need to find a blueprint or a description of Uncle Clive's mansion. It's famous. There's got to be something in the library."

"So what?"

"We need to find out where Uncle Clive's office is so we can find the Will tomorrow night. The mansion has fifteen bedrooms. We could be wandering like Moses in the desert until we find his office."

He made a face. "I hate libraries."

"You've got to come with me."

Sonny dropped the basket with silverware on the kitchen counter, took out a dirty fork and stuck it in the chocolate cake. "Books are in libraries," he said and chewed. "You write." Another bite. More chewing. "I take pictures."

"We're a team."

He nodded. "Exactly. You do what you do best, and I do what I do best."

Sonny was right, but it was annoying. He really had to stop watching the self-help TV shows with his mother.

He licked the fork and hummed. "Your gram makes the best cake."

There was only one way to reach Sonny. I picked up the chocolate cake and held it away from him. "Help me or you'll never eat here again."

"Some threat. I'm your best friend." Sonny stabbed at the cake. "Besides, your grandparents like me."

I grabbed his fork and threw it into the sink. "I'll wash. You dry."

Sonny picked up a dish towel. "I can't believe your grandparents don't have a dishwasher."

Marty and I had always lived in cheap motels or in his car. We'd never needed a dishwasher because we never had any dishes. Until I came here, I thought everybody ate cold stew from a can. "Get busy."

Sonny leaned against the counter. "When you move into the mansion, you'll never wash another dish again."

I liked the idea of grumpy old Pellam waiting on me hand and foot. I didn't like the idea of leaving the best home I'd ever known. "Not true."

"You could get a horse or a bunch of dogs. I've always wanted a dog." Sonny thought hard. "I'd name him Krypto. You know, like Superman's dog."

I liked dogs. I liked all animals. "I've always wanted a cat."

"No kidding."

"They're really cool. Like feline ninjas. They can live with people or on their own." Kind of like me. I washed another dish and put it on the counter. "They're really smart."

"When you move, we'll never see you again." Sonny traced the grout line on the tile floor with his foot. "You'll go to a different school."

Hadn't thought about that. "No, I won't."

His foot squeaked on the tile. "Play ball with new friends."

I'd lose the only friends I've ever had. "We'll still get a game together."

"That's what everybody says before they move." He folded his arms across his chest. "Once you're out of here, you're out of here."

Uncle Clive had a Rolls Royce. I'd look for the keys when I looked for the Will. "I'll be driving soon."

Sonny shook his head. "I'll be stuck with the twins again."

Malcolm and Robbie lived three doors down. When they were five, they'd talked their eighty-five-year-old babysitter into playing cowboys and Indians. The old girl had a heart attack when they tied her up and tried to burn her at the stake. Their skills have progressed since then and if they weren't in juvenile hall before they graduated from high school, there really were miracles. "You hung out with them before."

"Not the same."

"If you like being with me so much, go to the library with me."

"Nope." Sonny held his hands out in front of him and started backing away. "You're not going to guilt me into going with you."

I flicked some soapy water at him. "Listen, Dr. Sonny. You really need to lay off the daytime TV."

"Probably but I'm still not going." Sonny wiped his face with the towel and tossed it onto the counter. "I have to check my camera equipment." At the door he gave me a big grin. "See you tomorrow night."

CHAPTER NINE

The dishes went pretty fast, and I was out the door in a heartbeat. It had to be a whopping ten degrees outside, and I hustled to the library. Taking the front steps two at a time, I wondered if I'd ever be warm again. I'd read that people who lived in cold climates were kind of like ducks. The little guys had a layer of fat that kept them from freezing when they were swimming in cold water. After thirteen years of living in Las Vegas, I was just a skinny kid with no body fat. I'd never be a duck.

"Hi, Mrs. Shapiro."

Other than Mrs. Riley, Mrs. Shapiro was the only person in this town who'd ever liked my dad. Marty had conned her like he'd conned everyone else in his life. To this day, she thought he'd helped her at the library because he was a dedicated member of mankind. Little did she know, Marty had dedicated his time here to figuring out how much dough Uncle Clive and Olivia had so he could black-mail them. Marty had been a loser. Yet, here I am, following the same money trail.

Mrs. Shapiro slipped her harlequin glasses off her nose

and let them dangle at the end of a rhinestone chain. She rested her pointy chin on her hands and whispered, "How's your family doing?" Her eyes filled with tears, and she sniffed. "The rumors are horrible. I know they can't be true."

Oh, they're true all right.

"To take his own life," she sniffed again, "he must have been a tortured soul."

Right. I tried to look as sad as Mrs. Shapiro thought I should feel. "Gram and Pops are taking it hard."

"Of course." She reached for a tissue. "Is there anything I can do to help?"

Now we're getting somewhere. "Sonny and I," I began weakly hoping to sound like I might break down any moment and grab a tissue for myself, "are putting together a tribute for Uncle Clive." I scrambled for something more. "For his memorial service. We're calling it *This Is Your Life.*"

Mrs. Shapiro looked at me blankly.

I was blank, too, but kept talking. Like every good investigative journalist, I wasn't going to come out and ask for what I wanted. I'd be cagey and start with a smoke screen. "I want to look at some of the stories he covered so I can talk about his career."

Mrs. Shapiro nodded and reached for her pad and pencil. I took this as a good sign.

"And," I added like it'd just come to me, "I want to add some personal stuff."

"Personal?" She frowned.

"About his mansion. He really loved his mansion."

Mrs. Shapiro's pencil was in mid-air. Just like my plan.

"Do you have any blueprints for it? I heard Mr. Evans

built it, and it's famous..." for Olivia's murder, "...for its architectural design."

"I have just the information you need." Mrs. Shapiro beamed. "Mr. Coffey was the architect."

The name sounded familiar, but I let it go.

"Barbara," Mrs. Shapiro called softly to a stout lady stacking books on a shelf, "please watch the desk for me."

The woman gave a slight nod and went back to stacking books.

"Thank heavens for archives." Mrs. Shapiro got up, pushed back the sleeves of her cardigan, then marched away in her sensible shoes.

I let out my breath and followed. Thank heavens for lying.

In the reference room Mrs. Shapiro stopped at an oak table. "Sit here." She put a blue-veined hand to her heart and sighed. "A few years ago, Mr. Christopher invited all the county librarians for tea. We toured the mansion, and it was magnificent."

"He was a wonderful man," I mumbled. Here I am lying again. By now, the talk all over town was that Uncle Clive had killed Olivia—not that anyone blamed him. But, if the truth ever came out that he'd killed her for her money, Gram and Pops wouldn't be able to bury him fast enough. Most people drew the line at greed. "Was the tea for a special occasion?"

"Indeed, it was. Mr. Christopher had a vast collection of first editions." She closed her eyes for a moment. "He actually let us hold them."

"Incredible."

"The visit was an experience I'll remember for the rest of my life. The rooms. The furnishings. So much beauty."

Sounding sincere wasn't easy for me but I sincerely

needed to cut to the chase. "Mrs. Shapiro, I have a first edition of *Huckleberry Finn.*"

She gasped. "Was it a gift from your Uncle Clive?"

Because Mrs. Shapiro liked me and I needed her help, I wasn't about to tell her I'd won it ripping off a dumb, rich kid in a game of blackjack. I squeezed my eyes tight, wishing for the hundredth time in my life that I could cry on cue. Red-eyed was the most I could hope for, so I stammered out my first truth of the day, "It's my most prized possession."

"Of course, it is." Mrs. Shapiro nodded vigorously, and her bun bobbled like a gray pincushion. "Mr. Christopher's library is legendary."

Since all of Uncle Clive's stuff now belonged to Gram and Pops and I was their only grandkid, I hoped legendary was another word for expensive. "Where's the library? We had Thanksgiving dinner at the mansion, but I didn't see it."

"It's the first door on the left once you pass the foyer. Mr. Christopher always kept the door closed and a strict eye on the thermostat. Very important for rare books."

"Is the library also his office?" Please say yes.

"No."

Bummer.

She cast her eyes upward, a skinny finger to her lips. "His office is upstairs and quite different from the rest of the mansion. You must see it."

I'm counting on it. The second floor was about as big as a shopping mall. "Is it to the right of the staircase or to the left?"

"Mr. Christopher's office is in the left wing."

Olivia's rooms were in the right wing. It made sense Uncle Clive would stay as far away from her as possible but as close as possible to her money.

"Wait here. I have the complete set of blueprints for Evans Peak."

I watched her walk away and smiled. Mrs. Shapiro was going to be better than any set of blueprints. When she returned with them, I began, "Would you," I gave her my best smile, "tell me about the mansion? Something I could use in my story?"

Mrs. Shapiro giggled, pulled out a chair, and sat down. "I was hoping you would ask."

Keeping Mrs. Shapiro on track was like chasing bubbles. She bounced around from the pretty drapes to the pretty china to the pretty paintings. When she finally worked her way up the stairs and to the left wing, I pounced. "Do you remember exactly where Uncle Clive's office is?"

"Uh, about halfway down on the left, I think. Does it matter?"

It'll matter if I get caught looking for it.

Mrs. Shapiro brightened and reached for the blueprints. "Let's see what Mr. Coffey says."

That's when the penny dropped. During my search for Evans's body, I'd learned during his last trip to South Africa, he'd suddenly developed a conscience. After he returned to Evansville, he hired Coffey to build homes for the poor people in Mozembo. He'd even rewritten his Will, cutting Olivia out of it. When Evans explained his change of heart to Olivia, she'd objected to his newfound love of humanity by shooting him through the fickle organ.

Mrs. Shapiro unrolled the blueprints and flipped through a few sheets. "Here." Her finger tapped on a rectangle. "The seventh door down in the left wing."

"Perfect." I rolled the blueprints back up and handed them to her. "Is Mr. Coffey still in Evansville?"

Mrs. Shapiro's eyes filled with tears.

A box of tissue sat in the middle of the table. Instead of one tissue, I handed her the whole box to sop up the waterworks. The way she was going, Mrs. Shapiro was going to be seriously dehydrated.

"It was the saddest thing. First, Mr. Evans disappeared." Sniff. "Now we all know why." Sniff, sniff. "Then Mr. Coffey."

"He disappeared?"

"He went to South Africa to build homes for the people just like Mr. Evans wanted." She dabbed at her eyes. "But he was struck down with Black Water Fever."

"There's medicine for that."

Her thin shoulders sagged. "Not for Mr. Coffey."

"He died?"

Mrs. Shapiro blew her nose. "And was buried in South Africa."

"Before or after he built the homes?"

She wadded up her tissue. "After, I guess."

"Hmm," I said as casually as possible and pulled out my notepad and pen. Coffey dying like that seemed pretty convenient, especially since there was a big bag of Evans's money involved. Probably an interesting story but it would have to wait. Right now, I needed to focus on finding the safe.

"You said Uncle Clive's office was different from the mansion." I jutted my chin toward the blueprints, picturing a room with bars on the windows, a little man in a green visor counting money, and a bank vault. It was a cheery picture.

She looked around and then scooted her chair close.

This may be the good part. I waited.

"Mr. Christopher was giving us the tour," she

murmured, "and he was showing us his office, which he'd just remodeled. He'd had all of Mr. Evans's antiques removed."

Good. That will make the Will easier to find.

"Anyway, Mrs. Christopher came by, and she was in a vile mood. She said Mr. Christopher had some nerve getting rid of her father's things because it was her home. They had a vicious fight. Right in front of us, too." Mrs. Shapiro looked over her shoulder. "I'm sorry to say but your aunt was not a very nice person." She blushed a deep red. "Many people wondered what your uncle ever saw in her."

Her money, of course. "Love is strange, isn't it?" I quipped like I cared anything about that mushy, gushy stuff. Olivia and Uncle Clive had both been evil, horrible people and in many ways, they'd been a match. If nothing else, they'd saved two other people from being miserable.

"Mr. Christopher said Mr. Evans was gone and the mansion was his." Mrs. Shapiro was on a roll. "He said he was tired of the old man's things. He wanted everything modern. Only a worktable, file cabinets, computers and that was it."

I took a leap here. "And a safe."

"Safe?"

"He must've had a safe." The mansion was loaded with antiques. If the safe was one of those Old West types with eighteen combinations that robbers always had to blow up, I was sunk. In Las Vegas, finding dynamite would've been easy but in this dinky town, it'd be impossible. "He was a businessman. He needed a place for his important papers." Like his Will.

She shook her head. "There was only what I told you in the room."

"What about pictures on the wall?" The perfect way to hide a wall safe.

Again, she shook her head. "I'm sorry. Nothing."

"Oh well." I managed to sigh like this was the worst news I'd ever heard instead of the best news yet. From experience, I knew locks on file cabinets were cheesy. No need to even pick them. Just stick a screwdriver in the lock and give it a good whack with a hammer. "You've been really helpful." I put my notepad and pen away and started to stand up. If I hurried, I could get to Sonny's before dinner and tell him.

"You're in for a treat," Mrs. Shapiro beamed and stood up. "You'll love Mr. Christopher's stories."

"Uh." The trouble with not lying all the time was that I was getting rusty. I'd forgotten about my smoke screen. "Great."

Ten minutes later, I was sitting in front of the microfilm machine and surrounded by at least fifty boxes of microfilm. "Why aren't these on a computer?"

Mrs. Shapiro shook her head. "We haven't converted everything yet."

"I'm only interested in the stories Uncle Clive wrote," I said, hoping to get out of this altogether.

"He insisted on writing all the local stories himself."

"Gee, where did he find the time?" I glanced at the wall clock. The second hand had to be stuck. No problem. I'd fiddle around for a bit and then sneak out once her back was turned.

When Mrs. Shapiro plopped down in the chair next to me, I knew I needed to come up with a plan to get me out of here.

She patted the boxes like they were a faithful pet.

"These represent the nineteen years Mr. Christopher owned the newspaper."

"Amazing." It would take me that long to go through them all. I gave her a thin-lipped smile and reached for the first box. Only forty-nine to go.

Evansville was hardly the hubbub of breaking news, but I needed to maintain my cover. I started skimming stories and occasionally saying, "Oh," and "Check this out," and scribbling notes I'd never use. All the stories were boring. A new traffic light was installed on Hamilton. Mr. Patrizi added bacon burgers to the menu at Pat's. Mayor Lee did something to renovate the city. Mayor Lee did another something to renovate the city. After only two boxes, my eyes were beginning to cross. Time to pick up the pace.

"You're going a little fast," Mrs. Shapiro said as the stories whizzed by.

"I'm trying to find the right one." Forget that. I was taking the next story and calling it a day. "The one that shows the kind of man Uncle Clive was."

A photo zipped across of Uncle Clive shaking hands with Slimy. I paused and reversed the machine to get a better look. The date was April 12th, about six weeks after Evans had disappeared and not long after Uncle Clive married Olivia. And her money. Underneath the picture, the caption read:

Attorney Sylvester Mee Hired by Clive Christopher To Oversee Funding of Evans's African Project

---

Well, well, well. The two cons had joined forces again.

Both men were grinning like Cheshire cats and when I zoomed in, I could see why. In Uncle Clive's left hand was a check for two million dollars, made out to African Project. The check was signed by Jonathan Evans and dated February 24th, the date Evans and Coffey had met to discuss building homes for the people in South Africa.

"Architect Frank Coffey," I read the opening out loud, "will leave for South Africa to build homes in the tiny village of Mozembo."

A man in a white shirt, who had to be Coffey, was holding a set of plans. Olivia stood next to him, sour-faced and glaring at Uncle Clive. Her gloves were balled up in her fists like she wanted to deck somebody, and it wasn't hard to guess who or why. She was already seeing her two million bucks flying away.

Mrs. Shapiro sniffed and waved her tissue. "Mr. Evans dreamed of building homes for the poor people in South Africa." She pressed the tissue to her eyes. "Mr. Christopher shared his dream. When I think," she waved the tissue in the air and her voice caught, "how he took it upon himself," sniff, sniff, "to make sure Mr. Evan's money ended up in the right hands."

"What a guy."

"What?"

"What a guy to do that." And keep it for himself. Maybe Uncle Clive couldn't change the words African Project on the check, but he could change who ended up with Evans's money. Or at least two million of it. Back to the homes. "How do you know the homes got built?"

She gave me a gerbil blink.

"You said Mr. Coffey died. Did anyone check to see if the homes were built?"

"Mr. Christopher would've seen to it," she stuttered. "That's the type of man he was."

"That's him."

Uncle Clive would never have let poor people have two cents, let alone two million bucks. It didn't matter that the money was Evans's to begin with. Marrying Evans's spinster daughter had made it his. I drummed my fingers on the library table and thought. Two million dollars was a big bag of money, and a big bag of money would leave a money trail. Putting Slimy in charge of the African Project's money had been an excellent idea.

Sunlight streaked across the table, and I suddenly saw the light. I'd been so focused on Uncle Clive's missing Will that I'd missed the real case. Uncle Clive had put Slimy in charge of the money but where had the money gone? Had Slimy ripped off Uncle Clive? I'd bet my lucky dice that Slimy only wanted Uncle Clive's missing Will because it was somehow linked to Evans's missing money.

"This is perfect." I tapped the screen. "Can I print this out?"

Mrs. Shapiro perked right up. "I'm glad this helped. What are you going to do now?"

"Get to work," I grinned. On *The Case of the Missing Fortune.*

CHAPTER TEN

———

On Sunday morning, Father Flanders took forever to save our souls. When Mass was over, I jumped to my feet, told Gram and Pops I'd be home soon, and bolted down the aisle. Sonny was way ahead of me, and I had to push my way through the people hanging around on the front steps.

"Sonny, wait."

He turned around, and I caught up to him. "There's a new development."

"Let me see it." He looked down at my hands.

"You can't see it. You have to hear it."

"You can't hear a photograph."

I pulled him aside to let other people pass. "What are you talking about?"

Sonny ran both hands through his bushy hair. It bounced back. "What are you talking about?"

"We got a break in the case."

"Why didn't you say so?"

"I did."

He shook his head. "You said there's a new development. That's what you say when you develop a new picture."

I gave up. "When I was at the library, I was looking through some old microfilm and ran across a newspaper story. It was all about Uncle Clive hiring Slimy to oversee Evans's African Project."

"Uh-huh."

"In the picture, Slimy and Uncle Clive are holding a check for two million bucks and grinning like thieves."

"So what?"

"Remember how Evans hired Coffey to build homes in South Africa?"

"Yeah."

C'mon, Sonny, connect the dots. "Coffey was to use the money to build the homes but he," I made air quotes with my fingers, "died."

"Everybody knows that."

"Yeah, but everybody doesn't know what happened to the money. There's no proof that the people of Mozembo ever got their homes."

Sonny shoved his hands into his pockets. "What are you saying?"

"I bet Slimy and Uncle Clive got their mitts on the two million. I bet the two million and Coffey never made it to South Africa." I told Sonny about Slimy and Uncle Clive forging the Will for my great-grandfather's farm. "Uncle Clive put Slimy in charge of the money for the African Project. Making it look legit. South Africa is thousands of miles away. They could've said the homes were built and who could say any different?"

"What really happened to Coffey?"

We thought about that for a minute. We both knew the real Uncle Clive and there was only one answer.

Sonny's eyebrows came together like one long red crayon. "What's this got to do with your uncle's missing Will?"

I don't know. "Since Slimy was Uncle Clive's lawyer, maybe he managed bank accounts and investments for him." Another thought came to me. "The second Will says only what Uncle Clive is giving away."

"So?"

"Doesn't say how much money Uncle Clive had. Maybe the first Will does."

"I don't get it."

I'm betting Slimy did. Get the money that it is. "Maybe Slimy was skimming money from Uncle Clive, and Uncle Clive found out about it."

Sonny frowned. "How are we going to prove it?"

"We'll compare what Uncle Clive had when he made the first Will and what he has now." I nodded like this made perfect sense. "Then maybe we can nail Slimy for ripping him off."

"That's a lot of maybes."

Maybe but my inheritance was definitely at stake. "That has to be why Uncle Clive turned on him. All this has to be about money. Money is the only thing Uncle Clive cared about."

Sonny squinted into the December sun. "What happened to honor amongst thieves?"

"That's only in movies."

"Sorry to interrupt, boys." Gram came up beside me.

"Hi, Mrs. Christopher. You look really nice today."

Gram smiled. "That's kind of you to say."

"When do you want me to come over tonight?" Sonny grinned at me. "I don't want to be late for the memorial service."

"Kiss up." I knew Sonny was asking because he wanted to be invited for dinner.

"I talked to your mother," Gram said, "and invited you to dinner."

"What are we having?'

"Sonny!"

He rubbed his stomach. "I like to mentally prepare myself."

Gram took her gloves out of her purse. "Lamb chops, mashed potatoes and gravy, green beans, and homemade rolls."

Sonny and I both waited for the best part.

"Red velvet cake for dessert." Gram slipped on her gloves. "With homemade whipped cream, of course."

"Gram never serves anything from a can." I smirked at Sonny. "Not like someone I know."

Gram patted my arm. "Hurry along. You still have homework to finish."

"Okay." We waited until she walked away. "We're all set. I found out where Uncle Clive's office is. We'll be in and out."

"I don't know about this."

"C'mon, Sonny." A headache shot between my eyes. "I've got this all figured out." Almost.

He rubbed his stomach again. "Good thing we're eating first. I hear jail food sucks."

I waved goodbye and headed home.

A little before seven o'clock, we parked our bikes in front of Lincoln Mortuary. Underneath my winter jacket, I was all decked out in church clothes, lock picks, a flashlight, a screwdriver, and a hammer. Everything I'd need for a little burglary.

Sonny was traveling light with a small backpack

crammed with camera equipment. He pointed to the crowded parking lot and then to Lincoln Mortuary. "Told you the whole town would turn out for this. I hope I brought enough film."

"It's not every day the town's saint becomes the town's sinner."

The front double doors stood open to welcome guests and lights blazed from all the windows. The most beautiful Christmas tree I'd ever seen, shining bright with bulbs and twinkling lights, stood in the foyer. Classical music was playing. Men in black pants and white shirts were offering food on silver trays to the people already crowded inside.

"Looks like a Christmas party," Sonny said.

"Nothing brings people together like a good scandal." The people of Evansville may have been cheated out of Uncle Clive's trial, but they weren't going to be cheated out of his service.

We pushed our way inside. People touched my arm and told me they were sorry about Poor Clive. "Me, too." Right. The mortuary was stuffy, and I unzipped my jacket, hoping my burglary tools wouldn't fall out. Gram and Pops were nowhere in sight.

Sonny pulled out his camera and started clicking away. "Might as well get started."

A tall, skinny guy with a scraggly beard and jet-black hair came up to us. "Are you here for the deceased?"

We nodded and he handed each of us a thin pamphlet. On the front was a picture of Uncle Clive, maybe twenty years ago and many pounds lighter.

"I'm his nephew."

The guy looked at Sonny.

"I'm not."

He nodded. "Service will begin in fifteen minutes. You

will wish for some quiet time with your loved one before then." He raised a thin white hand and pointed. "Please follow the hallway. He is resting in the last room on the right."

I turned to Sonny and mouthed resting. We both knew Uncle Clive was down for the count.

Sonny held the pamphlet up to me. "Why didn't your grandparents use a recent photo?"

"His mug shot might've spoiled the mood."

The man was still pointing so we threaded our way through the mourners and down the hall, passing rooms called Heavenly Angel, Peaceful Shepherd, and Serene Contemplation. There was still no sign of Gram and Pops and that was good. I could say I'd missed them and for once I wouldn't be lying.

Outside the last room, I stopped and turned back to Sonny. "Did he say the last room?"

"Yeah. Why?"

I showed him the room's name. "Holy Virtue. This is a joke, right?"

Sonny shook his head and put his hand on my shoulder. "Sage, this memorial service isn't about you. Your grandparents are mourning the passing of a loved one and require closure. Try extending yourself and exhibiting a little empathy for them."

"Cut the TV baloney, Benson. Do you even know what empathy means?"

"If you didn't waste all your time doing homework, you could learn a lot from TV."

"At least I'm going to graduate from high school."

"Me, too." Sonny held a little silver thing up to test the light. "The nuns never fail anybody."

"Why not?"

"Because the tuition at Holy Cross costs a fortune." Sonny adjusted something round on his camera and peeked inside the room. "There are a few people here. Do you want me to get their photos now?"

"Yeah."

"While I'm doing all the work," he gave me a little shove toward the casket, "go pay your respects."

I wasn't sure what that meant but I didn't want another lecture from Dr. Sonny. The mahogany casket was closed and covered in yellow roses and white pompom flowers so big they should've come with a cheerleader. I had to admit they made the casket look pretty. I leaned closer to read the simple, brass nameplate: Clive Callen Christopher. In its reflection my freckled face stretched long like in a fun house mirror but that was better than seeing Uncle Clive's face. Three weeks of Catholic school had done its best to teach me the power of forgiveness, but I wasn't there yet. Sure, he'd made me rich, but that would never make up for what he'd done to Gram and Pops.

The mortuary guy must've sent everyone to the viewing room. When I turned around, the room was crammed with shoulder-to-shoulder looky-loos and waiters. Sonny was standing next to the door, holding up his camera. I guessed that meant he'd gotten enough photos. I made my way over.

Sonny slipped his camera into his backpack. "I got close ups of people in the viewing room, pictures of the casket, and about a dozen pictures of people in the foyer."

"Great." I scanned the crowded room one more time. "As soon as Pellam gets here, we'll take off. I'll tell Gram and Pops we looked real hard for them and had to get a seat in the back."

"I don't know." Sonny was slowly shaking his head. "I think we should see them before we go."

"You're trying to get out of this."

"Got that right." Sonny took his camera out of his back-pack again. "Okay. Five more minutes." He gave a little wave, but not at me. A whiff of cherry came my way, and I knew who it belonged to.

"Hi, son."

I turned around. "I told you not to call me that."

Faith grinned. "You did."

"This is Sonny."

"I know. It's my job to know." She shifted a purse the size of carry-on luggage from one skinny shoulder to another. "You and your pal," she jerked a thumb at Sonny, "are now on the job."

"What do you mean?" Something told me I wasn't going to like this.

"Whiny's got the flu, and you need to cover the memorial service." She snagged a stuffed mushroom from a passing tray. Mozzarella cheese dropped onto the carpet. "I need fifteen inches on Clive's life."

"Fifteen inches?"

Faith sighed. "Just write a lot. No doubt it'll be all drivel, and I'll have to rewrite it anyway." She spit her bubblegum into a napkin and began nibbling on the mushroom. "I want to know who came to see him off." She popped the rest of the mushroom into her mouth. "Sonny can take pictures. Is it open casket?"

"No."

Her face fell. "Too bad. Open caskets sell copies."

"That's pretty cold." I tried to look offended, but she was right.

Sonny snorted. "You two are going to make a good team."

Faith tapped the program in my hand. "I told your

grandparents they did a good job putting this together. Suicide is so inconsiderate. Such short notice."

Panic arrowed through me. "They're here?" I looked around for a tiny woman with a big man. "You've seen them?"

"They're in the foyer. Your grandmother is doing the meet and greets, and your grandfather is going over the program with the orchestra. They said they'll see you soon."

"Okay." If they came in now, we'd never get away. "No problem."

Faith pulled her iPad from her purse. "See what you can do to ham this up. Remember, newspapers are in business, and that business is to make money." She gave me a two-finger salute and hurried off.

Sonny suddenly looked happier. "We'll have to stick around."

Not a chance. "Just start snapping pictures like crazy. I'll talk to a few people and later throw in a bunch of words to go with it."

Sonny shifted his backpack. "Jimmy Olsen would never do that."

"That's because he always had Superman to save the day."

"Oh yeah? I'd like to see Superman pull this off."

Me, too. From the doorway, the twins, Malcolm and Robbie, gave me a big wave and that gave me an idea.

"We're in luck," I said and motioned them over. "They're going to save our bacon."

"Are you nuts?" Sonny made a face. "They're crazy."

Exactly.

———————

CHAPTER ELEVEN

"Hey, guys." I grinned at Malcolm and Robbie like I hadn't seen them in a week. "Thanks for coming."

"Our mom made us," Robbie said. "She says lending support to others in their time of sorrow will make us sensitive, caring individuals."

Their mom must watch TV with Sonny's mom.

"I'm here for the free food," admitted Malcolm, holding up a chicken wing. "You gotta try the little pizzas and tiny sandwiches."

Sonny looked around. "What about dessert?"

"Guys, guys," I waved my hand in front of their faces to get their attention. I was losing them, but I wasn't a con man's kid for nothing. "Sonny and I have been given two, big jobs tonight."

"Oh yeah?" Malcolm turned to Robbie. "Want to get something to drink?"

"We're covering the story for the newspaper." Sonny held his camera up.

The twins weren't impressed.

"That's one of the jobs." I dropped my voice. "The other one is really, really important."

Sonny lowered his camera and cut his eyes to me.

"Like what?" asked Robbie.

"Gram and Pops are real upset about Uncle Clive. Gram especially." I drew the twins closer. For all I knew, mortuaries and churches might have the same rules about lying. In case a lightning bolt came my way, I wanted it to hit the twins first. "She's afraid Uncle Clive isn't wearing his St. Christopher's medal."

Sonny's eyes popped behind his glasses.

The twins frowned.

"It's a lucky medal because Christopher is our last name." I scrambled to think of what the nuns had told us about St. Christopher. "He's the patron saint of travelers."

"Well, he's traveling now," laughed Robbie and pointed skyward.

"Ha!" Malcolm laughed. "Down below is more like it."

The twins were having too much fun. I looked to Sonny for help.

Sonny smirked. "You're on your own."

Thanks a bunch. "Since Uncle Clive's going a long way," I stammered, "Gram's worried. If he's not wearing his St. Christopher's medal, he might not get there." I turned sad eyes in the direction of his casket. "Gram wants me to see if he's wearing it."

Robbie's eyebrows shot up. "You're going to look inside the casket? Wow. You get all the fun."

Sonny stepped on my foot. It really hurt but my eyes didn't even tear up. I swear, if it killed me, I was going to learn to cry. "Except we have to interview these people for a story for the newspaper." I managed to choke a little, hoping it sounded like a sob. "We have to do that first," I squeaked out a tearful sound, "but I told Gram we'd let her know before the service starts."

"We could do it." Malcolm looked at Robbie.

Finally. "Gram told me to do it." I chewed hard on my bottom lip. Blood but no tears. "She's counting on me."

"She'd never know," insisted Malcolm.

"What are friends for?" Robbie hung an arm around Malcolm's shoulders.

Identical faces bobbed up and down. Their eyes were four shiny, brown dots. Nothing like the macabre to brighten their day.

I pretended I hadn't heard them, chewed on my lip some more, and gave the casket a really sad look. "What if," I struggled to find the words, "I can't do it?"

"Just lift the lid," said Malcolm.

"Whoa." Sonny started backing up. "Are you insane?"

I grabbed his backpack and pulled him back. "Knock it off," I hissed. He was ruining the moment.

Sonny shook himself free.

I turned back to the twins and tried to remember how I was feeling. Oh yeah. Very sad. "He's probably all gross from hanging himself." I shuddered.

The twins licked their lips.

Robbie stuck his fingers in his eyes and pulled down. "He's going to be all stinking and skin will be rotting off his bones."

Malcolm smacked his hands away. "Hasn't been dead long enough."

I choked back a laugh and hoped it sounded like a sob. "I'll manage to do it. Somehow."

"Forget about this," Sonny warned.

"It'll be hard," I made my lips tremble, "but I promised Gram."

Sonny gripped my arm. "Pellam."

Time's up. I plastered on what could pass for a miserable but brave face. "Thanks for coming guys. We have to start interviewing people." I patted Malcolm on the shoulder and rubbed my forehead like this was more than I could bear. "We'll catch up later."

Sonny did an eye roll.

Halfway to the door, a scream split the air, followed by a soft thump. And a big crash.

"Holy, moly, joly!" Sonny grabbed my jacket and spun me around. "What was that?

The crowd parted. Mrs. Kirkpatrick was flat out on the floor near the casket, covered in yellow roses and white pompoms. Her black, sturdy shoes were tips up.

"Water! She needs water!" someone shouted.

A waiter handed a tray of cookies to a woman and pushed his way to the casket. "Nothing to worry about," he soothed, holding his hands out in front of him. "Just a little excitement, folks." He searched the room for the cause, saw nothing and went back to calming the crowd. "She must've slipped."

Sonny and I made a break for it, but at the door I couldn't resist another look. Next to a vase of pink roses, Robbie and Malcolm gave me thumbs up and then disappeared into the crowd faster than ghosts.

"Mrs. Kirkpatrick's got to be a hundred," gasped Sonny, making the sign of the cross. "What if she croaks?"

"Relax."

"We'd be murderers."

"The twins did it." I grinned. "We're only burglars."

"What's the difference?"

About twenty years in the pen. Maybe life. "Let's go."

Outside, the night was raw and damp. Above us, wispy black clouds inched over the moon like fingers across a milky white face. The wind whistled, and we hustled over to our bikes.

"Why can't we do this in July?" Sonny stamped his feet and pulled his wool cap over his ears. "When it's warm?"

"Because it'll be too late." Memorial services may not be as fun as wakes, but Gram and Pops were Irish. That meant lots of alcohol. I pulled out a small bottle of vodka from my coat pocket. "This will keep you warm."

"Where'd you get that?"

"The bartender. I told him Mrs. Kirkpatrick fainted, and it was a matter of life and death."

"It will be if we get caught."

Sonny was already giving me grief, and we hadn't even left. "Not going to happen. I've got a plan." Sort of.

He grabbed the bottle, twisted off the cap and took a long swig. "Good stuff."

I did the same while I had the chance. When it came to devouring food and knocking back booze, Sonny was no slouch.

We pushed off. Except for the biting headwind threatening to freeze our faces off, everything was going perfect. It'd been a bonus when Mrs. Kirkpatrick fainted, making it easy to slip away in the excitement. The night was quiet and thanks to the whole town seeing Uncle Clive off, the streets were deserted. The only sounds were our bike wheels whooshing through the puddles on the road. Still, time was tight tonight, and I pedaled faster.

When we reached Uncle Clive's driveway, I slowed to a

stop. "This is weird." I said over my shoulder and then pointed to the dark mansion.

Sonny dragged a sneaker until he came to a stop next to me. "What?"

"Pellam always has the outside lights on at night."

"Maybe he forgot."

"He never forgets anything." The clouds parted and, in the moonlight, the mansion looked deserted.

"Maybe he was in a hurry to get to the service."

"That old geezer's never in a hurry for anything."

Sonny looked around. "Maybe we should forget this."

Forget that. Pellam was gone. There was nothing to worry about. "Fifteen minutes." I tried for upbeat. "We'll be in and out in fifteen."

"Uh."

Sonny was about to bail, and I needed to save this. "Fifteen measly minutes. That's it."

Sonny shifted his backpack. "Fifteen isn't very long."

Fifteen years is, if we get caught. "We're wasting time. Let's go."

Sonny didn't budge. "Where should we park?"

Good question. If we parked in front of the mansion, Pellam would see our bikes when he pulled into the driveway. If we parked in the back, Pellam would see our bikes when he pulled into the garage. It was a crapshoot. "By the front steps. C'mon."

Two larger-than-life sphinx statues guarded the twenty-five steps leading up to the mansion's massive front door. We parked our bikes in their shadows.

Sonny chewed on his lip. "Are you sure this is a good idea?"

No. "Absolutely." If Pellam came home early, we'd need a quick getaway.

We trudged up the front steps. On the landing, I unzipped my jacket and got out my lock picks.

Sonny stepped in front of me and reached for the doorknob. "When will you learn?"

I bumped him aside and tried the door. Unlocked.

Sonny grinned. "Gotta love Evansville."

CHAPTER TWELVE

A perfect night was getting better. We slipped inside, and Sonny turned the wall light on. "No!" I shut it off. "Use your flashlight."

"Why? Pellam's at the service."

"Because the cook or the staff might be here." I thumbed my flashlight on low. "I'm not taking any chances."

"Chances?" Sonny stammered. In the dim light, his eyes danced around the foyer and then landed on the front door. "You said no problem."

That's because I wanted your help. "Nothing to it. Let's go."

We made our way to the stairs and headed up. I tried listening for any sound that might tell me someone else was here. Not an easy thing to do with Sonny clomping behind me. "Can you keep it down?"

"I can always leave."

"Sorry." Relax, I told myself. Everything was going great, I told myself, but my heart was banging around in my chest. My hand shook, sending out zigzags of yellow light. At the top of the stairs, I motioned for Sonny to follow me.

The long hallway faded before us into darkness. We crept down, counting doors until we came to Uncle Clive's office. Locked.

"This is it," I whispered and reached inside my jacket for my lock picks.

"Sage."

"Quiet." I put a finger to my lips.

"But."

"Not now." Blood was pounding hard in my ears. Maybe it was better to work solo. I put the flashlight in the crook of my arm and sorted through my lock picks.

"You've got the wrong door."

"No, I don't."

"Yeah, you do."

I looked over my shoulder toward the staircase, but it was too dark to see anything. "This is the seventh door."

"The sixth."

Cripes. "Why didn't you say something when we were counting?"

"You were counting. I was following."

I clocked Sonny on his shoulder with the flashlight. "You're an idiot."

"Ow! Maybe but I can count to seven."

"Stay here."

I retraced my steps. After six doors I found myself at the top of the stairs. I couldn't believe Sonny was right. I turned around and doubled back. When I caught up with him, I kept going. I wasn't apologizing. "Move it."

We got to the seventh door. Locked. Grabbing Sonny's flashlight, I trained the beam on the lock. "Keep it steady." I took out my lock picks again and went to work. In seconds, a soft click made me want to shout.

"That was good." Sonny patted me on the back. "How'd you do that?"

"Easy." Truth was, picking locks on TV was simple. In real life it was time consuming work, and I wasn't that good at it. I got all happy inside. This had to be the best night of my life. Everything was going my way.

I turned the knob slowly, pushed the door open with my finger, and we went inside. Moonlight sifted in from the bare windows, making everything a fuzzy gray.

"It's really dark in here." Sonny turned on the light.

I snapped the light off and rounded on him. "Didn't we just go through this?"

"Nobody's here."

"We," I pointed to him and me, "Are. Breaking. And entering."

"Oh, yeah."

I waved my flashlight through the air to get an idea of the room. Mrs. Shapiro had been right. This room was different. The rest of the mansion was like a museum and crammed with stuff you'd need maids to polish. Uncle Clive's office could've been in a warehouse. His desk was a huge worktable with a computer and two screens. Beige, metal file cabinets lined three walls. A workstation with a copier, paper supplies, and a coffee machine was in one corner. The only personal touch was a sign on the wall that read, "A newspaperman always tells the truth.'"

My happiness rocketed. I'd been worrying for nothing.

"There's a million file cabinets in here."

I sent another beam of light around the room. "More like twenty-six."

"How do you know?"

"I know Uncle Clive." He may've been a murderer, but he'd also been an organized journalist. "One file cabinet for each letter of the alphabet." I went over to the first file cabinet and aimed my flashlight. "See?" A neatly typed label on the top drawer said Aaronson Lighting Company - Agate Land Development. "These are the As."

"What if he had more A files than B files?"

I ignored Sonny and moved over to the second file cabinet. "Here are the Bs."

"What do these names have to do with anything?"

Don't know. "Uncle Clive liked computers. The file cabinets probably hold notes and research about the stories he wrote. Maybe business projects. A wild thought popped into my head, and I returned to the first cabinet. I took out my hammer and screwdriver and was about to haul back and whack the daylights out of the lock. At the last minute, I gave the top drawer a little tug. It slid right out. Tonight was getting better. I trained my light inside. The African Project file greeted me. I'd never believed in luck before, but maybe there was something to it after all. "Look what we have here."

Sonny peered over my shoulder, squinting at the file. It was huge and heavy. "Why didn't he hide it?"

Thirteen years of living with Marty, the champion of two-bit con men, had taught me it was always better to hide stuff in plain sight. Most people overlooked the obvious. He'd also taught me to cover my butt. "We need to take the file." I grabbed for Sonny's backpack.

"No."

I tried one more time. "Give it."

"Unh-unh." Sonny held it high and away. "My camera equipment is inside."

"You have more at home."

Sonny tightened his grip. "No."

"We'll come back for it." Maybe.

"No." Sonny hugged his backpack to his chest.

"It's the only way we can take the file."

"It's been safe here this long," Sonny argued. "What's the big deal?"

The big deal was whether Slimy knew the file was here. Even if he had a copy, he might be waiting for the right time to do a little burglary of his own to destroy the original. If this file proved he and Uncle Clive had pulled a scam and ended up with the two million dollars meant for the poor people, Slimy could wind up giving free legal advice in prison. In the darkness a clock chimed eight. Sonny was still clutching his backpack. He may have the brains of a rabbit, but I'd never convince him to trade his camera equipment for the file. Somehow, I'd have to leave the file and find a way to get back for it. "Help me."

"We're not taking it."

"We're hiding it. Go over to the S cabinet."

"Why?"

"Sonny, just do it. We don't have all night."

I hefted the file and followed behind him. "Open the drawer." Using the beam of my flashlight I found the Scaffington and Scarborough Shopping Mall files. "Make room."

Sonny did, and I slid the file in between them.

"Why did you put it there?"

"The African Project was a scam. Scam comes between Scaffington and Scarborough. In case we can't get back right away, we don't want to forget where we put it."

"There you go with that *we* business again."

"I could ask the twins," I sighed, looked him straight in the face, and went for sincere, "but you're my best friend."

Sonny shook his head, but he placed his backpack at his

feet. "Five minutes and then I'm out of here. This place gives me the creeps."

Five minutes wasn't much but at least he was still with me. I eased the drawer shut and aimed my flashlight beam down the row of cabinets. "We need to get Uncle Clive's Will. Start down there. Shout when you find it."

"How?" He waved his arm around the room. "This is impossible."

Sonny was back to whining, and back to getting on my nerves. "Look for a file with personal information."

"Why can't I start with W for Will?"

I snorted. "Because that would be stupid. A Will is a very important document. Uncle Clive wouldn't put it where anyone can look for it."

"We're looking for it."

Not the same thing. "Just to show you how dumb your idea is, let's look."

We found the drawer marked Waverly Nursing Facility – Witson Bank. Happy to prove him wrong, I yanked it open. Putting my flashlight between my teeth, I finger-walked through the files. The files jumped from Wilk Realty to Wimes Construction Company. No Will of Clive Christopher. "Ha! See what I mean?"

I straightened up, but Sonny was gone. He was in the middle file cabinet and rifling through the first drawer. "Got it."

"Got what?"

Sonny waved me over with his flashlight. "His Will. It's in the Ls."

"What?"

He parted the folders in the drawer with his free hand. "Last Will and Testament of Clive Christopher." Sonny straightened his glasses. "Geez, Sage, you're the investigative journalist. I'm only a photojournalist. You should've thought of looking in the Ls."

"Maybe I did." I snatched the file and slammed the drawer shut, almost taking Sonny's fingers with it.

"Hey!"

"Come over to the table," I was already walking, "and get your camera out."

"We need to turn on the light or the pictures will be too dark."

"Use your flash." And hope it's enough.

Inside the file were several documents. On top was Uncle Clive's Will in eight neatly typed pages. I skimmed through it but there were too many wherefores and whereases for me to understand. I skipped to the end and saw Uncle Clive's signature scrawled across the last page. Underneath the Will were pages stapled together with titles like Bank Accounts, Investments, and Real Property. One said Olivia and that was interesting. I hadn't thought about Olivia having a Will, but she must have. That meant Uncle Clive would've inherited her stuff. Olivia had been rich. Uncle Clive was even richer with her gone. Which meant I was even richer than I'd imagined. This night was on a roll, and my heart beat happily. Of course, Uncle Clive had murdered her so that might be a snag.

"Sage, let's go."

Sonny was getting twitchy, and it was catchy. My guess was we'd been gone about forty-five minutes. I rifled through the Will again, itching to read it, but it was time to go. "Start taking pictures of everything. We'll read them later."

Sonny pointed to the copier. "We could make a copy."

"It'll take too long to warm up and make too much noise."

"Why not just take the Will?"

Sonny and I were still kids with no criminal records, so burglary would be a slap on the wrist. Taking pictures of the Will wasn't a crime but stealing the Will would bump everything up to some serious jail time. Since I didn't want Sonny to cut and run, I decided to leave out the part about ending up in the slammer. "The pictures are insurance."

"For what?"

"In case Slimy gets back here before we do and destroys the Will." I put the papers in front of Sonny and trained my flashlight on the papers. "I'll turn the pages, and you can take the pictures."

Sonny aimed his camera and started snapping away. "That's it," he said after the last one. "C'mon."

"In a minute." I put the file away. "In no time we'll be back at Lincoln Mortuary and scarfing down dessert."

The overhead light blasted on and a deep voice boomed, "Hold it right there. Hands in the air."

Uh-oh.

A cop was leveling his gun right at us. "Now boys."

Sonny's hands flew up so fast, I felt a breeze. "Sage, do something."

"Calm down," I whispered out of the corner of my mouth. This wasn't so bad. The cop had called us boys. He was almost friendly, except for the hunk of gleaming, black metal he was pointing at us. Putting on my best polite kid's face, I decided to kiss up and call him by name. "Officer," I began but quickly shut my mouth when I caught his name tag. If Sonny saw it, this perfect night would be over. I stepped in front of him, hoping to block his view.

Sonny's right hand shot over my shoulder. "See that?"

My hope shot to the floor.

The cop flicked the safety off the gun. "Got something to say, boys?"

"No." I shook my head just in case he was hearing impaired.

"Sage." Sonny's finger rapid tapped my shoulder. "His name is Krypto."

I backed up in case the cop was a good shot.

"Officer Krypto to you." He kept the gun leveled at us.

"It's all right." Sonny stepped around me, a big, goofy grin on his big, goofy face. "I'm a photojournalist, just like Jimmy Olsen."

"Who?"

Sonny barreled on. "Sage is an investigative journalist like Clark Kent. You know, Superman's friend."

The cop kept the gun steady.

"We're on assignment for *The Evansville News*," Sonny said, like this explained everything. He turned to me. "This is like a sign or something."

"A sign you're going to get us arrested." I shuffled a few steps away from him.

The cop turned his flashlight on and shined it in our eyes. "Are you boys high?"

"Krypto," Sonny laughed. "Don't you get it?"

I did but I kept my face blank, praying Sonny would get the hint and shut up. If I ever got out of this, I was going solo.

"Krypto." Sonny started laughing again and looked from the cop to me. "Super Dog."

The cop stared at me, and I rolled my eyes. No way was I a part of this.

"Guys," Sonny pleaded, holding out both hands. "Superman's dog,"

That's when the cop cuffed him.

CHAPTER THIRTEEN

"Superman's dog?" I stepped over a snoring, stinking guy in a trench coat lying face down on the jail floor and collapsed onto the first cot. "You had to bring up Superman's dog?" The mattress felt like it was stuffed with gym socks and smelled worse. I wiggled my shoulders and butt, trying to get comfortable, but it was no use. Just like me to get thrown into a low-budget jail. "Honestly, Sonny. Why did you start with that Krypto dog stuff?"

Sonny put his backpack on the floor, sat down on the edge of my cot, and sniffed, "I thought it was a chance to bond, to build relationships."

I kicked him in the thigh. "Life isn't a TV show, Dr. Sonny. In case you haven't noticed, we're in jail. They're going to call Gram and Pops." I didn't care if they called his parents. For all I cared, he could stay in jail and rot. From here on out, I was on my own. "They'll have to leave Uncle Clive's memorial service to bail me out." I raked my hands over my face, taking a few freckles with me. "I wouldn't blame them if they bounced my sorry hide out for good this time." I sat up and gave his shoulder a hard jab. "This is all your fault."

Sonny dropped his face into his hands and made snuffling sounds. "That's not very Christian talk."

The pillow on the cot was as solid as a ham, and I flung it at his stupid head. "Well, excuse me. I've only been Catholic for three weeks." I fell back onto my elbows and tried to think. Forget that. I snatched the pillow back, stuck it under my head, and closed my eyes.

"This was your dumb idea." Sonny bit his lower lip.

"My dumb idea?" I catapulted myself forward and grabbed his scrawny neck. He was right, so I shook him hard.

Sonny slapped at my hands, but I held fast, squeezing my thumbs into his windpipe. Sonny was making gurgling noises and turning as red as his hair, so I shook harder. He palmed my face, and I bit his hand.

"Yeow!" Sonny shook his hand in the air. "My hands are delicate instruments."

"Oh right. I forgot. You're Jimmy Olsen, hotshot photojournalist."

"You thought so when you needed me and my camera to help you tonight."

"Yeah? Thanks to your big, fat mouth, I now have a criminal record." I lunged for him again. Sonny put his hands up to his face, so I smacked him up the side of the head instead.

"Hey!" Sonny scooted back on the cot. "Thanks to you, I'll probably get kicked out of Journalism Club."

"You can start one in prison."

"Prison!" Sonny yelped. "You didn't say anything about prison when you asked me to help."

Because you would've turned me down flat.

Sonny pulled his backpack onto to his lap and busied himself arranging camera equipment on the mattress. And sniffling.

I needed a plan and quick, but Sonny's drippy nose made it hard to think. "Stop sniveling." I bounced a foot on the mattress and the camera lenses slid into a heap. That made me feel better. "Why didn't they take your backpack away when they booked you?"

Sonny blew his nose on the hem of his shirt. "Maybe they thought the strip search was enough punishment."

A fart blasted from the drunk on the floor, and I covered my nose with my arm. The guy flapped his trench coat, bounced his buns up and down a couple of times and in seconds, went back to snoring.

"Holy, moly, joly," Sonny gasped.

Enough was enough. I rolled over onto my side and stared at the puke-green, cinderblock wall. There had to be a way out of here.

"Sage."

"Do me a favor. Get your stuff and take it over to the other cot."

"Sage."

"Shut up."

"You've got company," a male voice announced.

Great. I'd been hoping to get a couple of hours of sleep and a decent breakfast before Gram and Pops threw me out onto the streets but maybe it was better this way. I swung my legs over the edge of the cot just as an officer unlocked the cell.

He slid the door back and pointed to us. "All yours."

A whiff of tutti-frutti came my way, followed by Faith planting herself in the cell opening, hands on her hips. "When I told you to do fifteen, I meant fifteen inches of newspaper story. Not fifteen years." She hefted her shoulder bag and stepped closer to the drunk sprawled on the floor.

"Shut up." I should've been embarrassed about being in jail. But since I didn't like Faith, it didn't matter.

Sonny sighed. "For an investigative journalist, you have a small vocabulary."

I scowled at Sonny, and he backed off. "How'd you know we were here?"

"Didn't." Faith nudged the drunk on the floor with the toe of her Doc Martens. "Wake up. Party's over."

The man rolled over and blinked. "Mom?"

She gave him another kick. "Mom never posts bail for you. Get up, Whiny."

Whiny looked about as bad as a guy could look and still be alive.

"He's your brother?" It didn't seem possible.

Faith pointed at me. "You're quick. Have you ever thought of going into journalism?"

Sonny said, "You told us Whiny had the flu."

"I lied." Faith rolled her eyes. "He gets stinking drunk every weekend, and every weekend I bail him out."

"You're just enabling him to do bad," warned Sonny.

"Enough Sonny," I shouted, whirling around. "Lay off the TV psychobabble."

"Sonny's right," Faith blew a bubble and popped it, "but my mother would kill me if I didn't." She sighed and opened her purse. "Might as well spring you too."

"Thanks." Sonny pumped his fist in the air. "I'll get my stuff."

"Thank Sage. Bail is coming out of his inheritance."

"Good thing I'm rich," I grumbled. Something was wrong here. "Where are Gram and Pops?"

Faith stopped rooting around. "At the front desk with Sonny's parents, filling out paperwork. You're both getting arraigned at nine o'clock tomorrow."

Sonny grinned. "No school. Perfect."

"Perfect," I mimicked. My perfect night had gone in the dumper. "Only you would think that's perfect."

Faith was back in her purse and fishing around. "There's just enough time to get this in for the morning edition." She came up with her iPad. "Why did you and Sonny break into the mansion tonight?"

My heart sank and my Irish went up. "You can't write about this." I didn't care, but Gram and Pops had to live in this town. "Have a heart."

"Have to sell newspapers." She waited, her fingers resting on the iPad.

Sonny, who'd never volunteered once in class, charged over with his backpack and suddenly became the star pupil. "It was all Sage's dumb plan."

"Shut up." This was becoming my mantra.

Sonny ignored me and poured everything out from start to finish, Faith tapping like crazy on the keyboard. When he finally wound down, she looked up. "Sonny's right. That's a dumb plan."

My plan was a lot dumber when said out loud, I could see that now. I could also see the headlines, ***Evansville Newest Millionaire Arrested for Burglary***. It was a good story and would sell a ton of papers, but when the story hit, Slimy would know twenty years of scamming was about to blow up in his face. The idea of him rotting in jail for the rest of his miserable life had real appeal. But I was pretty sure he'd end mine before he'd let that happen.

"You can't print this story."

"I'm the boss," she grinned, "and I can."

"I can change that." Faith was a head shorter than me and too skinny to cast a shadow. Grabbing her bony shoulders, I tossed her onto the cot and covered her face with the stinking pillow. Snuffing her lights out would be easy. My only witnesses were Sonny and Whiny. I could take them both.

"No!" Sonny hauled me back. "Wait until she bails us out first."

"Oh, yeah." I lifted her off the cot by her jacket and put her on her feet. "There." I said, smoothing out her collar. I held out her iPad. "You're fine."

She clobbered me with her purse. "You're nuts."

More like desperate. Except for the fact she was going to ruin everything, I had to admit I liked the way she latched onto a story. The only way to save my skin and solve this case was to give her something better. "Right now, you only have a story." I gave her a look like I felt sorry for her intelligence. "People will forget it by tomorrow."

"Small towns forget nothing." Faith grabbed her iPad and waved it in my face. "This is a headliner. I could milk it for days."

I'd always dreamed of having my first headliner, but it was pretty depressing to think it'd be about my own arrest. Well, they're always saying to write about what you know.

"Chump change," I declared and pulled Sonny closer. "We've uncovered a huge story."

Sonny tried to wiggle free. "We?"

I tightened my grip. "Maybe even a Pulitzer. Right, Jimmy?"

Faith frowned. "I thought your name was Sonny."

"Jimmy Olsen was Superman's friend," said Sonny. "Huh?"

"I'll explain later." I raised both hands like I was trying

to stop traffic. "Back to the story. We're talking scams, crimes, intrigue. We're calling it *The Case of the Missing Fortune.*"

Faith remained stone-faced.

No one was around but I leaned in and lowered my voice. "This story will sell newspapers."

"Sell newspapers?"

I finally had her attention.

Faith snapped her iPad shut. "Start talking."

"Slimy and Uncle Clive's felonious partnership started years ago," I began in my best, dramatic voice, "when they forged my great-grandfather's Will and swindled Pops out of his rightful inheritance, the family farm."

"Your grandmother mentioned that at Slimy's. Can you prove it?"

No. "Absolutely." I imagined what came next and thought it could pass for the truth. "Not long after that, Slimy and Uncle Clive saw their chance to join forces again when they learned Evans was going to build homes for poor people in South Africa."

Faith gave me a hurry up hand gesture. "Why?"

"Because two million dollars was involved." I told her about the newspaper article and the check. "The snag was they could only get their hands on the money if they got rid of Coffey."

Faith was coming around. "A story is only a story unless you have proof."

"We've got proof," said Sonny.

"Really?" She slanted her eyes at me.

"Really." Maybe. "We can prove Coffey and the money never made it to South Africa. When Coffey died, everyone just assumed the homes had been built but no one ever checked."

"Coffey's not dead?"

"He's dead," Sonny laughed. "Just not dead in South Africa."

"Without a body, you have no proof."

Faith was like a one trick pony. "We do have proof," I argued. "We found the file when we were, uh, at Uncle Clive's."

"You mean when you broke in."

I shrugged. "Found. Broke in. Just a technicality."

"Technicality is not synonymous with triviality," Faith corrected.

"What's the difference?" asked Sonny.

Faith smirked. "Two years in the pen."

Sonny teared up. "I'll never be a famous photojournalist."

Faith eyed Sonny's backpack. "Do you have the file?"

"We hid it in Uncle Clive's office." I began to flounder around, my arms waving in the air. "I need a little more time. If you write the story now," I screwed up my face and tried to look like the world could fall apart, "Slimy will cover his tracks. We'll never find out what happened to the money."

Faith stared at me.

"The story will be lost forever. Like the Pulitzer." I went for her weak spot, "Worse yet, some other newspaper will write the story."

"How much time do you need?"

Now we're getting somewhere. "How soon can you spring us?"

Faith jammed her iPad into her purse. "Come on." She grabbed the back of Whiny's trench coat and helped him to his feet. "Do you have everything?"

Whiny's eyes looked like bloody eggs, but he squinted

and gave the cell a slow look. "Yup." He swayed a bit and yawned. "Can we get breakfast?"

"Pull yourself together," Faith ordered. "You're a mess."

"You're bossy."

We watched for several long seconds while his pudgy fingers tried pushing one button at a time into a buttonhole before giving up and going on to the next one. When he'd tried all without any luck, he wrapped the coat around him and then fumbled with the belt, trying to get the fabric through the buckle. No luck there, either. Tying both ends of the belt together, he patted his stomach and burped. "Ready."

Sonny bolted out of the cell. Faith linked one arm through Whiny's, and they shuffled ahead of me. I wasn't in a rush to meet Gram and Pops and took my time walking down the hall to the reception area. Shoving my hands into my pockets, I walked on knowing there wasn't anything I could do about anything. I had no proof Uncle Clive had stolen the money and even if I had, so what? Thanks to Sonny's big, fat mouth, I was going to get kicked out of the only decent home I'd ever known. Rats. I'd been this close to getting a Christmas tree. Maybe even seeing snow fall. This made me so lightheaded I had to stop and lean against the wall. Ever since I'd gotten here, all I'd done was screw up. That bothered me but what bothered me more was knowing I was just like Uncle Clive. The only thing I cared about was money.

Faith stopped and turned around. "Are you okay? You look like you've seen a ghost."

I opened one eye, checked the hall for Uncle Clive, and then snapped my eye shut. Nope. He was still dead.

"I'm fine." I shoved away from the wall and walked on. "Let's get this over with."

When I swung the door open to the reception room, the sight of Gram and Pops hit me hard. They were the only normal people in a family of losers. Marty had been a second-rate con man and Uncle Clive had been a scumbag murderer. I was nothing but a money-grubbing kid. Pathetic as that was, I brushed off the thought. Maybe in the grand scheme of things, I wasn't so bad. I managed to smile at my grandparents.

"Sage." Gram rushed toward me with her arms outstretched.

Pops was right behind her. Soon I felt Pops' big arms wrap around both of us. This would be the last time I'd ever see them.

"Sage." Pops' voice was low, and he slowly pushed me away from him.

Here it comes, I thought, plastering on a blank face, and looking straight ahead like I could care less. I shifted my weight. Just hurry up and get it over with.

"Sage," Pops repeated, "what were you thinking?"

I asked myself that all the time but was still waiting for an answer.

"What Jack means," Gram said, "if you wanted to go to Uncle Clive's, why didn't you just ask?"

CHAPTER FOURTEEN

After getting arrested, I should've had a lousy night. I should've tossed and turned and beaten myself up for being so stupid. Gram had been right. Since they now owned Uncle Clive's mansion, I should've just come up with some stupid excuse to go to the stupid mansion instead of coming up with a stupid plan that ended up getting my stupid hide thrown into a stupid jail.

And now I had a criminal record. Stupid, stupid, stupid.

Long ago, Marty had taught me guilt was a wasted emotion. So, I decided there was no sense in crying over something that was a done deal. Sure, I was in trouble but now all I had to do was come up with a plan. And I would. After breakfast.

"Sage," Gram called. "Breakfast in ten minutes."

Wonderful words. "Be right there." I threw off the covers and felt a huge grin take over my face. There was nothing so wrong in this world that Gram's breakfast could not make right. After splashing some water on my face and brushing my teeth, I hustled off to the dining room.

Sliding into my chair, I tried to guess what was coming.

Bacon, eggs, and pancakes or waffles? Didn't matter, I liked both.

"Good morning." Gram came into the dining room with a basket of blueberry cinnamon streusel muffins and a pitcher of orange juice. "Help yourself."

The muffins were my favorite and normally I could put away four or five. "Uh." I looked over to the sideboard for the rest of my breakfast. Nothing.

Gram put the muffins down, poured my orange juice, and handed me my napkin. "We've eaten."

My stomach rumbled, and I gave the sideboard one more try. The food fairies hadn't appeared.

"Jack will meet us at the courthouse. He had to go by the plant to tell them he needed time off."

Because I messed up.

She wiped her hands on her apron. "Be back with your breakfast."

"Okay." I smiled like I wasn't responsible for anything.

Gram started to go but turned back and put her hand on my shoulder. "We're glad you're all right."

A twinge of something that might have been guilt tore through me. Watching her walk away, I wondered for the millionth time about Gram and Pops and why they put up with me. They weren't normal.

Halfway through my third muffin, Gram came back with a mushroom and cheese omelet and a plate of waffles smothered in homemade whipped cream and sliced strawberries. I sat up straighter to see if chopped walnuts were sprinkled on top. Yup.

She checked the table. "I'll get the syrup."

I didn't wait for Gram but dug into the omelet. Gooey, white cheese and sautéed mushrooms oozed onto my plate. In Las Vegas, I'd only had American cheese slices wrapped in plastic. I shoveled in a mouthful and warm strings of cheese slid down my chin. A couple swipes with my tongue, and it was gone. Brie, my favorite.

Gram came back with the syrup and took her place across from me. She poured herself some orange juice and waited. I didn't. I cut a large bite of waffle, smeared it with whipped cream and strawberries, and stuffed it into my mouth. Chewing happily, I reached for the syrup. Sooner or later, she'd bring up the arraignment.

"Sonny and his parents are meeting us at the courthouse."

"Uh-huh." Okay so that explained why Sonny wasn't mooching breakfast from us this morning. "Does this mean I have to dress up?"

Gram blinked and put her coffee cup down with a clatter. Apparently out of all the questions I could ask, that wasn't one of them. "Wear what you would wear to church."

I didn't think that included a tie but didn't ask in case Gram thought it did. "Okay."

Gram cleared her throat. "We called several lawyers this morning, but everyone refused to represent you. No one, it seems," she picked up her coffee cup but paused halfway, "wants to risk his career."

I looked at the perfectly golden omelet on my plate and my stomach churned. I must really be in deep trouble if a lawyer would turn down money. If there was ever a time when I needed my strength, it was now. I attacked my food like it was my last meal. Through a big mouthful, I asked, "I'm innocent until proven guilty, right?"

Gram paled.

I went back to the waffle, sawing off a big bite. "I'll be fine," I mumbled.

For the next few minutes, Gram tried making small talk, and I tried avoiding it, hoping she'd get the hint. She didn't and by the time I finished my last bite, I still hadn't a clue how I was going to fix anything. I tossed my napkin onto the table. If worse came to worse, I'd hotwire a car from the courthouse parking lot and make a break for it.

"Go get ready." Gram reached for my plate. "I'll take care of the dishes. We're leaving in half an hour."

Terrific. Now she was doing my job. The whole guilt thing bubbled up again. I knew I should say I was sorry for everything, but the words stuck in my throat. Instead, I pushed back my chair and shrugged. "Okay."

The ancient, two-story brick courthouse hadn't changed since Uncle Clive's murder trial. It still had a million steps leading up to its front door. My calves burned as I trailed behind Gram who had no problem with the climb, and she was in high heels. No doubt the steps gave the criminals plenty of time to think about where they'd screwed up.

On the six o'clock news, it was always the same. The bad guys hung their heads before the judges, moaned how sorry they were for what they did, and threw themselves on the mercy of the court. That wasn't going to be me I decided as I puffed behind Gram. I wasn't sorry for what I did. I was only sorry I'd gotten caught.

We stopped to ask for directions from a bailiff with enough muscles to bust through titanium. He gave me a hard look like I'd never see sunshine again and pointed down the hall to Room 107. In the crowd of people waiting outside, Sonny was easy to spot because his hair always looked like it was on fire. Mrs. Benson frowned when she saw me and maybe I couldn't blame her. Since I'd arrived in Evansville, I'd gotten Sonny involved in murder and now arrested. Still all this was really good training for when he became a photojournalist. I waved at both of them but only Sonny waved back.

A very tall female bailiff opened the double doors wide. "Good morning." She gestured everyone inside. "Sit down. No talking. The clerk will call your case at nine o'clock sharp."

"Hey, guys." Whiny shouldered past us and stopped in front of the bailiff. "Morning, Esmeralda. You're looking good."

"I see your sister posted bail again."

"When are you going to go out with me?"

She stared down at him. "You're always in jail Saturday night."

"There's six other nights."

"I carry a gun, remember?"

Whiny smiled. "That's what I like."

She glared at him but let him pass.

People filed in looking guilty and bewildered. Mrs. Benson steered Sonny to a row near the front. I started after them, but Gram shook her head. We slipped into the row behind them.

"Where's Pops?" I whispered to Gram.

"He'll be here."

A pretty woman in a navy suit sat on one side of a long, scarred oak table, working on the stack of files in front of her. Opening a file, she scanned its contents and made a note before tossing it aside and going onto the next. At the other end of the table, a guy who looked like he could have his own TV show swiveled in his chair. He also had a huge stack of folders, but they sat neatly in front of him. He tried to talk to the woman, but she waved him off, never looking up from her files.

The judge's bench was empty but an older woman with

white hair and wearing a baggy, beige dress sat in the attached clerk's corral. She was muttering over a list in front of her. Pencils stuck out at odd angles from her frizzy hair. The harsh, fluorescent lights gave her a peculiar green tinge, making her look kind of like the Statue of Liberty. She stopped muttering, checked her work, looked satisfied, and after putting the paper in a stack, put another pencil in her white hair. A second later she frowned, looked at the stack, and moved the piece of paper to another stack. This seemed to be the rule here. Everyone had to have a stack of something.

The courtroom clock on the wall moved from nine o'clock to nine fifteen, to nine-thirty. By nine fifty-five, the crowd had grown restless and was shuffling its feet and ignoring the no talking rule. Ringing came from the woman's desk, and everyone craned their necks to see. She pushed some papers aside, found the telephone, and after a few words, gave a nod to the bailiff.

The bailiff rose, hitched up her gun belt, and announced, "All rise for the Honorable Neal Hampton. Court is in session."

"Oh no," Gram moaned.

"What," I mouthed.

"Before he became a judge, Neal Hampton represented the Evans' family for years."

As in Olivia Evans. Who had been married to Uncle Clive. Who Uncle Clive had murdered. For her money.

This morning was off to a bad start.

The wooden floor shook as a man with silver hair and a long, black robe pounded his way to the bench. He frowned at the wall clock, dropped himself into his seat, fixed wire rimmed glasses on a beaky nose, and rapped his gavel once.

"You may be seated," said the bailiff.

"Counselors," the judge began. "Are you ready to proceed?"

"Your Honor." The man got to his feet and flashed a smile as dazzling as his white shirt. "Alec Malone, District Attorney."

The woman rose. "Good morning. Cassandra Hampton for the Public Defender's Office."

Wait a second. "Hampton," I whispered to Gram.

Behind me, Whiny drilled a finger into my shoulder. "The judge's daughter. You're dead."

Gram explained, "The judge and his daughter had a falling out years ago."

I slumped back against the hard bench. Could this get any worse?

The judge turned to the clerk. "Mrs. Lovato, let's get started."

When Mrs. Lovato barked out the case name, a defendant came forward, hung his head before the judge, and stumbled through a sad tale of woe. None of the cases were a big deal. Mostly disturbing the peace, a couple of petty thefts, and one guy who thought he could get out of a drunk driving ticket.

"But Your Honor, I didn't cause no trouble." He ran a hand through his hair. "The cop is just rousting me for no reason." He stood taller, straightened his jacket, and spread his hands out in front of him. "I wasn't even speeding."

Whack! Judge Hampton banged the gavel down on the desk. "You were drunk and driving on the sidewalk."

"Yeah," he looked around the courtroom for support, "but I didn't hit no parking meters."

The crowd roared but the judge didn't. The guy got a hefty fine, his license suspended, and the fun of wearing an orange jumpsuit in the county jail for the next ninety days.

"But Judge," he pleaded.

"Bailiff," Judge Hampton ordered, "remove this man."

"Aloysius Benson and Sage Christopher," Mrs. Lovato called.

Sonny's real name always cracked me up but today wasn't the day for it. Mrs. Benson and Gram got to their feet and the four of us approached the bench.

"Do you have a lawyer?" Judge Hampton asked.

"No," Gram and Mrs. Benson said together.

Judge Hampton sighed. "Which one of you is Sage?"

"He is." Sonny piped up. "This was all his idea."

"Shut up," I whispered.

Miss Hampton agreed. "That's good advice."

The judge read some papers and looked up. "I understand you're the nephew of Clive Christopher."

"The owner of the property," Miss Hampton added.

"Miss Hampton, the Court is aware of the obvious." Judge Hampton removed his glasses. "The Public Defender's Office is hereby appointed as counsel for the defendants."

Miss Hampton sorted out two files from the sloppy pile on the table and reviewed them briefly. "I'll need to confer with my clients regarding a plea."

"Don't know why," the judge grumbled. "You always plead not guilty."

She grumbled back, "Don't know why you're always in a hurry to set a trial date."

"Now, Cassie."

She stiffened. "Miss Hampton."

Crack! Crack! The judge aimed the gavel at her.

"There's the matter of bail." Miss Hampton reached for a pen.

Alec Malone cleared his throat. "Your Honor, burglary

is a serious offense and the District Attorney's office is strongly opposed to bail. Sage Christopher is the son of a con man, has few ties to this community, and has recently come into a large amount of money. Obviously," he nodded to me, "that adds up to a flight risk."

"But--" I spoke up.

Crack! The judge sounded his gavel. "Quiet, young man."

Mr. Malone wasn't done. "Your Honor, Sage was caught by Officer Huckleberry last Friday night fleeing Evansville in a stolen car."

Okay, so he had me there. "Your Honor, I can explain."

"Be quiet," the judge warned again, "or I'll find you in contempt of court."

The District Attorney wouldn't let it go. "It is our recommendation that the defendants be held until their trial date. If," he turned to the Public Defender, "there is so much concern for their wellbeing, you can agree to waive time and proceed to trial immediately."

Miss Hampton remembered why she was here. "The defendants are thirteen-year-old boys. Sage lives with his grandparents, Jack and Frances Christopher, longtime residents of Evansville. Aloyisus Benson has lived in Evansville with his parents all his life. There's no reason to deny bail."

Panic was all over Sonny and he grabbed my arm. "Can they really send us back to jail?"

"We're kids." I forced a laugh and peeled off his fingers. The only exit was behind us, but I could be fast when my life depended on it. Sonny was on his own.

CHAPTER FIFTEEN

The courtroom doors opened behind us. Pops strode down the aisle, followed by a tall, skinny guy who looked vaguely familiar. "Judge Hampton, sorry we're late."

"The Court recognizes Jack Christopher."

"I have hired an attorney for the boys."

Mr. Malone and Miss Hampton jumped up, for once in agreement. "Your Honor!"

Crack! The judge's gavel bounced out of his hand.

The skinny guy hustled forward and put a shiny new briefcase on the table. "Your Honor, A. B. Lincoln for the defense. May I have a few minutes with my clients?"

Hope surged through me. My lawyer was Abe Lincoln! He had to be the great, great, maybe even great, great, great grandson of the great man and looked like he'd just stepped out of a history book. His black beard was uneven and sparse over a craggy face, and his black suit hung on him like it was still on a coat hanger. Bony wrists dangled from white shirt cuffs, and his shirt collar was two sizes too big. The only thing missing was the stovepipe hat but there was probably a rule about wearing one in court.

"What are you doing here?" The judge scowled.

"Uh," he swallowed hard, his Adam's apple bobbing up and down like an elevator.

My hope dipped a bit at the judge's harsh words but popped back up. Judge Hampton was probably afraid of our lawyer, since he was such a great man.

Judge Hampton banged his gavel. "You got ten minutes. Take it out in the hall."

"Thank you, Your Honor."

The judge turned to his clerk. "Seems anybody and his dog can get a license to practice law nowadays."

That didn't sound like fear talking, but Mrs. Lovato called another case, and we followed Pops and the lawyer down the aisle. Gram and Mrs. Benson fell in behind us.

"Sage! Over here."

A flash from Whiny's camera caught me between the eyes. "Gotcha," he grinned through the light show.

"I'm firing you tomorrow."

Whiny laughed. "You'll be in jail."

Out in the hall, we gathered around a small table, and Pops pulled out chairs for Gram and Mrs. Benson.

"You're Abe Lincoln?" I asked.

"A.B. Lincoln," Gram, Pops, Mrs. Benson, and Sonny chorused.

The lawyer handed me his card. "Aaron Benjamin Lincoln."

Above his name was a picture of a brick building and rolling green lawns.

"Lincoln Mortuary," Sonny added. "The guy handing out brochures last night."

"The undertaker?"

"My parents own the mortuary." A.B. flipped the card over to show his name and the scales of justice.

"You moonlight as a lawyer?" My head was spinning.

He cleared his throat. "I'm building my practice."

"Mr. Lincoln is," Pops paused, "new to the legal profession."

Up close, A.B Lincoln looked about ten years older than me. "How new?"

Red shot up Lincoln's neck. "About eighteen days."

I turned to Mrs. Benson. "Get up."

She did, and I collapsed into her chair, dropped my head into my hands, and stuck my fingers in my eyes. This couldn't be my life.

"Sage," Gram put her hand on my shoulder, "all the other lawyers turned us down."

"Okay," I sighed, looking up. The good news was we had a lawyer. Someone to fight for us. He had to have an ace up his sleeve. "What can you do?"

Mr. Lincoln pulled a file out of his briefcase and opened it. "I've read the police report."

This was a good start. "And?"

"You're guilty."

"Don't I keep telling you Sage is nothing but trouble?" Mrs. Benson griped at Sonny.

"Mindy," Gram snapped. "You're not helping."

Pops held both hands up. "Let's hear what he has to say."

"That," Mr. Lincoln's voice wavered, "is what I have to say. They were caught at the scene." He closed the file. "Guilty."

Gram, Pops, and Mrs. Benson started talking at once.

"Sonny," I groaned. "This guy's a joke."

"The joke's going to be on us, if we get convicted."

Good point. "Not if I can help it."

Sonny sent a look my way. "You got a plan?"

This is the moment where the lawyer pulls a rabbit out of a hat. Trouble was, I wasn't a lawyer, didn't have a rabbit, and thanks to Abe who was really A.B., I didn't even have a hat. I gave Sonny's arm a friendly punch. "Don't I always?"

Sonny's eyes got watery. "Your last plan landed us in jail. Your uncle killed your aunt in the one before that."

"That one wasn't my fault." Not exactly.

"I'll never graduate from high school."

Sonny didn't look all that sad about that. "You hate school."

"It's gotta be better than jail."

True.

The bailiff opened the door and motioned us forward. "Time's up."

We trooped back into the courtroom and Pops, Gram, and Mrs. Benson slid into the first row. Mr. Lincoln, Sonny, and I went to the counsel table and stood between the lawyers.

"Well?" asked the judge.

"We're pleading guilty," said Mr. Lincoln.

Mrs. Benson cried out from the front row.

"No, we're not," I argued.

Sonny grabbed my arm. "We're not?"

Judge Hampton hunched forward in his black robes, looking like a very large, very bad-tempered raven. "You were arrested at the scene."

"We're innocent," I boasted.

"Your Honor," Alec Malone interrupted, "this is a classic example of guilty defendants wasting the court's time."

"I can prove it." My words trailed off just in case I couldn't.

"Mr. Lincoln, control your clients," warned Judge Hampton.

"Yes, Your Honor."

"Judge," I continued, "you don't have all the facts."

"That's what they all say." His fingers drummed the bench.

Marty had taught me all cons were better when they ran closer to the truth. I was hoping the truth would set me free.

Judge Hampton made a rolling gesture with his hand. "Let's hear it."

"Sonny and I were at Uncle Clive's mansion."

Sonny gaped at me. "Your plan is to tell the truth for once?"

I hung my head and scrambled for something to get me out of this. "My uncle died last Friday." I decided to leave out the part about him committing suicide. Why let a few facts get in the way of a good story? Instead, I chewed on my lower lip but, as usual, no tears came. "Tomorrow is his funeral."

"The Court is aware."

Part of me hated me for what I was about to do but a bigger part of me would hate jail more. I took a deep, shaky breath. Wetting my lips, I stole a look at Pops. He was staring at me, and I hoped he wouldn't see through me. "I went to Uncle Clive's office to find some of his newspaper stories."

The idea that his stories would be at his home office and not at the newspaper sounded lame even to me. The judge wasn't rapping his beloved gavel, so I rushed on.

"I was going to use them to say a few words at his funeral." I let my shoulders slump and traced the wood grain on the table with my fingers. When I'd milked that as long as I dared, I looked at Pops again. "I wanted it to be a surprise." I choked a little, hoping I sounded like I could fall apart any second. "You said it was going to be hard for you to give his eulogy." My finger was back to tracing the grain. "I wanted to help."

Pops reached into his pocket for a handkerchief. "You're such a good boy."

Sonny rolled his eyes. I wanted to belt him.

"We've been patient," the District Attorney argued. "Where's the defendant going with this?"

I gave Judge Hampton a trembling smile. "In his Will, my uncle left my family everything." I rubbed my dry eyes with the back of my hand. If they couldn't be wet, at least they'd be red.

"This is all very interesting but not relevant," Mr. Malone cut in. "As the Court knows, burglary is the intentional breaking and entering the dwelling of another with the intent to commit a crime therein. The defendants were arrested at the scene. Case closed, Your Honor."

That was a lot of gobbly gook but lucky for me, I was good at gobbly gook. "Mr. Malone's right."

Sonny rounded on me. "If this is your plan, it sucks."

I squared my shoulders and tried to remember the District Attorney's exact words. "Mr. Malone says burglary is breaking and entering."

Judge Hampton cocked his head to the side. "What's your point?"

To get out of this. "We didn't break in."

"You were arrested at the scene."

The judge was having a hard time with gobbly gook, so I explained. "Uncle Clive's mansion isn't the dwelling of another because now it belongs to my grandparents and me." I frowned hoping I wouldn't come off cocky. "There's no breaking and entering. No burglary." I paused and then couldn't help myself, "Case closed."

Judge Hampton folded the stems of his glasses together and tossed them aside. He studied me for way too long before reaching for his gavel. "I trust the District Attorney's office has learned a valuable lesson today." He rapped once but with none of his usual enthusiasm. "Case dismissed."

Sonny shook my arm. "What happened?"

"We won."

"How?"

"Sonny, Sonny, Sonny," I said patiently, like I did this every day. "I *told* you I had a plan."

"Does this mean I'll graduate high school?"

Only if I do your homework. "Yeah."

A.B. Lincoln picked up his briefcase. We followed him down the aisle and this time it was a much happier trip. Pops was hugging Gram and for once, Mrs. Benson looked like she didn't want to kill me. We pushed open the heavy, wooden doors and A.B said goodbye. I promised insincerely to keep in touch.

Flash photography blasted us. There were easily two-dozen photographers and reporters outside, arms and voices raised, all wanting attention.

"Over here."

"Look this way."

I was totally amazed that news of my legal debut had traveled so quickly. If I did say so myself, winning my case was an incredible victory and I couldn't wait to see my story in my own newspaper. Questions from reporters were flying in from all over the place, no doubt wanting to know how I came up with a brilliant strategy when my lawyer couldn't. I put a humble smile on my face, happy for my first interview.

A photographer bumped into me. "Sorry." Then he rushed past, disappearing into the crowd.

"Hey," Sonny yelped when another photographer muscled his way forward, his camera high above his head, taking photos of anything.

It took me a second to realize that none of this was for me. I rose up on tiptoes to see Police Chief Murphy was center stage. I worked my way closer through the press.

"Attorney Sylvester Mee was found dead today at 8:07 a.m.," he announced.

"Did you hear that?" Sonny gasped. "Slimy's dead."

"Quiet."

"What happened?" a man in a brown suit asked.

Police Chief Murphy hesitated. "We're waiting for the coroner's report."

A pretty reporter waved her iPad in the air. "Who found the body?"

"Mrs. Steffens, his housekeeper."

"Geez, Sage." Faith appeared out of nowhere and gave me a punch to the shoulder that knocked me forward. "Ever thought of working for a newspaper?"

"Uh?"

"Chief," her hand went up, "do you have time of death?"

"We're waiting on the coroner's report."

Faith pushed. "You must have some idea."

He shifted his weight. "Mr. Mee had an appointment around eleven o'clock last night, so sometime after that."

Faith was right. It was time to get my career in gear and grab my first byline. "Who'd he meet last night?"

"No comment."

"No comment means you know who it was," I argued, "or you wouldn't know he met with anyone."

The other reporters agreed, voices shouting over each other to be heard.

Chief Murphy raised both hands. "No comment."

This was fun. I was already feeling like a hotshot investigative journalist. "You said that already."

Chief Murphy paid no attention to me. "Next question."

"How did he die?" I was hoping for slow and painful.

"Mr. Mee was found seated in his office chair, still holding the gun in his right hand. One shot to the right temple."

"He left a note," Faith called out. "What did it say?"

The press jumped on this faster than fleas on a dog. "Suicide?"

"Foul Play?"

"Help us out here, Chief."

Chief Murphy hitched up his gun belt. "We aren't releasing the contents of the note at this time, Miss Mackie."

Sonny touched Faith's arm. "How did you know there was a note?"

Faith's eyebrows shot up to her spiky hair and she gave a thirty-two teeth grin. "Didn't. Just a wild guess."

I had to admit, she had guts. "Are you saying suicide?"

"Better." She grinned again. "The Chief didn't say it wasn't."

Two suicides of two partners in crime in four days was a crazy coincidence, but being a gambler's kid, I didn't believe in coincidences. Only luck. Something told me Uncle Clive's and Slimy's had run out. My hand shot up. "Chief, are you investigating other leads?"

"The police department is capable of doing its job, Sage."

"Ouch! That's stepping on his toes." Faith winked. "I'm proud of you."

Questions fired in from all directions, but the chief's patience was up. "We'll release more info when we get the coroner's report."

"That's the third time you mentioned the coroner's report," Faith reminded him. "Can't wait to see it." She turned to us. "Want to bet it wasn't suicide?"

Sonny cocked his head. "But you said."

"Sage." Faith scanned her iPad and wrote something. "Doesn't all this seem a tad bit convenient to you?"

"None of this has anything to do with me." I hoped.

Chief Murphy tipped his hat, signaling the interview was over. Reporters and photographers shouldered past us, and I searched the crowd for Gram and Pops. They were at the far end of the hall with Mrs. Benson. She was red-faced and pointing in our direction, probably telling them Sonny was on restriction for the rest of his life.

"Don't be so sure." Faith snapped her iPad shut and dropped it into her purse. "Slimy and Clive were thick as thieves, if you'll pardon the cliché."

Nerves began a tap dance in my stomach. "So?"

Faith was getting impatient. "Three can keep a secret if two are dead."

"What are you saying?"

"Actually, Ben Franklin said it."

"I don't get it," said Sonny.

"Your uncle committed suicide last Friday." Faith jabbed a red-polished nail bitten to the quick into my chest. "You inherit everything." Another jab. "You discover a scam between Clive and Slimy that leaves two million floating around."

"And?"

"Slimy sues you for a fortune, but now you've got nothing to worry about."

Sonny got it. "Because Slimy's dead."

Faith blew a bubble. "Two out of three." She popped the bubble, tried a grin but failed. "That leaves you, son."

CHAPTER SIXTEEN

The next morning, after a breakfast that could feed a football team, I followed my grandparents into the foyer. Pops helped Gram on with her coat.

"I put the prime rib in the oven on low, so it'll be ready when we come home." She buttoned the top button and took her gloves out of her pocket. "Mrs. Benson will be here in an hour to take you to Lincoln Mortuary."

"Are you sure you don't want to go with us?" Pops shrugged into his own coat and pulled a burgundy muffler from the coat rack.

Here I go again, forgetting Uncle Clive had to actually be buried. Seemed like a waste of real estate. "I've got homework to do."

Pops knotted the muffler and tucked it inside his coat. "I can call Sister Gonzaga and ask her to forgive the work."

A laugh flew out of my mouth, but when I saw their shocked faces, I managed to turn it into a sob. If Sister Gonzaga ever cut me some slack, it would be the first recorded miracle in Evansville. "It'll help me take my mind off," I made myself look sad, "things."

They both looked ready to cry, so I patted their shoulders before shooing them out the door. In case they changed their minds, I turned the lock and bolted for my room. They never locked the front door and probably didn't even carry a key. If they wanted back in, they would have to huff and puff and blow our apartment building down.

Since Chief Murphy's press conference, questions had been boomeranging around in my head, but not one answer had come back. Marty had always taught me that when things didn't make sense to look for the common denominator. Other than greed, Slimy and Uncle Clive didn't seem to have anything in common. I rummaged around in my desk for paper to make a list. I liked lists. They helped me focus. Ten minutes later I was staring down at the blank sheet, stumped.

The doorbell blasted through our quiet apartment, and I jumped a foot. Gram and Pops were the best people in this world, but if they were on the doorstep, I was going to scream. I stomped to the front door and yanked it open. "What?"

Sonny pushed past me, shook off his coat and let it fall on the floor.

"Where's your mom?"

"She's in bed with a migraine, shoveling in cherry chocolate chip ice cream and watching an old movie." He whipped off his hat and tossed it onto the pile. "She says she'll never recover from yesterday. We're riding our bikes to the funeral."

It was eight o'clock in the morning. "How much ice cream does she have?"

"Half a gallon."

It'd better be a short movie. "Gram and Pops already left."

"I know." He waved a manila envelope in my face. "I developed the photographs. While I was waiting for them to dry, I looked out the window and saw them leave."

In all the excitement, I'd forgotten about the pictures Sonny had taken of Uncle Clive's first Will. I snatched them out of his hand and hurried to my room. Without waiting for Sonny, I settled myself on the hooked rug in front of my bed. The investment pages were the last ones, and I put them on the floor. Sonny went to my desk and started opening drawers and slamming them shut.

"Stop." I was trying to read but the noise was getting on my nerves.

"Your room's boring. It's too neat." Sonny banged one more drawer shut. He ambled over and plopped down in front of me, crossing his legs. "What does it say?"

"Hold on." When I finished, I wasn't sure if I knew anything or not. I sorted through the photographs on the floor. "The first Will leaves everything to Pops and Gram, too."

"Was your uncle loaded?"

"I guess." I picked up a photo. "This is a list of property and bank accounts, and where they're at. Not how much anything is worth." I slumped back against my bed. "The Will he just wrote says I get everything. It doesn't say how much money or anything else."

"How do we find out?"

No idea. "Slimy must have that information."

"He's dead, remember?"

About that. "None of this makes sense. Even Faith says so. First Uncle Clive and now him."

We thought about that for a moment.

"Why," Sonny began, "would a guy with tons of money

and who's got the town in his back pocket want to kill himself?"

I sat up straight. "Seems strange he didn't leave a note."

"What if--" we said at once and stopped.

Sonny made a face. "Remember what Faith said about three people keeping a secret?"

I'd been having nightmares about that. "This doesn't have anything to do with me."

"Your conscious is afraid to admit it does," Sonny reasoned and stood up. "But your subconscious," he argued, "knows the truth."

"Cut it out, Dr. Sonny." His psychobabble was getting to me. My hands shook a little as I gathered up the photographs and put them back inside the envelope. "Do you have a copy of these in a safe place?"

Sonny grinned. "In my room."

Which meant they were gone for good. Last week we'd forgotten to do a science project. It had been worth a hundred points and could make or break our grade. No problem. Under Sonny's bed, we'd found a plate with half a baloney sandwich. A glass of coke had spilled on it and eaten most of the baloney. It was pretty gross. We'd added a picture of a toothless kid and gotten an A.

Looking around my room, I had to admit Sonny was right. My room was really neat because Gram came in every day and cleaned. Even if I did hide the photos, they wouldn't stay hidden for long. "Be right back."

"Where are you going to put them?"

"Away." I'd learned from Marty never to tell the number two man everything. Sonny was my best friend, but I was still a con man's kid at heart.

I took off down the hall to Gram and Pops' bedroom and tossed aside the quilt on top of her cedar chest.

Opening the lid, I took out Gram and Pops' wedding album. Underneath were some pictures of Marty. One was of him in a baseball jersey, holding a ball and glove like he was winding up for a pitch. In the picture he was about twelve, younger than me, but he was tall and thin like me. He had dark brown curls like mine, and they were sticking out from under his baseball cap. Looking closer I saw he had freckles across his nose, like me. Marty had been my dad for thirteen years but there were so many things I didn't know about him. What was his favorite color? Did he ever want to be anything other than a low-life con artist? My finger traced a crooked smile that would later turn cruel. That, I knew for a fact.

The duffle with my reward money was next. Every time I unzipped it, I expected it to be empty. It still blew me away that Gram and Pops didn't use a bank. In Las Vegas a stash of cash wasn't even safe in a vault. I slid the photos inside, zipped the duffle, and put everything back where I'd found it.

"Hey, Sage," Sonny called.

"What?"

"Gotta go."

For a moment, I was blank. Oh yeah. The funeral. I'd hated Clive Christopher and had wished him dead. Today should be a happy day, proving that wishes do come true, but here I was dragging my feet. "Must be my subconscious," I muttered and suddenly went lightheaded. I was beginning to sound like Dr. Sonny. "Coming."

The morning was bleak and raw. At the bottom of our apartment stairs, the wind slapped us in the face. Sonny rubbed his gloves together and started toward our garage where I kept my bike.

"Wait." Sonny lived five doors down, and I pointed to

the Bensons' car parked in their driveway. It was a ten-year old, baby blue Chrysler and not my style but neither was freezing my buns off. "Let's drive."

Sonny stopped dead. "Are you serious? That's stealing."

"Borrowing."

"We just got out of jail."

The air was so cold, I felt like I was breathing ice. "Where do you keep the keys?"

"Nuh-uh." Sonny backed up.

"Go get them." My eyes were watering, and my eyelashes were sticking together.

"Can't." He looked almost happy. "My mom keeps them in her purse."

I pulled my hat down over my ears, and for the millionth time I wondered why anyone would want to live in Connecticut on purpose. "I'll hotwire it."

"You *are* serious," Sonny's gloved hand flapped in the direction of the Chrysler, "about taking *my* car?"

I hitched one shoulder and let it fall. "We should take something better but it's getting late."

In the end, Sonny talked me into dragging my bike out of the garage. I concentrated on peddling, partly because I was mad but mostly because I'd forgotten my gloves. Again. The wind raced up the sleeves of my jacket, numbing my arms. Someday I'd live somewhere warm, and I'd stay there forever. It was a happy thought, and I could almost feel myself getting a tan.

Twenty miserable minutes later, we arrived at Lincoln Mortuary. A kid in a red valet vest hustled over. "May I take your, uh, bikes?"

"What's all this?" The parking lot was crammed, and other red vests were parking cars on the street. "This is supposed to be for family and a few friends."

"The whole town has turned out." The kid grinned and a mouthful of silver brightened the gloomy day. "People are here whether they've been invited or not."

"Nothing brings a town together like a good funeral," Sonny mused.

"Very philosophical," Valet Guy agreed. "That's why you should take care of people generously while you're here on earth." He held his hand out, palm up.

"Here's five." I slapped my hand down, giving him five fingers instead of five bucks.

"Hey!"

"Get a real job."

We walked our bikes to the bike rack by the front steps, and Sonny nosed his into the rack. "I can't believe he wanted money to park our bikes."

"You're thinking about getting a red vest so you can do it, too."

Sonny shrugged. "I don't have money coming out my ears like you."

"Your family isn't poor."

"Your family is rich."

"Look, I'm not going to apologize for having money." This must be bothering him a lot, but it had to stop. "While you were growing up all happy with parents who loved you, I was living with a drunk in Las Vegas who beat the stuffing out of me whenever he felt like it. You," my voice snapped like a whip, "should apologize for being jealous. Haven't you learned anything from those stupid psycho-nonsense TV shows you watch?"

Sonny's eyes watered up behind his glasses, and I hoped it was only the wind. I couldn't stand it when people cried. They always expected you to hug them and say, "There, there." Maybe that's why I couldn't cry to save my life.

Whenever I'd come close to sniveling, Marty would always give me something to cry about.

"You're right." Sonny wiped his glasses on his sleeve. "I'm sorry."

"Forget it." I tried smiling but my chapped lips cracked and started bleeding. "You're my best friend."

"Really?"

"Yeah, really."

"Thanks."

He nodded at me and put his glasses back on. Realizing I had a friend for the first time in my life always surprised me, but I didn't say anything. With Sonny, when the fight was over, it was over.

Sonny pointed to a two-story brick building the size of a bed and breakfast hotel. "That's the mausoleum."

We ignored the Do Not Cut Across the Lawn sign and fell in with the throng of people making their way through the heavy morning mist. Everyone was bundled up in black or gray woolen coats with the exception of a tall, slender lady with wild red hair, wearing a bright yellow coat. Over her shoulder, she gave me a shy smile and a finger wave.

"Who's that?" Sonny jutted his chin in her direction.

No idea. "Probably someone who worked with Uncle Clive."

We hunched forward into the cold wind and walked past crumbling headstones that rose up from the patchy grass like decaying teeth. The wind howled, and I pushed my bare hands deep into my pockets.

"Here." Sonny handed me a fur-lined glove. "We'll share."

"Thanks."

From the size of the crowd shivering in front of the

mausoleum, my guess was Uncle Clive's death was now an official Evansville holiday. Mrs. Shapiro from the library and Mr. Patrizi from Pat's called out to me, and I managed a one-handed glove wave. People I knew from school and around town smiled or waved. I tried not to return a big grin, after all I was supposed to be in mourning. Most people were standing together and talking quietly. When Mr. Weinstein arrived with his basset hound Chester, they stood apart from the others. He gave a quick look around and then reached into his overcoat pocket for a flask. I fought the urge to scamper over. He always drank peppermint schnapps.

I scanned the crowd. "Why isn't Pellam here?"

"Huh?"

"Pellam. He should be here."

"Make up your mind. Either you want the old guy gone or you want him here. Which is it?" Next to me, Sonny was like the mayor and waving to anybody who looked. "Don't you think this is a great funeral?"

My teeth had stopped chattering about a quarter of a mile back, completely frozen in place. "I think," I said through clenched teeth, "this is like either Walt Disney's funeral or Samuel Goldwyn's."

"Huh?"

"Thousands of people turned out for Disney's funeral because he was a popular guy. About a thousand people showed up for Goldwyn's because they wanted to make sure the movie tycoon was dead."

Sonny stared at me. "That's really cold."

"So's murder."

I blew on my bare hand and looked around for Pops and Gram. They stood in front of the mausoleum with Father Flanders and a tall man in an expensive black overcoat who kept looking at his watch. The tall guy looked familiar. "Is that Abe's dad?"

"Yeah. He owns the mortuary."

The mausoleum was a miniature of Evans Peak, right down to the marble sphinx on either side of the doorway. They looked real enough to devour small children. In case the townspeople needed reminding who the town was named after, Evans was chiseled in the stone above the doorway. Young girls with big wicker baskets mingled with the crowd, passing out single, long stem red roses.

Under a canopy, a woman in a long red dress and a black velvet coat struggled to balance a violin and keep sheet music on a rickety stand. Next to her a man wearing a charcoal wool coat and a red rose in his lapel was tuning a cello. A woman with long hair bumped across the frozen lawn, pushing a harp on a dolly. She staked out the spot on the end and slid the instrument off with a soft *thump*. Flinging back her hair, she unfolded a stool, settled down, and together they launched into "Stairway to Heaven."

Sonny elbowed me. "Your uncle was a Led Zeppelin fan?"

I burst out laughing.

"What's so funny?"

"Uncle Clive." My eyes were watering but this time, not from the cold. "Thinking about heaven when he picked out this music was so," I searched for the right word, "optimistic."

Gram and Pops looked our way and waved us over. The music trio caught the cue and softened the last strains. I turned to Sonny. "This is it."

He hung back. "I'm staying here."

"Don't even think about it." I snagged his arm. "Best friends, remember?"

When we reached Gram and Pops, Father Flanders nodded and stepped away to address the crowd. "Thank you for coming today. Your support means a lot to the Christopher family."

The trio switched to "You Can't Always Get What You Want."

Sonny's eyebrows went up. "And a Stones fan?"

"News to me." The pallbearers appeared, guiding Uncle Clive's magnificent casket along the pathway. This time it was smothered with enough red roses to be a float in the Rose Parade.

Sonny gave a low whistle. "That's a lot of roses."

"No joke." Even I knew the price of roses in December was outrageous. "I hope he paid for them before he died." If not, it would put a serious dent in my inheritance.

Gram gave us both The Look.

Maybe it was some kind of law that all priests loved public speaking. People were immediately captivated by Father Flanders's rich voice that swelled and fell like waves coming into shore. Unfortunately, in less time than it took to say Hail Mary, everyone soon realized he hadn't known Uncle Clive. At all.

Where the young priest had gotten his information was anybody's guess but it wasn't from facts. "Clive Christopher," he boomed, "was a man of humble means who came to Evansville with nothing but hope, dreams, and a burning desire to succeed."

People shifted around me and cleared their throats, knowing Uncle Clive had been a liar and a murderer. A cheat was added to the list when he'd committed suicide before the jury could convict him, but no matter. Arrested was pretty much as good as convicted. Before long the gossip will say he hanged himself on death row instead of in the city jail.

"For Clive Christopher, there was nothing greater than his love of family."

In front of me Gram and Pops were huddled together. Gram's head jerked up.

"He'd better not mention the family farm," I said to Sonny.

Sonny nudged me. "Be quiet."

"Hey, it wasn't me who cheated Pops."

Gram had her arm around Pops' waist. He was leaning heavily on her, sobbing into his hands, but she managed to turn around and give me The Look. This made me angry all over again. Pops was a good man, and Uncle Clive had been a rotten scumbag.

"Next to family, Clive Christopher loved journalism and devoted his life to making *The Evansville News* what it is today." Father Flanders smiled at me.

I smiled back but muttered, "He left out the part about Uncle Clive blackmailing Olivia into marrying him so he wouldn't have to buy the newspaper."

This time when Gram turned around, her pretty face was grim, and her mouth was set in a hard line. Bright pink flushed her cheeks, but I knew it wasn't from the cold.

"Sorry," I managed even though I'd bet she really was on my side.

Around me, voices were low, and eyebrows were raised. The mourners were taking in every word and not buying any of it.

"This is getting bad," Sonny said. "Somebody needs to stop Father Flanders."

"Not me." I grinned like a jack o' lantern, chapped lips, and all. This was getting good.

With each distorted fact, Father Flanders' voice got warmer, and the crowd got more steamed. At last, he paused, lifted his arms, and proclaimed to heaven, "We'll all remember Clive Christopher's love for his brother Jack, to whom he gave and gave and gave."

"Say what?" Gram cried out. She let go of Pops so quickly Sonny and I had to spring forward to catch him.

Suddenly everyone had something to say and didn't mind saying it. Some people fall from grace, but Uncle Clive had taken a running leap off the cliff. I handed Pops over to Gram and turned to Sonny. "You're right. This is a great funeral."

"Geez, Sage," Sonny shook his head, "Father Flanders will probably leave the priesthood after this."

"I, I," Father Flanders's uplifted hands fluttered in the air like a wounded bird and then dropped to his sides.

"Father Flanders," Mr. Lincoln stepped forward and shook the priest's hand. "Thanks so much for those, uh, stirring words."

Mr. Lincoln pivoted on one shiny black loafer. At the snap of his fingers, men in dark suits started ushering people away.

A few people lingered, talking amongst themselves. Minutes dragged while we waited for the pallbearers to slowly wheel the casket into the mausoleum.

"Immediate family only," Mr. Lincoln announced, holding both hands in front of him in case anyone should charge forward for one last look.

The mausoleum was damp inside and the air smelled like wet paper. Sonny's glasses fogged up. He took them off and wiped them with his muffler, making a mess. The chandeliers were giving off small sizzling sounds, and I looked down to make sure I wasn't standing in water.

"I could say a few words," Father Flanders began.

"No!" everyone exclaimed.

The men slid the casket into the vault, and Mr. Lincoln shut the door softly.

After a moment, Pops murmured, "I guess that's everything." He dried his eyes with a rumpled handkerchief and squeezed it into a ball. "Clive's really gone."

And good riddance.

Outside, we said goodbye to Mr. Lincoln and Father Flanders. The wind whistled across the cemetery, but the sun was beginning to peek out. Uncle Clive was finally buried. I raised my happy face to the sun. All was right with the world.

Gram tucked her arm into Pops' arm. "Let's go home."

I started to follow, but Sonny was turning his pockets inside out.

"Wait. I must've dropped my glove." He went back inside the mausoleum.

"We'll catch up," I called after Gram and Pops. With the service was over, I knew Gram would be anxious to get home to the prime rib she'd left in the oven. She was a wizard in the kitchen, but five minutes was the difference between mouthwatering and beef jerky.

"Sage."

I turned around. It was the redheaded lady in the yellow coat. She'd been leaning against a tree but pushed herself away and came toward me. Maybe she worked at the newspaper as a reporter or in the office. She definitely wasn't a teacher from school. All we had were hundred-year-old nuns. I'd spent a lot of time at the police station lately, but she didn't seem the type to wear a uniform and ugly shoes.

The woman stopped in front of me. She was pretty with

huge, blue eyes. "Sage," she repeated. She started to reach out but gave a little laugh instead. "Sorry. It's been so long."

Behind her in the crowd of departing mourners, I caught sight of Pellam watching me. He must've slipped in after the service started. For an old guy, he had the creepy habit of appearing from out of nowhere. He gave me a rare smile before turning the collar up on his overcoat and shuffling away.

"Do I know you?"

She took a deep breath and looked down. When her eyes came back to mine, they were filled with tears. "I'm your mother."

CHAPTER SEVENTEEN

"Awesome!" Sonny was standing over me and laughing. "I've never seen anything like it. You hit the ground so fast I thought you were dead."

"If I were dead, I wouldn't be looking at your ugly face." Sonny's red freckles danced out of focus. I struggled to my elbows but fell back, whacking my head on the hard ground. "Ow."

Sonny helped me into a sitting position. "What happened?"

I searched the grounds. "Where'd she go?"

"Who?"

"That lady. The one with," I waved my hands about my head, "the red hair. She was right here."

"All I saw when I came out was you falling on your face."

"She...." I looked around again. "I've got to find her."

Sonny's stomach growled. "Do it later. I'm starving."

Working my fingers through my hair, I found a bump but no blood. Deciding I was going to live, I got up and brushed off my pants. A white envelope with my name printed on it crackled under my feet, and I snatched it up. "See?" I waved it in Sonny's face. "I'm not crazy. She was here."

"Okay, she was here. So what?"

"She's," the words locked in my chest, "my mother."

"Get out!" Sonny snorted. "You've got a mother?"

My thoughts exactly. Marty had never mentioned her. Sure, every kid had one, but I'd always thought she'd run away from him when she'd had the chance. What was she doing here? Maybe she'd gotten the news mixed up and thought this was Marty's funeral. I rubbed the back of my head again. She was going to be really disappointed to hear she'd missed it.

I ripped open the envelope. My fingers trembled when I took out the note.

Dear Sage,

I can explain everything. Meet me at 2 p.m. today on the bench in front of the library.

Love,

Mom

PS If you don't want to see me, I'll understand. 555-1929

"Are you going to call her?"

"I can't. Not from home." What would I tell Gram and Pops? "I need to buy a cell phone."

"You need to be sixteen. Maybe eighteen."

"I'll get one."

Sonny's eyebrows shot up. "How?"

"I know a guy. C'mon." I started walking. The world

spun once, but I was okay and kept going. I needed to think. I needed a plan. "I need to get home."

The great thing about Sonny is that food always came first. Mystery Mom was forgotten, and we hurried toward our bikes. In no time flat we were parked outside my apartment and jogging up the stairs.

"Hi, Gram," I called, opening the front door. "We'll wash our hands and be right in."

"Hurry. It's getting cold."

I turned to Sonny. "You heard her."

Sonny didn't like being clean, but he didn't like being hungry, either. He tossed his coat and hat on the floor and hustled toward the bathroom.

When we got to the dining room, I slid into my chair and put my napkin on my lap. Gram passed the prime rib platter to me. I helped myself and started to pass it to Sonny but put two slices on his plate instead. Then I handed the platter to Pops.

"Hey," Sonny's eyes tracked the prime rib like it was about to disappear.

I gave him the mashed potatoes. "Work on this."

We settled into the meal, nobody saying much. I felt sorry for Pops, but I had my own problems. This whole mom business was hard for me to imagine. I'd never thought about having a mom, never thought about wanting one. Maybe there was something wrong with me. All kids wanted a mom.

"Sage," Gram was looking at me, "I asked what you and Sonny are going to do this afternoon."

"Um." Looking down, I was surprised to see I'd eaten everything on my plate. I licked my fork clean and tried to think of a plan. This was my chance to get out of the apartment. "We're going to the library. Mrs. Shapiro is there."

Okay, so that was sort of true. Mrs. Shapiro was the librarian, and we were going to the library. "I, uh, need to get some information."

Pops folded his napkin. "Frances, I think we're ready."

Gram smiled and got up from the table. "You're right."

"I'm ready for dessert." Sonny sat up straight and looked to the kitchen.

"Me, too." I pushed my plate away and wondered what I'd eaten.

Gram came back in and placed a large package on the table. "We were saving this for Christmas, but now seems a better time."

I'd never gotten a present before and wasn't sure what to do. "For me?"

Pops nudged it closer to me. "Open it."

The box was wrapped in silver paper and tied with a red bow. I tugged at the ribbon and the bow unraveled. Inside was an Apple laptop computer and carrying case. I couldn't believe it. "For me?" I repeated.

"It'll help you with your schoolwork," Gram said.

"And when you start working at the newspaper," Pops added. "Do you know how to use it?"

Something told me my grandparents might not be impressed with my hacking skills. "A little."

Sonny grinned. "Now we both have one."

"You've got a computer?" I thought about all my trips to the library to dig up information about Evans so I could collect the million-dollar reward. "Why didn't you tell me?"

Sonny shrugged. "You like going to the library."

I put the computer on the table and opened it. The keyboard lit up like an alphabet runway, and my fingers danced over the keys.

"We had email and the basic apps installed," Pops

explained, "but you can change the screen saver and password to whatever you like."

"What's the password now?"

Gram laughed. "Pulitzer."

Sonny punched me in the arm. "Perfect."

Yeah, it was. Even better would be if I could think of the perfect words to thank them. I closed the computer.

Gram and Pops waited.

"It's perfect." So was the plan that popped into my head. "Can I show it to Mrs. Shapiro this afternoon?"

My grandparents were great. They were nice people. They loved me. And they seldom questioned me about stuff I said that didn't make sense. Anyone else would've asked why I needed to take my computer to a library. Anything I needed from the library I could now Google.

"Sounds good." Pops nodded to Gram. "I think we're ready for dessert."

Eating kept Sonny quiet through dessert but he started complaining when I said we'd clean up.

"I can do this, if you want to go to the library," Gram offered.

I gathered the plates and stacked the silverware on top. "It's my job."

"Not mine," Sonny grumbled.

Pops stood up. "Thanks. It's been a long day."

When they left, I turned to Sonny. "Grab something. We have to hurry."

Sonny picked up his cloth napkin and trailed behind me to the kitchen. "What's the rush?"

I filled the sink with soapy water and slid the plates in. "I want to get there before she does." I'd learned from Marty it was always better to be the first one to arrive.

"Are you nervous?"

"Try angry." I flicked a soap bubble at him. "What makes her think she can pop up after thirteen years and expect me to be happy about it?"

"There you go again. Always thinking about yourself." Sonny sighed. "Try putting yourself in her place."

He backed off when I glared at him. I wasn't in the mood for this. "You really have to give up daytime TV."

"Did you ever think," Sonny said quietly, "she might be sorry? Most kids would be happy to find out they had a mom."

"You don't get it." I stabbed the air between us with a dirty fork. "She. Left. Me. With Marty."

"Maybe she had no choice. Maybe she wants to make it up to you. Give her a chance."

"Right." I tossed the fork into the soapy water and faced him. "Can she make this up?" I traced the scar above my right eye. "Marty gave this to me for calling him Dad. I did that one time. One lousy time and I'll be wearing it forever." My voice dropped. "She can't make anything up to me."

Sonny folded his arms across his chest. "You've got trust issues."

"Not true." I didn't trust anybody. I stuck my hands into the soapy water. "Anyway, she's too late. I like my life just fine."

"She's your mom. You'll have to live with her."

That bothered me the most. "Not going to happen."

"You're a kid. You can't say no."

"Wanna bet? I'm never leaving Gram and Pops. Nuh-uh. Never."

Sonny's eyebrows shot up. "Whoa. I know that look. Do you have a plan?"

Almost. "Always."

"Does this involve burglary?" He stepped back. "Doing anything illegal? Getting thrown in jail? Again?"

"Of course not." Maybe. I tossed him a dishtowel. "Start drying. What are you worried about?"

"If I mess up one more time, I'll be on restriction until I go to college."

"That's not going to happen."

"Yeah?"

"Yeah." Sonny would never get into college with his grades. "Get busy. We gotta get out of here."

When we finished, we bundled into our coats, hats, and gloves. Gram and Pops weren't in the living room, but I shouted a goodbye and pushed Sonny out the door.

CHAPTER EIGHTEEN

"Hi, Sage." She raised a hand in my direction and stood.

Sonny elbowed me. "She got here early. How about that?"

Yeah, how about that. "Hi."

Her smile was quick, and two dimples appeared. "I can't decide if I'm really nervous to meet you or it's really cold."

"It's really cold," Sonny chimed in. "Sage is always complaining about it."

"Stop it," I muttered.

"You," she said, "must be Sonny. Sage's best friend."

Sonny's face went as red as his hair. "How'd you know?"

The wind blew her hair across her face, and she brushed it out of her eyes. "I asked some people at the funeral." This time she blushed. "You want to be a photographer."

"Photojournalist," Sonny stammered. "Like Jimmy Olsen."

"Superman's friend?"

"Right." Sonny's face lit up. "Sage wants to be an investigative journalist. We're going to work at *The Evansville News*."

"Really?" Her blue eyes sparkled. "You must be good. I'd love to see some of your work."

This was more than I could stand. "Can we get on with this? You wanted to meet and here I am."

Sonny surprised me by turning to mush. "You're so lucky, Sage. She's pretty."

The dimples were back. "Thank you."

I'd had enough. "Wait for me inside, will you? This won't take long."

"I'm going," Sonny shifted gears, becoming Dr. Sonny, "but try to be receptive and listen to your mom with an open mind. This is a chance to settle the past and start fresh. Resist being," he arched his eyebrows, "you."

I resisted punching his lights out. "Go."

She waited for Sonny to leave. "He's a little intense for a kid."

I shrugged. "He watches daytime TV with his mom to get out of cleaning his room."

"Smart."

That cracked me up, but I kept it to myself. Sonny was my best friend, but smart he wasn't. "What are you doing here?"

"Can we sit?"

The wrought iron bench was freezing cold. When I put my computer case at my feet, I pretended I had a watch and faked checking the time.

"You must have lots of questions." She fumbled in her purse, took out a folded piece of paper, and held it out to me. "Here."

"I don't want anything from you."

She pressed the paper into my hands. "Please."

My fingers ignored me and unfolded it anyway. The top line read *Certificate of Live Birth*. In the first box, neatly typed under Father's Name, was Martin Christopher. I skipped over it and zeroed in on the next box: Mother's Name.

So, it was true. I had a mom. Just like any other kid.

And she'd walked out on me.

The words in the box blurred. It took everything I had to read it. Tess Langley. My mother's name is Tess.

"So what?" I tried to sound like I didn't care but slipped the paper into my coat pocket.

Her blue eyes filled with tears. "I'm your mother."

"So. What." I kept my face hard, refusing to give her an inch.

Tess sighed and rubbed her hands together. The temperature had dropped since this morning. It was probably five degrees out here, and she wasn't wearing gloves. For some reason, that bothered me.

"When you were born," she began, "I was thrilled." She smiled but let it fade. "Marty wasn't."

Not hard to imagine.

"You were," she paused and gave me a radiant smile, "the most beautiful baby."

"Yeah, right."

"I know every mom says that, but it was true." She pulled a photograph from her purse and handed it to me. "See?"

The picture was faded, and the edges were worn. I'd never seen a baby picture of me before, but there I was. She was holding me in her arms, her face turned from the camera, and she was kissing the top of my head. I frowned. I'd been fat. Really fat.

"Not long after you were born, Marty got in with a bad crowd. The more I begged him to get away from them, the worse he became. He drank nonstop and gambled money we didn't have. He owed a lot of money to dangerous people. I was scared all the time. Somebody was always knocking on our door, looking for him."

I didn't bother telling her nothing had changed. Marty had been a mean, nasty drunk and a loser until the end. In Las Vegas we were always dodging someone named Guido or Vito. Not exactly crime bosses, but close enough. Instead, I put the photograph in my pocket.

"I told him I couldn't take it anymore and threatened to leave him. Take you away." She took a deep breath. "He said if I ever tried anything that stupid, he'd kill me." Her lower lip trembled. "By then, I knew he meant it. I stayed, but he got worse. We fought all the time. He liked being mean."

My finger traced the scar above my right eye.

"I had a part-time job at a private school, teaching piano. Look." She touched my sleeve and held out small hands with long, slender fingers for me to see. "We have the same hands."

I looked at my hands and my chest tightened. It was true. They were just like hers.

"One day your babysitter couldn't watch you. I should've known something was up when Marty said he would. When I got home from school, you two were gone. Just gone." She burst into tears, covering her face with her hands.

There should be some kind of rule that people can't start crying in the middle of a good story. They should only be allowed to cry when they're done. Still, I was impressed she could start crying so fast. I couldn't boo-hoo to save my life.

She sniffed and wiped her eyes with the back of her hand. "No note. Nothing." New tears ran down her face. "I thought I'd die."

I was having trouble with this one. Sure, I'd wondered my whole life why Marty had kept me around, but then he did a lot of crazy things. Hearing it had been his idea to be saddled with me was too bizarre. "This doesn't make sense. What are you leaving out?"

She looked down at her hands. "I had some problems. Depression."

Okay, being with Marty could do that.

"Things were pretty bad for me," she took in a breath, "but I'm better now. I got counseling." She smiled. "I'm teaching music at a high school in California, and I even have a little house with a vegetable garden."

Good for you. While you were planting tomatoes, Marty was using me as a punching bag. "Did you look for me?"

"I hired a private investigator. He'd get some leads, but they never panned out. Marty knew people with connections. The kind that could make people disappear. He must've gotten help from them." She looked away and then came back to me. "I never stopped searching for you." She bit her lower lip. "There's no reason for you to believe me, but it's true."

The thing was, I was starting to. A little. "How'd you find me?"

"The investigator found out Marty had died and sent me an email. By then you'd been turned over to the Children's Home Society. He talked to a woman named Mrs. Spears. She said you were living here."

Even I knew there were laws about keeping kid information private, but I wasn't surprised the old biddy had spilled her guts. She'd been glad to get rid of me. Too many kids in the system. Too much work for her.

"Now what?"

"My school is on winter break. I thought," she studied my face, "we could use this time to get to know each other. You'll want to ask your grandparents, of course."

Never. The less they were reminded of Marty, the better. It would kill them to find out Marty had a wife, and she was here. "Sure, Tess."

She handed me a business card. "I'm staying at the Evansville Hotel. I see you have a computer." She flipped the card over. "I've written my email on the back. Think it over and let me know." She stood up.

"Okay." I slung the computer strap over my shoulder and headed toward the library. For some reason when I got to the steps, I looked back. When I did, she waved, and my heart skipped.

CHAPTER NINETEEN

"How'd you find me? I just moved in."

I patted my computer bag. "The internet is a wonderful thing."

Bongo Feltzer peered over my shoulder. "Where's pumpkin head?"

"Sonny's mom is out of ice cream." I hooked a thumb over my shoulder. "He went to get some."

The furniture in Bongo's place was modern. All chrome, glass, and sharp edges. My eyes were watering from the fresh paint fumes. Looked like his forgery gig was a money-maker. "You've come up in the world."

"Yeah, I was wasting my time at Holy Cross."

Since I needed his help, I didn't say Sister Tarbula had expelled him for fighting--with me. Bongo had gone through every grade at least twice and had been the only eighth grader with a five o'clock shadow, a truck, and old enough to vote. "Right."

Bongo led me to an open door down the hall. "My office." He slid into a big chair behind a bigger desk. "Why are you here?"

The great thing about a short story is that there wasn't much to tell. Twenty seconds later I was placing my birth certificate on his desk.

Bongo examined its front and back carefully. "It says you were born in Newport Beach, California. I thought you were from Las Vegas."

"Me, too."

"Sounds like a ritzy place. How'd you end up in Las Vegas?"

Good question. "They had a fight. Marty was gambling, drunk all the time and hanging out with really bad people."

"How bad?"

"Bad enough. Anyway, she told him she was leaving. He threatened to kill her, so she stayed. One day he took off with me."

He leaned forward, putting both elbows on the desk. "Why'd he want to be stuck with a kid? Doesn't make sense."

"Marty was mean." Just mean enough for this to make sense.

"Do you believe her?"

Yes. Maybe. "I believe Marty." I tried to shrug his memory off, but my gut twisted. I'd never forget him.

"So?"

I moved closer to the edge of my seat. "Is the birth certificate real?"

Bongo turned it over and held it up for me to see. "It's certified. Looks to be legit."

A stupid grin shot across my face. "So, she's really my mother."

"Don't know."

"You just said so."

"I said this looks like a legit birth certificate. Birth certificates are public record, and anybody can get a copy. Doesn't mean this woman is your mother. Before you get all worked up, what other proof do you have?"

"Proof?"

Bongo put the certificate on his desk. "Got any DNA?"

"Like what?"

Bongo scratched his chin stubble. "Smoked cigarette. A soda can or water glass she drank from."

"She cries a lot."

"Not helping."

I pulled out my baby picture. "Here."

Bongo barked out a laugh. "You were really fat."

"You have a head like a meatball."

"Whatever." He rubbed the picture between his fingers before holding it up to the light. "The picture may be real, but the photograph isn't."

"Huh?"

"This paper isn't old enough." He tossed it to me. "They weren't using this paper when you were a kid. It's too new."

"Are you sure?"

Bongo smirked. "I'm in the business."

"She could've made a copy."

He leaned back in his chair. "Or not."

I leaned forward. "Can you find out if she's legit?"

"It's not what I do but I know a guy. Cisco Rogue." Bongo nodded once. "He can find out anything."

"That's good right?"

Bongo wagged his head back and forth. "He's not cheap."

I slid my computer case onto my lap. Bongo watched while I pulled out a short stack of Ben Franklins and put it on his desk. "When can he start?"

"I'll set it up. He'll need a way to get in touch with you." He glanced at my computer case. "Email?"

"Unh-unh." Too easy for Gram and Pops to catch on. "Can you get me a cell phone?" I thought about Sonny. "Make it two."

"Sure thing." Bongo got up. He stopped at the door and turned around. "What if she's a fake?"

My internal elevator dropped a few floors, but I held it together. "Then I'll know."

I leaned back in my chair and huffed out a breath. My head was swimming, and I couldn't figure out what to do next. Having a mom would change everything. Life was weird. Two days ago, I was sure my grandparents wouldn't want me anymore and I wanted to stay here really bad. Now my mom showed up and I would have to leave.

Because Sonny was right. Moms and kids were supposed to live together. That's how it worked. But California was a long way away. Outside Bongo's window the trees were bare. No flowers bloomed. Evansville was gray and depressing. I shivered.

I didn't know where Tess lived in California, but it had to be warm. I could finally get my boat and that made me happy. If things didn't work out, I'd cruise the Pacific Ocean and try out Mexico. Mexico was warm and had beaches, tequila, and mariachi music. My happiness disappeared. I didn't speak Spanish.

"All right." Bongo came back in and handed me two cell phones. "I taped your phone numbers on them. Since you're rolling in dough, I went with top of the line. You got voice and text, and data can be stored up to a year. After that you can buy more time with prepaid cards. You want to buy the cards at convenience stores." He dropped into his chair. "You don't want to buy online—ever. Use a website and the cards can be traced back to you. Then you're nailed."

"I thought burner phones couldn't be traced."

"Yes and no. Stuff like bank accounts, credit cards and home address can't be traced from your phone to you. But if you commit a crime, the cops can get a warrant and you're busted."

"No sweat." I'd pulled my last burglary job. Maybe.

"The beauty of a burner is that it's anonymous. But if you forget and login to a website like Facebook or hop onto a Wi-Fi network, like at a coffee shop," he snapped his fingers, "it's over. Your location data and other private stuff is known."

I didn't know that. "Who'd want to know about me?"

Bongo swiveled in his chair. "You tell me. Two people in your life suddenly commit suicide. A new Mom pops up outta nowhere. That's gotta be no coincidence."

You gotta be right. "You know about that?"

Bongo rolled his eyes. "This is Evansville. Everybody knows."

Hmm. "What about Cisco?"

"Gimme." Bongo held out his hand and I tossed him my cell phone. He punched in a number. "I'll set it up now, so you'll have his number in your contacts."

The number rang four times. "What?" a voice snarled.

We heard a crash and a lot of shouting.

"It's me. Bongo." Bongo hit FaceTime. "Are you in a fight?"

"Yeah. Hold on."

Bongo propped my cell phone against a coffee mug. The cell phone screen danced, and a biker guy's ugly face filled the screen. Then a man's hand slammed Biker Guy's face down and pushed it across a filthy table, knocking beer bottles and ashtrays out of the way. The man's hand grabbed Biker Guy by the hair and hauled him back before decking him. Biker Guy crumpled to the floor and stayed there.

A second later Cisco came into view, a little out of breath. "It's all good." He shook out a bloody hand before running it through thick, black wavy hair. When he gave us a slow grin, he looked like a modern-day pirate. "What's up?"

Bongo told me to scoot my chair closer. "Meet your newest client, Sage Christopher."

Cisco squinted at me. "Are you twenty-one, kid?"

I laid a hand on the stack of Ben Franklins sitting on Bongo's desk. "My money is."

"Close enough. Why do you need me?"

My story didn't get any longer the second time around.

Cisco studied me for ten seconds. "Smoke and mirrors." Then he was gone.

"He's a little strange," I said.

"He's a lot strange," Bongo agreed.

"What did he mean by smoke and mirrors?"

"The guy talks in riddles all the time. He's weird." Bongo jerked a shoulder in a shrug. "But he's good. He'll contact you when he's got something. You can trust him."

I don't trust anybody. "Okay."

"Anything else," Bongo put his number into my cell phone and handed it to me, "call me." He didn't get up.

"Thanks."

I wrapped my muffler around my throat and found my own way out. I thought about life as my boots crunched over the frozen ground. Except for getting sued for three million big ones my life was going okay. I had a computer, cell phone, a private detective and possibly a mom. I walked faster and gave my life a B+.

Better yet I had a plan. Sort of.

I checked my cell phone for the time. I'd have to hurry to catch Sonny between ice cream runs for his mother. Angling my bike helmet over my wool cap, I shoved off. If I cut down Main Street, I'd make it to his house in fifteen minutes. Then we'd have a solid two hours to do some serious internet sleuthing before dinner.

My bike skidded to a stop when I turned onto Main Street. Cars clogged both sides of the street, looking for parking spaces. Holiday shoppers spilled out of stores. I waited, stuck between American SUVs loaded with kids and import cars balancing Christmas trees on their tiny roofs. This was the middle of the afternoon. Didn't anyone work?

I thought about buying Christmas presents for Gram and Pops but drew a blank at what. When I was skipping out of town, I'd left them twenty grand to hire an attorney and eighty grand to cover the Mustang. The Mustang was back in the garage. Nothing clashed with cash and most people would be pretty happy with a hundred thousand. That should be more than enough. Except most Christmas gifts are wrapped in paper, not wrapped with a currency strap from a bank.

To keep my blood circulating I used both hands to ring my bike's bell. Drivers looked in their rearview mirrors and gave me friendly waves. Waiting was making me cranky but just in case someone recognized me I waved back. Criminy. I could be sitting here until Christmas.

My plan took a detour when I caught sight of Ambrose Ashton's, Attorney and Counselor at Law sign. It was in a storefront window dripping with garland and lit up by red and green lights winking merrily. I gave Main Street one more glance, but nothing had changed. Hopping off my bike, I coaxed it between a Dodge Ram truck and a BMW decked out in reindeer antlers with a big red felt nose on its grill. The BMW's driver was a pretty lady in a Santa's hat. I gave her a quick wave.

Mr. Ashton's office didn't have a bike rack in front. I thought about taking my ride inside but there was probably some law about that. Besides, this was Evansville. We didn't have thieves, only murderers.

When I pushed through the front door, a tiny bell tinkled out my arrival. I was surprised to see Mr. Ashton's office looked more like an old-fashioned home library than a stuffy office.

An elderly woman with glossy jet-black hair that started low on her forehead and swept up high on her head sat at a carved desk, hunched over a computer. Everywhere leather-bound books filled floor to ceiling shelves and a fire burned in the fireplace. A sign on her desk said "Violet."

She turned away from her computer and trilled, "May I help you?"

Violet was wearing a fuzzy white dress with huge black buttons going down the front and she looked a lot like Frosty the Snowman. Behind her the fire crackled and a log fell sending up a burst of embers. I considered warning her about sitting too close to the fire. She could melt.

"I, um." That's when I spotted the black fur curled up next to a telephone on her desk. "Is that a cat?"

Without thinking I put out my hand. A pair of green eyes stared back at me. Then a long sleek front leg slid out and opened its paw. Tiny sharp claws wrapped themselves around my fingers and gave a slight squeeze.

"Meet Merlin. He belonged to our client Mr. Vickers,

but Mr. Vickers passed away. Merlin is very sweet and likes to be petted." Violet ran a plump hand down the cat's back which rippled under her touch like a furry slinky toy. "We're trying to find him a home. No one should be alone at Christmas."

I gave Merlin a scratch under his chin. He kept his unblinking eyes on me but opened his mouth in a jaw cracking yawn.

"Merlin likes you. You're great with cats."

Merlin tipped his head, and I moved the scratch to his left ear. "They're awesome." I worked my way around to his other ear. I surprised myself by saying, "I've always wanted one."

"He's available," Violet reminded me and smiled. "Is there something you wanted?"

"I'm Sage Christopher. Can I talk to Mr. Ashton?"

Two micro thin drawn-on black eyebrows shot up and her red lipstick mouth formed a perfect O. She reached for the phone on her desk, nudging Merlin aside. "Mr. Ashton, Sage Christopher is here to see you." Keeping her eyes on me she listened for a moment before replacing the receiver. She waved toward the open doorway. "You may go in."

"Thanks."

Mr. Ashton glanced up from a yellow legal pad on his desk. "Sage. This is a surprise. Please sit."

I sat in the dark green leather chair across from him but kept my computer case on my lap. "I've never been here before."

"You're welcome any time." He waited.

"I need to ask you a legal question. I can pay you."

"Well," Mr. Ashton drew out the word, "I charge four hundred dollars an hour."

Wow. Whoever said talk was cheap never hired a lawyer.

Mr. Ashton leaned back in his chair and steepled white well-manicured hands on his chest. "What is this about?"

Light from his desk lamp glinted off his shiny nails and I wondered if he was wearing nail polish. "Slimy's lawsuit."

"I'm sorry," he warbled, shaking his head slightly. Not one white hair fell out of place. "Your grandfather talked to me about the lawsuit. I can't help you. It would be a conflict of interest."

"Why? Slimy's dead."

Mr. Ashton's forehead creased in thought.

I kept going. "Slimy was the one suing me. He doesn't have any family. He didn't have any law partners. There's no one to take over the case." I hope. "That means the case dies with him, right?"

He tapped his bony fingers together, pursed his lips and thought in silence for a long time. The only sound was the *tick, tick, tick* of his desk clock.

"Mr. Ashton?" At this rate he was using up a chunk of my four hundred dollars an hour.

"That's true," he agreed. "In theory."

"I'm interested in reality."

A slow smile spread across his face. "I heard you argued your own defense at your arraignment and won. Most impressive."

I was pretty proud of it myself. "Thanks."

"Do you want to be a lawyer?"

"Me?" For a split second I saw Marty rolling over in his grave and I laughed. Still, it was good advice. And Ashton charged four hundred bucks an hour. The way my life was going, being a lawyer would save me a lot in legal fees. "Maybe."

Mr. Ashton went back to thinking. After a minute he said, "We'll make a motion to dismiss the case. We will argue that because Mr. Mee is dead, he is unable to continue."

No joke.

"That would be the easiest way to handle this."

Was that the same as the cheapest? Now that I had money, I wanted to keep it. "Okay."

Mr. Ashton wrote something on the legal pad. "I'll start on this first thing tomorrow morning."

"Great." I started to reach inside my computer case but remembered I'd given Bongo all my money. "Can you bill me?" I asked like I did this every day.

"Certainly." He gave me a reassuring smile. "Please try not to worry. I'll take care of everything."

I smiled back. In ten minutes, I'd added getting a lawyer and keeping three million dollars of my inheritance to my list of happiness. My life was turning out better than okay and I bumped it up to a solid A.

CHAPTER TWENTY

"Some friend," Sonny grumbled. "You were supposed to come over yesterday. I waited for you all afternoon."

"I said I was sorry." We were sitting cross legged on the floor. It was the only clean spot in his room. I wiggled my butt but couldn't get comfortable, so I grabbed Sonny's pillow off his bed and sat on it. Much better. "After I left Bongo's, I went to see Mr. Ashton."

"Whatever." Sonny sent a glum look my way. "*And* you didn't show up at lunchtime today *and* I had to sit with the twins in detention."

"You knew I was in the library working on my English assignment." I reached for my computer case. "You got stuck sitting with the twins because you mouthed off to Sister Gonzaga and got detention."

"She took my Superman comic book away. So rude," Sonny huffed out and straightened his glasses. "I was reading it."

"During a history test."

"Big deal," he grumbled. "I didn't study."

You never do. "I got this for you." I pulled out Sonny's

cell phone and handed it to him. "Your number is taped on the back. I put my number in your contacts."

Sonny's face lit up. "This is so cool." He turned the cell phone over and over in his hands. "Thanks."

The great thing about Sonny was that he didn't keep score. His mad was gone and forgotten.

"This is really important," I said when he looked up. "Only use it to text or call me. Never use it to log in to a website. If you do, then it can be traced back to you."

"Are we doing something illegal?" Sonny's face went dead white. "I can't get arrested again."

"Not gonna happen." Not yet anyway but I made up my mind to get a law degree someday. "We need to be careful." I changed the subject, hoping to distract Sonny. "When I was at Bongo's I hired a private investigator to, uh, help us."

"With *The Case of the Missing Fortune?*"

For a moment my mind went blank. I'd been so focused about getting a mom that I'd forgotten about the case. "Yeah." I decided not to tell Sonny the real reason I'd hired Cisco and hurried on. "Uncle Clive is dead and so's Slimy, but we still don't know where the missing two million went."

"Hiring an investigator is good. He probably knows a lot of people in the police department."

More like in jail.

Sonny opened his computer. "What do we do now?"

"Before we get started," I said like the thought had just occurred to me, "I want to check out Tess on Facebook."

Bongo had given me the idea. Facebook was a site old people used to post pictures of their kids, their vacations and what they ate for dinner. Since Tess was around thirty-five, I was betting she was on the site. If she posted pictures, I could learn a lot about her. Like if she lived at the beach.

"Why?" Sonny frowned. "She's your mom."

Maybe. "Yeah."

A few seconds later we were staring at Tess Langley on Facebook. How about that? She was real. Tess was really my mom. "I'll take the pictures. You look at everything else."

"Under About," Sonny read out loud, "it says Tess was Miss California."

"Oh?" My tone was casual, but something warmed inside me. I sneaked a peek. It wasn't a great picture, and it was taken from a distance. Tess looked kind of the same, just prettier. Happiness fluttered in my stomach. Every kid wanted a pretty mom.

"It says she graduated from Juilliard in New York City."

"Whoa!"

Startled Sonny looked up. "I've never seen you impressed."

"Tess impressed a lot of people to get into Juilliard. It's," my hands waved in the air, "like the best performing arts school in the world."

"Huh?"

"Juilliard's famous for singing, music, dancing and theatre."

Sonny's mouth dropped open. "She went to school and just sang?"

"She plays the piano." I felt a flash of pride. Maybe I'd learn to play. "We have the same hands."

"Yeah, but you pick locks," Sonny snorted and went back to reading. "If she was so great how'd she end up with someone like your dad?"

Interesting. Marty had been a loser. "Opposites attract." I'd read that in a fortune cookie, so it had to be true.

Tess's Home Page was crammed with pictures. One picture showed her in jeans, a T-shirt, and working in a garden. Thick vines loaded with fat red tomatoes climbed trellises and lots of green things stuck up from the ground. Behind her fluffy white clouds floated across a light blue sky. I looked closer and my breath caught. There it was. California sun glinting off dark blue water.

"It says," I turned my computer so Sonny could see, "she lives in Laguna Beach, and she has a garden."

"Big deal."

"Laguna Beach," I repeated. "That's on the water."

Sonny went back to his own screen and kept his eyes down. "So go live at the beach already and get a stupid boat."

"Geez Sonny. You act like I'm already gone."

He shrugged. "Have you told your grandparents she's here?"

Are you nuts? "I'm waiting for the right time." Like never.

"Mm-hmm."

I scrolled down the page. Most pictures showed her with friends, others showed her in classrooms surrounded by teenagers, and one showed her bicycling. The wind was blowing her red hair away from her face and she was smiling for the camera. "She looks happy."

Sonny stopped reading and glanced over. "Who took the picture?"

The question surprised me, but I let it go.

"She got the Teacher of the Year award three years in a row." Sonny turned his laptop around to show me. "This says she's the most popular teacher at Laguna Beach High School."

"Really?" My heart double-timed. Tess was pretty, nice and people liked her. She was so different from Marty. "Keep reading."

I found a picture of her holding a large black cat with mouser paws and long whiskers. The cat was giving the camera an intent green-eyed stare. The next picture showed the cat nuzzling its whiskers against her cheek. Tess had written, "Beethoven, my furry friend." I showed Sonny. "She has a cat. I've always wanted one."

Sonny's eyebrows knitted together. "Who'd give a cat a dumb name like Beeth oven?"

"It's not Beeth oven, you moron." Honestly, the kid really had to read more than Superman comics. "It's *Bay toe van.*"

"It's still dumb."

"Beethoven was—still is one of the greatest composers of all time. He's probably her favorite since she named her cat after him." I wiggled my long fingers. They were just like hers. "Makes sense."

"I guess."

I moved to the next picture. Tess was in a homey living room with friends, and they were playing Scrabble. Her finger was on her word play: Jacuzzis. "She plays Scrabble. She likes words," I crowed, "just like me." One more thing we had in common. "Look at that word play. It's," I counted, "thirty-five points."

Sonny rolled his eyes. "Check out the chocolate cake."

Tess was wearing an apron and icing a chocolate cake that had to be a foot tall. Wow. Tess baked. I ran my finger over the picture, and I felt a pang. Did she ever bake a birthday cake for me? "Nice. Keep going."

"Later. I'm hungry." Sonny tossed his laptop aside and it clattered onto the hardwood floor. "Mom left us a snack in the kitchen. Want some?"

"Sure." I put my laptop in its computer case and followed him. "What is it?"

"Hostess Snoball Cupcakes. Do you want milk or soda to drink?"

I put my computer case on the counter and eyed the box of blue and pink cupcakes. Hostess Snoball Cupcakes were gross. They were a small ball of dry chocolate cake with a fake cream center and covered with a quarter inch of dense, probably totally fake, colored marshmallow.

"Milk." I went to the cupboard and got out two glasses before going to the fridge.

By the time I'd poured the milk, Sonny had broken into the box of cupcakes. He picked a blue one and peeled the rubbery thick marshmallow off in one piece. Two big bites later and Sonny had a blue ring around his mouth. He held the box out to me.

I shook my head. "I bet Tess never buys this junk."

Sonny licked some blue dye from his fingers. "You like her."

No. Maybe. Yes.

"You like her," Sonny repeated.

I took a swig of milk. "She's okay."

"Admit it," he pressed.

"Why are you being a butthead?" I scanned the kitchen for something to eat that wasn't artery clogging.

"Stop biting my head off."

"I'm not."

"Are too."

I drained my glass of milk and banged it down on the counter. "I don't get it. You wanted me to like her.

Remember all that noise about giving her a chance? Feeling sorry for her?"

"That was before she turned out to be perfect."

She really was. Tess liked everything I liked. We were alike. My heart skipped. She wasn't like Marty.

"Your grandparents live here," Sonny said flatly. "You can't have it both ways. You can't have a mom in California and live here."

I know. "So what?"

"Everything's changing." Sonny reached for another cupcake. "First you were moving to the mansion. Now you'll be moving to California." He tore off the plastic wrapper. "Either way I'll be stuck here," he tossed the wrapper aside, "with no best friend."

His words slammed into me. "You can come visit."

"Get serious."

"This is crazy." I picked up my computer case and slung it over my shoulder. "I'm outta here."

"What about *The Case of the Missing Fortune?*"

"It'll still be missing tomorrow."

I banged the front door shut on my way out and trudged home. Late afternoon shadows were giving way to night-time. I stopped in front of Mrs. DeLuca's house. A fat Christmas tree loaded with ornaments filled the bay window and colored fairy lights popped and twinkled like electric sparks. A jolly Santa in a sleigh led by Rudolph and eight reindeer was on her roof, ready to dash off into the night sky. Below elves, candy canes and gingerbread men littered her front yard. The only thing missing was snow.

Snow. My heart sank to my knees. If I left Evansville now, I'd never see snow fall.

A hard choice was in front of me, and I didn't know what to do.

If I lived with Tess, it would be at the beach in California. Nice. And she had a cat.

But I couldn't just leave Evansville. In three weeks, it had become home. Sonny and I were on *The Case of The Missing Fortune*. We were professionals. And I needed to finish school.

But Sonny said I couldn't have it both ways. I thought about that.

Maybe I could have it both ways. It only seemed fair, I reasoned, that Tess wait until summer for me. After all, I'd been waiting for her all my life.

The hiccup was Gram and Pops. They were the only family I've ever known. Sure, I had to tell them about Tess sooner or later but waiting until summer would get me off the hook now. The way I saw it the later Gram and Pops found out about Tess, the better.

Yep, waiting until summer to tell Gram and Pops was absolutely the right thing to do. I wasn't being a coward. I just didn't want to hurt their feelings. I was only thinking of them.

That settled I felt better about the whole thing.

I shoved my hands into my pockets and started walking. When I reached our apartment building, my heart was lighter. I could have it both ways and now I had a plan. I took the stairs two at a time. I'd start by sending Cisco a text tonight. The Facebook pictures proved Tess was legit. I didn't need him spending my money to tell me the same thing. My plan skipped ahead to where Sonny and I solved *The Case of The Missing Fortune*. Somewhere along the way I'd collect my inheritance. If I had to go to California, no sense going flat broke.

Okay so my plan was a little fuzzy in the middle, but I was all right with that.

I let myself in and marinara sauce and garlic smells greeted me. My plan was quickly replaced with happy thoughts of spaghetti. I shrugged out of my jacket, shook off the cold and then stopped. Gram and Pops were talking to someone in the living room.

"That's Sage now." Pops raised his voice. "Sage, come join us."

"Okay." Sometimes Father Flanders came for dinner during the week. I hurried toward the living room but froze when I heard a woman's voice.

"Getting acquainted has been fun," she said.

Oh no.

CHAPTER TWENTY-ONE

"Look who's here," Gram exclaimed and put down her glass of sherry.

"Hey, son," Faith smirked. "About time you showed up."

I resisted clutching my hammering heart. Truth was I was so happy to find Faith sitting in our living room instead of Tess, I almost smiled at her. "Why are you here?"

Gram sent me The Look.

"You're not going to believe this." Pops was in his favorite chair next to the fireplace and a glass of whiskey was on the end table. No girly drinks for him. "When Frances was in high school, she used to babysit Faith's mother."

"Lacey was such a darling girl. I loved taking care of her." Gram smiled warmly at Faith. "Small world."

Too small. "So?"

Now Gram and Pops both gave me The Look. My manners were on thin ice. "So amazing," I managed to add. "Sorry I'm late."

"When Faith's mother was nine, her family moved to

Hartford," Gram went on, "and we lost touch. I always wondered what happened to her."

"We can catch up over dinner." Pops looked to Faith. "Frances always makes plenty. Please stay."

Please say no.

"I really wish I could. It smells wonderful." Faith closed her eyes and breathed in the aroma of tomatoes, spices, and baking bread. "But I have to get back to the newspaper." Faith didn't make a move to get up. Instead, she settled back in her chair and crossed one skinny leg over the other. A Doc Marten kicked the air in my direction. "Son, you're now on the payroll. Report to work at eight o'clock tomorrow morning."

"But." I sank into the chair next to Pops.

"No excuses." She held up a hand cutting me off. "Holy Cross closed today for winter break. You belong to me and the newspaper until January."

What a sneak. I stopped myself in time from reaching for Pops' glass of whiskey. Instead, I scowled. I'd been looking forward to no nuns, no memorizing Latin verbs and no getting up at the crack of dawn for the next fourteen days. Still, I had to admit Faith was good at her job. She'd done her research.

"You and Sonny are joined at the hip so bring him along," she went on.

My brain kicked into high gear. Tess was in town. Sonny and I had *The Case of the Missing Fortune* to solve. Working every day would seriously cut into both. "Sonny's mom won't let him."

"Nice try." Faith shook her head. "I called Mrs. Benson on her cell phone two minutes ago. Her exact words were, 'You can keep Sonny forever'." Faith pursed her lips. "What do you think she meant by that?"

Gram and Pops hid their smiles by taking big sips of their drinks. We knew Mrs. Benson was always thrilled to get Sonny out of the house. She just wasn't so thrilled when it was with me. Obviously two weeks of quiet had changed her mind.

"Faith has a great idea." Pops started to say more but caught himself. "Perhaps she should tell you."

"Twenty years ago," Faith's Doc Marten seesawed the air again, "Clive took over the newspaper from Jonathan Evans."

More like Uncle Clive blackmailed Evans's daughter Olivia into marrying him so he wouldn't have to pay for the newspaper.

"Evans was old school. People don't know this, but back then the newspaper never made a dime. In fact, it was bleeding money. It would've gone under, but Clive pumped his own money into it."

More like he pumped Olivia's money into it. Geez. What a sleaze.

"Clive got rid of the outdated equipment and the newspaper went high tech. He brought in the latest computers and equipment and streamlined the whole operation."

I thought about his office in the mansion. She was right.

"Clive had vision. He turned a dying newspaper into a golden business. He was smart and kept the small-town appeal by writing local stories himself. But he got new readers by hiring gifted reporters and journalists, and their readers became our subscribers. Newspaper columns became syndicated which is a nice word for making big bucks. With all the changes Clive needed people who could run the new equipment and repair it."

"At the time," Pops cut in, "Evansville was mainly ma and pa businesses. Unemployment was high. Clive used local labor to build a new building for the newspaper. Then Clive sent people to school to learn about the new equipment and how to keep it running smoothly."

"Clive put the town to work. Soon the newspaper beat out its competition for the highest circulation in the county." Now Faith reached for her glass of sherry and took a sip. "Everyone loved him for it."

Until he killed Olivia. I slid a look to Pops and saw him wipe his eyes. Even now Pops still loved him. I cut to the chase. My winter vacation was on the line. "What do we have to do?"

"In a few months it will be the twentieth anniversary of Clive becoming editor in chief. Every week for the next twenty weeks we'll feature a major contribution since his takeover. The story will be a tribute to Clive and his leadership."

This was a great idea. I was impressed Faith thought of it.

"After twenty weeks our readers will be up to date."

She'd better leave out the murder trial. It was old news. Then I changed my mind. Murder and greed were always news.

Faith gave us a big grin. "The readers will eat it up."

"And it will sell a ton of newspapers for twenty weeks." My words sounded cold even to me.

"I'm sure Faith has more than that in mind," Gram said gently and gave Pops a quick smile.

I was sure she didn't but who was I to argue? Once again, I was impressed. She was investing in my inheritance. No wonder Uncle Clive put her in charge.

Faith caught the look between Gram and Pops. "Since Sage is the new owner, it's time he started learning the business." She turned to me. "I'll teach you how to write. Once a week you'll write a story. You'll get your own byline. This way the readers will get to know you."

Not bad for a thirteen-year-old kid. I thought I'd have to wait until I was twenty-one for a byline. My Pulitzer was getting closer. "Okay."

"Not only will the readers get to know you, but they'll come to know you're in charge." Faith's expression went serious, and she looked me straight in the eye. "*The Evansville News* was Clive's legacy. You have the chance to make it yours." She waited a beat. "What do you say Boss?"

Wow. She was good. We both knew she only cared about selling newspapers, but I wasn't about to blow it for her. Or me. "Sure."

Gram and Pops smiled at each other and then at me. Tears were in Pops' eyes again. Gram sniffed and her lower lip trembled.

"Great. See you and Sonny tomorrow morning." Faith uncrossed her legs and planted both Doc Martens on the ground. "Sage, walk me out."

"Why?" I caught Gram's look, and my manners took over. "Okay."

When we got to our front door, Faith took her time putting on her coat, hat, and muffler. "Don't be late tomorrow."

"I won't." For some reason I blurted out, "I'm excited."

"You should be. Any idiot would kill for this opportunity."

Uncle Clive had done just that, but he hadn't been an idiot. He'd only gotten caught. "Right."

Faith frowned. "What I don't get," she said, buttoning her coat, "is why Clive left you the newspaper and almost everything else in his Will." Faith came up to my chin, so she had to look up at me. "Don't you think that's strange?"

Sonny had said the same thing. "He knew I wanted to be an investigative journalist."

"That's not it."

Faith and I locked eyes, playing an eyeball game of chicken. She caved first. "It doesn't make sense he'd reward the one who ratted him out." She reached into her pockets for her gloves. "There's a story here, you know?"

Faith was smart, I knew that. The fact that Sonny had come up with the same smart idea was downright scary. Realizing I hadn't thought of it first had me rethinking my career as an investigative journalist. "Bye."

Faith and Sonny were right. Uncle Clive's Will didn't make sense but there was something else nagging at me. Something I couldn't let go. The rattle of pots and pans came from the kitchen and sounds of the evening news came from the living room. Meals at the Christopher house ran on the clock. That meant I had about twenty minutes to check out my hunch. I grabbed my computer case where I'd left it near the front door and slipped past the living room and into my bedroom.

I opened my computer on my desk and grabbed paper from the drawer to make notes. It seemed a long shot the internet would have anything about a small-town newspaperman, but I did a search anyway. To my surprise I got a bunch of hits. I started with everyone's favorite, Wikipedia.

The info was pretty straight forward. I thought about Father Flanders and the mess he'd made of Uncle Clive's funeral speech. Poor guy. He should've checked out the internet.

There was the usual stuff like Uncle Clive grew up on a farm outside of Evansville, had an older brother and they'd both graduated from Holy Cross. Big deal. Marty had gone to Holy Cross. Even I was going to Holy Cross. It must be a

Christopher family tradition. I skimmed over the parts I already knew.

Hmm. This was interesting. Gram said Uncle Clive always wanted to be a newspaperman, but he'd gone to Yale and majored in business administration and finance, not journalism. I read on.

Then I hit the jackpot.

It started with the picture of Uncle Clive and Olivia on their wedding day. I'd seen it before when I was investigating Evans's disappearance. Uncle Clive had been a good-looking guy but Olivia, yikes!

I'd heard people say all brides were beautiful but clearly, they hadn't been invited to this wedding. Olivia's dress was straight out of Mary Poppins. She was clutching a bouquet of drooping roses so tight her bony knuckles showed and I didn't have to guess why. Olivia knew Uncle Clive was marrying her for her money. That might've been sad for anyone else, but they'd deserved each other.

More pictures followed but the interesting one was out of order. Uncle Clive and Olivia were applying for their marriage license at the courthouse. I got excited and zoomed in on their signatures. Olivia's was cramped and the letters so sharp they could've etched glass. Uncle Clive's signature was large and showy, practically sliding off the page. My hunch was paying off.

I opened my desk drawer and got out the lawsuit Slimy had served on me. I skipped to the exhibits at the end and found the one marked The Last Will and Testament of Clive Christopher. Slimy had called it a holographic Will because Uncle Clive had written it himself.

Uncle Clive had printed the Will in block letters but his signature on the last page was a messy scrawl. It was nothing like his signature on the marriage license application. I didn't know if handwriting changed over time, but I had an idea how to find out.

"Sage," Gram called. "Wash your hands. Time for dinner."

"Okay." I closed my computer and put everything away. Sonny had taken pictures of Uncle Clive's first Will. It would be easy to compare the signatures on the two Wills. Everyone assumed the first Will was real because Slimy had said so. But what if it wasn't?

Slimy could've easily forged it. He'd done it once before. That's how Uncle Clive had gotten the family farm.

Uncle Clive's second Will gave him nothing. But I was betting the first Will gave him a bunch.

That's why Slimy was going to all this trouble.

I needed more proof. Faith was right about Uncle Clive being the king of high tech. Still, I was betting his office at the mansion would have papers and notes he'd written. I'd think of an excuse to go there tomorrow.

I groaned out loud. Tomorrow I would be stuck working at the newspaper.

Then a slow smile spread over my face.

Tomorrow. The newspaper.

Oh yeah.

The answer was so simple I wanted to shout. Since I'd be working there, I could dig around all I wanted. No one would think twice about it. Besides, I owned the place.

Now I couldn't wait for tomorrow.

Happily, I dashed off to wash my hands and I slid into my chair in record time. When I looked up, Gram and Pops were beaming at me. "What?"

"You're now an investigative journalist." A flush swept over Gram's cheeks, and she tipped her head to Pops. "We're so proud of you."

"To celebrate," Pops picked up the basket of breadsticks and passed it to me, "let's get a Christmas tree tomorrow night."

My mouth dropped open, and I fumbled the basket. A Christmas tree!

Uncle Clive, Slimy and even Tess were forgotten. I sucked in a deep breath. My first Christmas tree. My breath blew out in one long whoosh. All of a sudden, the world was a wonderful place. Nothing could go wrong.

CHAPTER TWENTY-TWO

"Our first job at the newspaper sucked," Sonny grumbled and zipped ahead of me in the bike lane. He didn't bother putting his left arm out. Instead, he gripped his handlebars with both hands and rocketed across two lanes of traffic. Motorists slammed on brakes. Horns honked. Sonny kept going. Turn signals were for the weak.

"Hey, kid!" an angry motorist shouted from a red and white Jeep. "Watch where you're going!"

I waited for an opening in traffic before following Sonny into the left turn lane. I didn't want my first day on the job to end up in the newspaper's Obituary Section. At the stoplight I brought my bike alongside his and huffed out a breath sending small frosty clouds into the air. "At least it's over."

"Who," Sonny griped, "wants to read a story about dumb little kids making dopey macaroni necklaces?"

I peeled a sticky elbow macaroni off my shirt and ate it. Two hours with twenty-seven screaming preschoolers had left me with a splitting headache and starving. Miss Gamboa was a new teacher, and she'd cooked the pasta.

The kids couldn't string the limp stuff and had quickly become bored. Then one kid smashed a fistful of it into another kid's face. A food fight happened next, and macaroni necklaces were forgotten. Sonny couldn't take pictures fast enough. "Their parents and grandparents will be excited to see their pictures in the paper."

"I hate kids. They're like little savages. People shouldn't have them." Sonny shuddered. "They kept grabbing my camera. I put it down for two seconds and their grubby hands were all over it."

I pushed my hair out of my eyes and found another pasta shell smooshed above my left ear. I really needed a haircut. "Human interest stories sell newspapers like crazy."

Sonny shoved off again and into traffic. "I get why you're doing this but what's in it for me?"

Simple. Misery loves company. If I had to give up sleeping in for fourteen days, so would Sonny. "You're right. Stay home. Read your dorky old Superman comic books instead of becoming a famous photojournalist."

He bit his lower lip and rang his bike bell. "You don't have to be mean about it."

"I'm not." Maybe a little. "You're getting paid."

"Money isn't everything."

Of course, it is.

"I could stay home tomorrow." Sonny said without looking at me.

Uh-oh. I went for Sonny's weak spot. "What about Comic-Con? You've told me a million times how much you want to go but it's really expensive. Now you can afford it."

Sonny spared me a glance. "New York or San Diego?"

No clue. But the odds were fifty-fifty I'd get it right. "San Diego."

"My dream," Sonny sighed. "I've always wanted to go to Comic-Con."

The beauty about lying is that I could do it all day. "Since we work for the newspaper," I rattled on like I was already in charge, "I'll tell Faith to send us. We'll do a story on your favorite characters."

Sonny whipped his head around and gaped at me. "Serious?" His bike wobbled and came so close to a Tesla its driver blasted the horn. "We gotta go as Clark Kent and Jimmy Olsen."

Really? I would've gone as Iron Man. "Absolutely."

"You mean it? Oh man." Happiness was all over Sonny's face. "Do you really want to go?"

Do I really want to be with thousands of weird fans dressed up as their favorite comic book hero and video game character for four days? No way. But there was no way I was working solo for the next fourteen days. Besides I still needed his help on *The Case of the Missing Fortune.* "We're a team."

Sonny took the lead again, peddling even faster. Somehow, we managed to get to *The Evansville News* without getting run over or causing a three-car pile-up. Out front a MediaCom van was idling at the curb and the parking lot was about half full. I wondered how many people worked at the newspaper. A sudden thrill went through me when I realized I was one of them. Sonny wasn't the only kid with a dream. And today mine had come true.

We slid our bikes into the bike rack, strapped our helmets onto the handlebars and hurried inside. The sudden blast of heat made my nose run and I used my sleeve to wipe it. I had a whole drawer of handkerchiefs at home but never remembered to take one.

"About time you got here," Faith called from her

glassed-in office and came out to join us. "We've been going crazy trying to get the paper out." She watched two MediaCom techs take off a wall panel. Brightly colored wires immediately rained down. One tech slid all the switches to the right before putting the wires back inside. The other tech grabbed his power drill and replaced the wall panel. "Our internet and phones were down all day. We're finally up."

"Technology is great until it isn't," I said.

She came closer to be heard. Today's bubble gum choice was banana. "Makes a slow news day." She popped a bubble. "Did you get the story?"

Sonny raised his camera and I nodded.

"Follow me." Faith brushed past us.

"I can't believe she has a glass office," Sonny said under his breath. "How are we supposed to sneak in?"

"You don't," she tossed over her shoulder. "That's why I have it."

The newsroom was the size of a basketball court. Digital wall clocks displayed times in thirty-eight time zones. News in other parts of the world showed silently across six wall mounted big screens. The huge flat screen on the middle wall was blank.

Desks filled the room but only about eight were occupied. The men and women seated at them were very busy pretending not to notice us.

"The reporters come and go," Faith explained, "depending on what story they're working on. It's a pretty cool job."

"Yeah," Sonny patted his camera, "but not as cool as being a photojournalist."

"Reporters get paid to be snoopy," I pointed out.

"But they're not going to Comic-Con," Sonny insisted.

"That's a job for investigative journalists and photojournalists. Like Clark Kent and Jimmy Olsen."

Faith's eyebrows raised an inch. "Comic-Con?" She looked from me to Sonny before holding up a hand. "Forget I said anything."

I'd already forgotten I'd said something. I must be slipping in the lie department.

"We have nineteen reporters," Faith went on. "Every six months we rotate their beats, so it keeps their perspectives fresh. Want to try it?"

"Maybe." No. I only wanted to be an investigative journalist and chase down stories and bad guys in far off places I'd read about. Like Kathmandu in Nepal or Cappadocia in Turkey or Madagascar off the coast of South Africa or Machu Picchu in Peru. For a change of pace, I'd go to Borneo, an island in Southeast Asia. I'd see its rainforests and write about the habitats of the orangutans. Even an investigative journalist has to have some fun.

"Here you go." Faith stopped at two desks that faced each other. The desks were identical with two computers, two desk phones, two staplers and two tape dispensers. She faced the other reporters and clapped her hands twice. "Listen up, everybody."

Heads shot up and the reporters gave us their full attention.

"Meet Sage and Sonny. They'll be working with us." Faith jerked a thumb in our direction. "Sage will be covering human interest stories and Sonny will be taking pictures. Please help them all you can."

Sonny and I gave a little wave. A murmur of hellos mixed with thin smiles and quick nods came back to us. I'd bet my press pass they knew Uncle Clive had left the newspaper to me and were wondering if they'd be bossed around by a kid.

We dumped our stuff on the desks. Sonny used the hem of his coat to wipe a smudgy pasta fingerprint off his camera. I resisted the urge to plop down and swivel in my very own swivel chair. After all, I was a professional.

Faith got down to business. "What are you calling your story?"

Uh. "Macaroni Mania Madness."

"No," she said flatly. "That's a name for a punk band. Keep macaroni and dump the rest."

I stood up straight, glad to be a head taller than her. My career was at stake. "I like it."

"No," she repeated. "It's dumb and sounds like it was written by a kid."

"I am a kid." So there.

"Our readers aren't." She sliced a tiny hand through the air. "Change it or the story gets scratched."

"Whoa." Sonny frowned at her. "That's harsh."

"Listen up Jimmy Olson, uh I mean Sonny." Faith took a step closer. "If Sage's story gets cut, so do your pictures."

Sonny came around. "Faith's right. It could use a little work."

"Traitor," I muttered.

"Start your story with a catchy first sentence. Use short paragraphs but don't leave anything out." Faith blew a bubble. "Get the five Ws and one H in and get them in early."

"Huh?"

"Five Ws. One H. The who, what, when, where, why and how of your story." Sonny smirked. "You're the journalist. You should know that."

"I know that." Now. "I'm surprised you know that."

"Stop!" Faith gave us the time out signal. "Don't cram all the info into one sentence or paragraph. Only amateurs do that."

"Never!" I declared and looked offended. I still had no idea what Faith and Sonny were talking about. As soon as she left, I would find out. Hooray for the internet.

"Sonny, send me three or four of your best pictures, the ones with the most kids in them."

Now I smirked. "Because the families of those kids will buy a ton of newspapers."

Faith blew another bubble and popped it. "You're learning, son."

"Can we drop the son part? It's getting old."

"Not to me." She clapped her hands again. "Get to work. Email a rough draft to me tonight."

We were getting a Christmas tree tonight. I started to protest but my cell phone vibrated. Turning away from Faith, I slid it out of my jeans pocket. Cisco's name flashed across the screen. Ugh! I'd forgotten to text him about Tess.

Sonny tried reading over my shoulder. "What's he want?"

Faith was glaring at me.

"Sorry." I started to drop my cell phone into my pocket. Then I saw his message. "News. NOW."

"Let me remind you. You're on the clock." Faith crossed her arms over her chest and tapped her foot. "Is there a problem?"

"Um."

"Faith!" A reporter slammed the receiver down on his desk phone. "Henry just called." He grabbed the remote control on his desk and aimed it at the flat screen. "You gotta see this."

The picture jerked and a second later a female reporter filled the gigantic screen.

"Morris," Faith called to the reporter with the remote, "turn up the volume."

"Good afternoon. This is Hillary Jacobs, Channel Six, coming to you live from Evansville, Connecticut." Behind her news vans were jockeying for parking spaces. "In fifteen minutes, folks, we'll be talking with Police Chief Murphy and bringing you the latest on the *alleged* suicide of attorney Sylvester Mee. Stay tuned."

The flat screen shifted to looky-loos on the sidewalk, all craning necks wrapped in holiday mufflers for a better look.

Sonny whispered, "How'd Cisco know something was going down?"

"Dunno." I had a hunch Cisco was a guy who knew pretty much everything.

"We got scooped!" Faith shrieked and turned to a woman reporter with candy cane earrings. "Monica. How'd this happen?"

Monica was on her cell phone. Her eyes darted to Faith, but she kept talking. "Yeah, yeah. Thanks," she said and hung up. "An hour ago, the police department scheduled a press conference. We missed the announcement."

"You think?" Faith whirled around to a skinny reporter wearing a Notre Dame hoodie. "Press conferences are *your* job, Brian."

Brian stammered, "The internet's been down all day."

"It's up now! Get on this folks!" Faith ordered.

The reporters were already hurrying to get car keys, cell phones and iPads. One woman reporter slung her crossbody bag around her neck, grabbed her ski jacket off the back of her chair and yanked another reporter out of his seat by his collar. In an instant all reporters were running for the door.

"This has to be about the coroner's report and Slimy's suicide note." Faith's clenched fists punched the air. "I knew something was off when Chief Murphy dodged my questions."

"You were right," I said, "about Slimy leaving a suicide note."

"Don't get excited," Faith warned. "Just because the cops found a note doesn't prove Slimy wrote it. And a note doesn't prove his death was a suicide. Someone could've written it for him."

The killer. If Slimy's death wasn't a suicide, then it was murder.

"Remember what Faith said?" Sonny spoke up. "Three can keep a secret if two are dead." Color drained from his face. "What if someone really did want to shut your uncle up and made it look like suicide. Then he took out Slimy and made it look like suicide. Now you're asking questions. You could be next."

That didn't seem fair. I was just a kid who wanted to go to Borneo. "Nah."

Faith agreed. "Clive was in a lot of trouble. No one thought twice about him committing suicide. But then you come up with the two-million-dollar scam theory and what happens? Slimy, Clive's partner *in crime*, suddenly commits suicide."

"We're the only ones who know about the missing two million," I argued.

Sonny disagreed. "The killer knows."

My words tumbled out like dominoes. "Someone would have to go to a lot of trouble to make Uncle Clive's and Slimy's deaths look like suicides. Why leave a suicide note for Slimy and not for Uncle Clive? It doesn't add up."

"Doesn't have to." Faith put both hands on her hips.

"We're talking two million dollars. People have killed for a lot less."

"Slimy's eleven o'clock appointment..." I began.

"...is the killer," Faith and Sonny finished in unison.

"Two out of three," Faith mused. "You're the only one left who knows about the two million bucks. You're a loose end."

"Shut up."

A crackling sound came from the flat screen. The news camera shifted away from the crowd huddled together in the cold to a male reporter.

"Shh!" Faith focused on the screen.

"This is James Sullivan, Channel Eleven. We're coming to you live from Evansville, Connecticut." He touched his earpiece before continuing. "I'm told Chief Murphy has two important developments to share with us today in the *alleged* suicide of attorney Sylvester Mee." Sullivan spoke to the camera. "Chief Murphy will join us in ten minutes."

"Okay." Faith snapped to attention. "There's still time to get to the press conference." She stared at us. "Why are you still here?"

"But," Sonny stammered. "The reporters already left."

"It'll take them thirty minutes to get through the traffic on Main Street." Faith talked over him. "Get on your bikes and cut through the park. You're young. You can make it in two minutes."

"What about my story? You wanted me to email it to you tonight."

Faith cocked one eyebrow. "So?"

"The killer could be at the press conference. He could kill me."

"Gee. Murder story or macaroni story." Faith threw up both hands. "What do you think?"

"I think I have a target on my back, and I could be next!"

Faith perked up. "You're right! That's a much better story than macaroni necklaces!"

I gave it one more try. "What if we don't make it to the press conference in time?"

"That would be most unfortunate." Faith's forehead creased, considering this. "Because then I'd have to tell your grandparents you two have burner cell phones."

"Oh man!" Sonny yelped.

"That's blackmail," I protested.

"You betcha." Faith flashed us a grin and then growled, "Move it!"

"Okay, okay." We grabbed our stuff and hustled out the door.

CHAPTER TWENTY-THREE

"We made it." I jumped off my bike and we raced across the front lawn of the police station.

The double doors of the police station swung wide and Chief Murphy, followed by four cops and a grim-faced man in a long tweed overcoat, strode over to the reporters.

James Sullivan was first in the press lineup, but Hillary Jacobs shouldered her way past him. Sonny and I dodged them both and planted ourselves in front. Their curses were life-threatening but kept on the down low. Video cams were rolling, and no reporter ever got a Pulitzer for swearing at kids.

Around us handheld mics were thrust forward, and video cams zoomed in for closeups. People strolling by the station paused, took one look at the press, and stayed for the show. A second later their cell phones were up and videos rolling. Evansville was in the news.

"Chief Murphy! Sage Christopher, *The Evansville News*," I announced like I'd been doing this all my life.

Annoyance flashed across the Chief's face. "I know who you are, Sage."

"You're the newspaper's new owner," James Sullivan said. "Got any openings?" He handed me his business card. "Call me. We'll do lunch."

I cut to the chase. "What's the latest in Slimy's, I mean, Sylvester Mee's *alleged* suicide?"

We were so close I could smell Chief Murphy's coffee breath. Dark circles under his eyes told me he hadn't slept much, and deep frown lines were etched around his mouth. I pulled out my cell phone and hit record like the investigative journalist I finally was. "Take pictures," I told Sonny.

He nodded but he was already at it.

Reporters didn't believe in taking turns. Instead, they jumped in and wasted no time asking questions and demanding answers from the Chief. The six o'clock news was coming up and they needed a soundbite.

Chief Murphy would not be bullied and waited until their demands died down. "Thank you for coming. Joining me is Medical Examiner, Dr. Milton Lenox."

"Doctor," a woman reporter called out, "was Mr. Mee's death suicide?"

Hillary Jacobs pushed her cameraman forward. "Don't miss this."

But Dr. Lenox stared straight ahead and ignored the press. Only dead people interested him.

The Chief cleared his throat and referred to a sheet of paper. "I will read a prepared statement.

"Sylvester Mee was found by Mrs. Evangeline Steffens, his housekeeper. He was pronounced dead at the scene, a victim of an apparent suicide. It is believed Mr. Mee fired two shots from a nine-millimeter handgun. One bullet was recovered from the floor, eight feet from the body. The second bullet entered Mr. Mee's right temple. GSR," Chief Murphy looked up and explained, "that's gunshot residue, was discovered on Mr. Mee's right hand. Mr. Mee was right-handed. This supports the theory that the injury was self-inflicted."

Onlookers turned to each other, their comments buzzing louder than bees. This was juicy stuff.

I've read dozens of crime stories. The killer in the best ones staged the murder by putting the gun in the victim's right hand and pulling the trigger, making it look like a suicide. Along would come a really smart investigative journalist, like me, and discover the victim was actually left-handed—solving the case when the police couldn't.

The fact that Slimy was right-handed knocked the stuffing out of this.

Sonny summed it up. "No murder, no killer."

"And no story," I added, letting it sink in. I knew I should be happy. There was nothing for me to worry about. No one would be gunning for me. All I had to do was find the missing two million bucks. I could even take my time. Uncle Clive and Slimy weren't going anywhere.

Hillary gave Sonny and me a dirty look before shoving her mic between us. For Chief Murphy and the cameras, she smiled sweetly. "We know Mr. Mee left a note. What does it say?"

Everyone hushed instantly. This was the big moment.

Chief Murphy brought out another sheet of paper. "It says, 'I'm sorry.'"

Dismay rippled through the crowd. Slimy had clearly let them down by not giving them anything to gossip about.

"That's it? I'm sorry?" Lawyers were paid by the word. "Pretty lame," I snickered. Then I remembered I'd said the same thing in my note to Gram and Pops before I'd run off in their Mustang. But that was before I'd become an investigative journalist, so it didn't count.

"That's it," Chief Murphy agreed and started to go.

"Wait!" I moved closer.

"What!" Chief Murphy's cop eyes snapped to me.

"Can we see the note?"

Behind me James Sullivan gave me a friendly pat on my shoulder. "Thanks kid."

Chief Murphy held it up with both hands. Cameras flashed. "We're done here folks."

Almost. "What," I stammered, "about his eleven o'clock appointment?"

"That's right!" a reporter wearing a black fur hat with ear flaps boomed out. "Do you have any leads, Chief?"

"We believe his visitor was an out-of-town friend traveling through Evansville for the holidays. Probably stopped only long enough to say hello and drop off a gift. We found a wrapped bottle of Scotch on Mr. Mee's desk. This makes sense. If Mr. Mee's visitor lived in Evansville, he would've come forward by now."

"Did you find fingerprints on the gift?" Hillary asked.

"We did not."

Sonny put his camera away. "Do you think Faith will be mad when she hears there's no story?"

"I think she'll be ballistic." We watched Chief Murphy walk away. I pulled out my cell phone and pressed Faith's number. "I'll tell her fast, so it won't sound so bad."

"Okay."

"Tell me the good news," Faith sang when she answered. "Tell me it's murder."

I ran through it. As a bonus, I told her I wouldn't be hunted down by a coldblooded killer.

"That stinks!"

"Which part?" But it didn't matter. "I'll send you the recording and Sonny will send you pictures."

Faith let out a long sigh. "Don't forget to email your macaroni story tonight."

The last of the afternoon sun was disappearing and nighttime was creeping in. On the edge of the crowd, I saw a tall woman carrying a large shopping bag. She was bundled up in a yellow coat. Underneath a wool cap, I caught a glimpse of red curly hair.

"Send the story tonight," Faith repeated. "And--."

"Yeah, yeah," I interrupted. The woman was slipping away. "Gotta go." I ended the call.

"What's the matter?" Sonny asked.

"Over there. I thought I saw...." I searched the crowd, trying for a look. "Did you see Tess?"

"Nuh-uh." Sonny zipped up his backpack. "Let's go."

"In a minute. Tess!" I took off running. "Wait up."

She stopped and turned around, her blue eyes twinkling under the streetlights. "Sage. This is a surprise." She looked beyond me, saw Sonny, shifted her bag, and managed a wave. Little green and red pompoms danced on her glove.

"What are you doing here," I asked, happy to see her. "Were you at the press conference? Did you see me?"

"Press conference?" She raised an eyebrow. "I was Christmas shopping."

Oh. "Downtown is that way," I said, waving behind me to Main Street.

Sonny loped up. "Hey, Sage, you were right. It's your mom."

"Hi Sonny." Tess smiled and tipped her head to her left. "Yes, but my hotel is that way."

"You have a lot of stuff," Sonny said.

"I'm hopeless at Christmas and always buy too much." She gave a quick laugh. "I should've driven but I felt like walking. It was such a pretty day."

It was freezing and bleak, like something out of a Charles Dickens novel. For the hundredth time I wondered why people lived here on purpose.

"Do you want to come to the hotel? We could get hot chocolate."

"Thanks but I, uh, I have to go home." And get my first Christmas tree.

"Me, too," Sonny chimed in, "but we can come tomorrow."

I gave his arm a light punch. "We're working at the newspaper tomorrow, remember?" I filled Tess in.

"Oh Sage. I'm so proud of you." Tears shone in her eyes. She reached out to give me a hug and dropped her shopping bag.

Tess's hug was surprisingly strong for someone so thin. Without thinking I hugged her back and a silly grin escaped before I could stop it. Tess was proud of me!

"We could come on Saturday." Sonny picked up her shopping bag and handed it to her. He looked at me. "Right?"

"I guess." I held my breath in case she said no. I didn't want her to know I was excited. Sometimes I'm such a kid.

"Wonderful. We can get to know each other better." Tess gave us a beautiful smile. "I'll meet you both in the lobby at noon. The hotel restaurant is very good."

"Great," we chorused.

"Great," she echoed and waved goodbye, the pompoms dancing on her glove again.

We hustled back to our bikes. The parking lot was deserted except for the usual black SUVs that no one was supposed to know were cop cars. Fingers of fog traced the pavement and swirled up into the early night like smoke.

My cell phone vibrated in my pocket. I pulled it out and

read a one-line text from Cisco. *The night has a thousand eyes.* The guy was definitely weird. And not very original. I recognized the line from some ancient poem we'd read in English Lit class. I didn't get what it meant then and I didn't get it now.

"What?" Sonny asked.

"Cisco." I shoved the cell phone back into my pocket. "I need to tell him to stop doing a search on Tess."

"Do it later." Sonny put his bike helmet on. "Hurry up."

"Wait." I faced the police station. Inside lights were burning bright. All was quiet but something was bothering me. "We're missing something."

"Dinner."

I held onto my bike helmet for a second before jamming it on my head. "I was just thinking."

"You can think and peddle. C'mon." Sonny shoved off. He glanced back, saw that I hadn't moved, did a figure eight in the parking lot, and came back. "What?"

"Why did Slimy fire two shots?"

"Don't know. Don't care."

Sonny was a great friend, but his mind didn't turn many corners. "Chief Murphy said there were two shots. One shot—had to be the first one--went into the floor eight feet away from Slimy. The second one, the one that killed him--was to his temple."

"Yeah."

"Why did he miss the first time?"

Sonny made a face. "Because he was a lousy shot?"

That couldn't be it. "Slimy was sitting at his desk. The shot to his temple was close up. He couldn't have missed."

"He's dead." Sonny zipped his coat up to his chin. "We'll never know."

Probably. It was getting late, and I had to meet Pops at the Christmas tree farm. "Let's go."

We rode in silence until we got to the library. I promised to get him in the morning, and he rode off. I picked up the pace and by the time I got to Tiny Timmy's Tree Farm my calves were burning. Pops was parked near the entrance. I cruised over and hopped off my bike.

Pops got out of the Mustang and slammed its door. "How was your first day?"

"Good." I started with the macaroni story and ended with Chief Murphy's press conference.

"Talk of Slimy's suicide is all over town." Pops stared into the darkness. "I keep thinking what I said to him about karma." He drew in a deep breath. "I wish I could take it back."

For once I wished I could be Dr. Sonny and give Pops some encouraging TV words to make him feel better. Instead, I mumbled, "I'm sorry."

"I know you are. You're a good boy. You understand."

Not really but I nodded like I did. Maybe "I'm sorry" wasn't such a lame thing to say after all.

"We can't change the past," Pops shoved his hands into his pockets, and we started walking, "but we can make this a happy Christmas."

"Jack!" Tiny Timmy came out of the shadows.

"Meet my grandson, Sage." Pops put a hand on my shoulder. "We want the best Christmas tree on the farm."

Pops was six foot three and built like Godzilla, but Tiny Timmy had him beat. Tiny Timmy was somewhere between forty and sixty with a beard to his waist. He was decked out in a lumberjack wool coat and carried a power saw. "Frances called. She said you're to get a *seven-foot* tree." He put a beefy hand on top of his head. "This tall."

Tiny Timmy revved the power saw to make his point and his beard fluttered dangerously close to its blades. I held my breath.

"One time, Sage." Pops laughed. "One time *only* I brought home the wrong size tree. Frances won't let me forget it."

"I told you a nine-foot tree wouldn't fit in your apartment, but you wouldn't listen. Your ceilings are eight feet." Now Tiny Timmy laughed. "People make that mistake all the time. They forget about the little things like the tree stand, the ornament on top—getting the tree through the front door."

This was funny. "What did you do with the tree?"

"I put it in our front yard. We decorated it with fairy lights and ornaments. The neighborhood dogs loved it. Then Frances sent me back to get a seven-foot tree."

"Let's get started. I've got Blue Spruce, Balsam Fir, Nordmann, and Virginia Pine. " Tiny Timmy led us from one tree to another. "What do you like?"

The scent of pine was making me delirious. "Can we have one with lots of pine cones?"

"Coming up."

Tiny Timmy showed us two trees. Then I saw the one. Tall and straight, fat, and green, and loaded with pine cones.

"Are you sure?" Pops asked.

I nodded. The words were stuck in my throat. It was perfect.

Pops paid Tiny Timmy. "Frances has dinner waiting. Can you deliver it at seven?"

"Sure thing." Tiny Timmy touched his cap and his big face smiled at me. "Merry Christmas."

CHAPTER TWENTY-FOUR

I helped Pops put my bike in the trunk before hopping into the Mustang. I was so excited it took two tries to strap my seatbelt on, but I played it cool. "Now what?"

"We'll put up the tree tonight and decorate it. Tomorrow we'll decorate the apartment. Frances has one or two special ornaments she likes to put out every year." Pops eased the Mustang away from the curb and into traffic. "We argue over where they should go, make s'mores, and have hot apple cider. It's fun."

It sounded better than fun. "Okay." What were s'mores?

When we pulled into the driveway, Pops said, "Tell Frances that Tiny Timmy's coming and we need to have dinner right away. It'll take me five minutes to put the car in the garage and get your bike out of the trunk."

"Thanks." I knew I should put my bike away, but I couldn't wait to tell Gram about the tree. I ran up the stairs, taking them two at a time. Slightly out of breath I barged through the front door to our apartment. Or tried to. The door slapped me back in the face and I saw stars. Putting my shoulder to the door I tried again.

Nope.

I checked the number to the right of the door—24. We lived at 24 Kimberly Avenue. I was in the right place.

"One moment," Gram called.

The sound of tiny footsteps coming my way was followed by the sound of something being dragged away from the door. The door opened another foot, and I squeezed in. Boxes and plastic crates were piled high in the foyer. Pops said Gram had one or two ornaments but obviously he couldn't count. I shuffled my way over to Gram, avoiding the decorations spread over the hardwood floor. Two red plaid matching reindeer were hitched up to a hand painted sleigh the size of a Mini Cooper. A red and white striped pole pointing skyward said North Pole. To be sure I glanced around. No Santa. "Incredible."

Gram brushed a strand of hair from her forehead, but it fell back. She giggled. "The Christmas decorations were in the storage shed. I couldn't wait."

"You hauled these up by yourself?" The storage shed was really our garage. Since our apartment was on the second floor and Gram was the size of a fifth grader, this didn't seem possible.

"Don't be silly." Gram waved the idea away. "Officer MacDonald was walking his beat and I asked him. He would've brought everything into the living room, but he got a call. Something about a press conference at the police station."

"Yeah." I walked around a gingerbread house. "Faith sent Sonny and me to get the story. Chief Murphy says Slimy's death was suicide."

"That's sad," Gram murmured. "I didn't like the man but it's still sad."

It was but I wasn't. "Tiny Timmy is bringing the tree at seven and Pops said we should have dinner right away."

"Frances." Pops shoved the door open wider, squeezed through, and sidestepped a toy soldier. "You started without us."

Gram giggled again. I'd never heard her giggle so much. I wasn't the only one who was excited.

"There's still plenty for you to do." Gram shooed us toward the guest bathroom. "Dinner is ready. Wash up."

We raced through chicken noodle soup and grilled cheese sandwiches while Christmas carols played softly from our living room. When the clock on the fireplace mantle chimed seven, I put my napkin by my plate. Tiny Timmy would be here any minute.

"Christmas is my favorite time of the year." Gram stood up to clear the table. "I especially love Christmas Day."

"Me too!" Or I knew I would. I couldn't wait for it to get here.

"Marty was the same way." She reached for our soup bowls. "You'd never believe how much he loved Christmas."

"Uh." I was wondering where Gram was going with this, but she was right. I'd never believe Marty, the worst excuse for a dad, had ever loved anything.

"Remember all the presents we'd put under the tree, Jack?" She stacked the soup bowls, smiling at the memory. "Marty's favorite Christmas decoration was the electric train. It even puffed out smoke when it circled the Christmas tree. When it broke," she placed our silverware on top of the bowls, "he cried for a week. He was such a sensitive boy."

Marty, sensitive? Marty, crying? Never. I couldn't cry to

save my life, but I smiled back, distracted by the thought of presents. Who was I to mess up a good memory?

"Marty wanted the tinsel on the Christmas tree to be perfect," Pops went on softly, "so he'd hang it one strand at a time."

"No way."

Pops' eyebrows shot up.

"That," I stammered, "was his way." How these nice people ever had such a rotten kid like Marty was a mystery.

"Did Marty ever talk about Christmas?" Gram asked shyly.

Their hopeful faces made me feel bad, but I got it now. All this talk about Christmas was really their way to ask about Marty. They wanted me to tell them something nice. Something that would tell them he hadn't forgotten them after he'd run away nineteen years ago. Being a con man's kid, I prided myself on being a natural liar, but even I had my limits. Since I moved here, I'd been going to Catholic school, and this whole no lying thing was proving really inconvenient.

Gram and Pops were waiting.

"Well...." I struggled for something to say. "Last year when Marty and I saw the Christmas tree at the Hilton," I left out the part about it being on the way to the craps table, "he pointed out the tinsel." Then Marty had snickered and said the tree had more tinsel dripping from its limbs than a Las Vegas stripper.

"Marty loved tinsel." Pops turned to Gram. "It's one of our special memories."

Gram picked up her napkin and dabbed her eyes. Pops' big shoulders heaved a sigh. I held my breath afraid they'd both start crying.

Ding dong.

"Tree's here!" I exclaimed and hopped to my feet.

Gram and Pops both jumped.

"You and Jack help with the tree." Gram picked up the soup bowls and started for the kitchen. "I'll be right there."

Tiny Timmy didn't wait for us but flung open our front door. His left arm was wrapped around the upper part of the tree and his right hand gripped its trunk. He gave the tree a good heave ho and pushed forward. Pops and I stepped back and watched while the long lower branches of the tree strained against both sides of the door.

"Stand back," Tiny Timmy ordered and rammed the tree again through the door. Loose pine needles flew off, but he got it in. "Want it by the fireplace?" Tiny Timmy was already heading there, his Timberland boots somehow missing the decorations on the floor. He knew the routine.

"I put water in the tree stand," Gram crouched to smooth the tree skirt covering the stand, "so be careful."

"Jack," Tiny Timmy directed, "grab the middle."

Pops did and they set the tree in the stand.

Wow.

"Before you go," Gram held out two armloads of white fairy lights to Tiny Timmy, "please help Jack put these on, starting at the top."

"Sure thing." Tiny Timmy took them from her and passed one to Pops.

"Sage," Gram pointed to a cream-colored box on the fireplace, "please get the angel for the top of the tree. Tiny Timmy can put it on for us."

I removed the lid from the box and saw an angel with snowy white wings trimmed with gold threads. Her porcelain face was lightly painted, and blue eyes stared back at me. Long wavy reddish-brown hair lay against her creamy silk dress. She was beautiful.

Gram took it from me. "Everything okay?'

"Yes." The angel looked like Tess.

"She's been in the Christopher family for years. It wouldn't be Christmas without her." Gram handed the angel to Tiny Timmy. "Here you go."

After two tries Pops and Tiny Timmy got the angel positioned just right. "Good night." Tiny Timmy touched his cap. "I got more trees to deliver. I'll let myself out. Merry Christmas."

When the front door closed Gram picked up a battered box from the hearth. "We have a tradition. Before we decorate the tree, we hang our stockings at the fireplace."

That sucked. The only stockings I had were on my feet. I wiggled my toes.

"I made these many years ago." She opened the box and handed Pops a red, blue, and green velvet stocking with his name embroidered on it. Then she pulled out a white, silver and gold stocking for herself. Pearls circled her name.

"Nice," I said and wished I had one.

"I needlepointed this for you." Gram held up another stocking. A tall pine tree was set against a midnight blue sky ablaze with rhinestone stars. Deer, fat rabbits, and red foxes gazed up at a shining gold star on the tree. My name was embroidered across the top of the stocking in cursive. "I hope you like it."

My eyes stung a little, but I knew it wasn't tears. I'd never cried a day in my life. "Thanks."

"Told you he'd like it," Pops said to Gram. "You worried for nothing. Where are the stocking hangers?"

Gram gave them to him, and Pops positioned them on the mantle.

"Make a wish when you hang your stocking and your

wish will come true," Pops promised. "But only if you don't say it out loud."

That was easy. I wished to see snow fall. Everything else had already come true. "Okay."

One by one we hung our stockings at the fireplace and stood back to look.

It was really Christmas.

Pops rubbed his big hands together. "Tree trimming time!"

"Sage, start with the large bulbs first." Gram found two boxes and gave one to Pops. She took the lid off the other box. "It's important to space them evenly on the branches." She touched a branch here and there. "When it's absolutely right we'll fill in the spaces with the smaller ones."

I peered inside the box. No two ornaments were alike. Red ones, green ones, gold ones, silver ones, crystal ones, carved ones, and velvet ones. Getting this right was a big responsibility. I glanced at Pops. He'd hung three ornaments and had two more in his hands.

Pops waited for Gram to get busy with glass candy canes before saying, "Just stick them on the tree. Doesn't matter where. Frances will move them around anyway."

Got it. I set to work and had almost finished my box when our doorbell rang.

Ding-dong.

Gram glanced at the mantle clock. "It's late."

"I'll get it." Pops handed me a crystal dove and went to answer the door.

When I placed the crystal dove in front of a fairy light, the dove became a prism, sending colored lights dancing into the air. Amazing.

"Frances."

Turning around I saw Chief Murphy. His hat was in his hands and his face didn't look any happier than usual.

"What's the matter?" I asked.

"There was a break-in at Clive's mansion." His cop eyes latched onto me, and his voice was sharp. "It happened during the press conference this afternoon."

I cut him off. "Don't look at me. I was with you."

"That's terrible," Gram went to Pops. "Was Pellam hurt?"

"No. He was having dinner with friends in town."

"Pellam has friends?" I couldn't imagine that.

"Sage," Pops warned.

I could feel Gram's eyes on me, and I knew she was giving me The Look. "Why are you here?"

"The crime techs are working the scene. As far as we can tell nothing was taken from the mansion, but Clive's office was ransacked. I want Sage to meet me there tomorrow morning. He might know if anything's missing."

"Why me?"

Chief Murphy wasn't known for his humor, but he rolled his eyes. "Because you were the last person in his office."

One little burglary and I had a rep. "So was Sonny."

"You're right. Bring him with you."

"Sure." Then I remembered. "Can't. I'm working at the newspaper tomorrow."

Pops settled this. "Sage will do anything to help."

Chief Murphy took his cell phone out of his pocket, scrolled through contacts, then tapped the screen. He pressed speaker and handed his cell phone to me. "Tell Faith you'll be late."

I took it, wishing it weren't on speaker. "You know Faith?"

"I know everybody. I'm the Chief."

Faith picked up on the third ring.

I turned away slightly but it was no use. Gram, Pops, and the Chief crowded closer.

"Where's your story?" she barked. "You're late. If you're in jail again, you can sit there until I can get around to bailing you out. I'm busy."

So far, I hadn't written a word. I planned on coming up with something later tonight. Macaroni necklaces weren't that inspiring but a break-in at Uncle Clive's mansion was. I filled her in. "Chief Murphy wants me and Sonny there tomorrow morning."

"Absolutely!" Faith switched from cranky to happy and her words tripped over themselves. "Tell me good news. Did that old geezer Pellam get taken out?"

Faith's fascination with murder and violence was scary. I glanced at Gram and Pops' horrified faces. They felt the same way. "He was having dinner with a friend."

Faith's happiness deflated. "That's too bad."

I didn't bother catching my laugh.

"Is Chief Murphy listening?"

I nodded even though I knew she couldn't see me.

"That's okay," she hurried on. "Take lots of notes and tell Sonny to take lots of pictures. Call it all in and I'll write the story."

"Faith," Chief Murphy interrupted. "This is police business."

"First Amendment trumps police business," Faith snapped. "It's called freedom of the press, so back off. This will sell newspapers like crazy!"

CHAPTER TWENTY-FIVE

"The cops are still here." I cruised by three patrol cars parked in front of the life-sized sphinx statues guarding the steps up to the mansion. "We can put our bikes next to the statues."

Sonny and I jumped off our bikes and strapped our helmets to the handlebars. The stone steps were super steep, very wide, and very deep. Anyone over thirty would need an oxygen tank to make it to the top. We took a deep breath and started.

"This is like hiking up a pyramid," Sonny huffed. "Tell your grandparents to put in a ramp when you move in."

A ramp was a pretty cool idea. I could see myself zipping down it on my skateboard.

"Do you want to live here?"

Most people would jump at the chance. The mansion had everything anybody could want, including a grumpy old butler. But so far Gram and Pops hadn't said a word about moving.

I plodded up the steps and thought about living here. I couldn't see it happening. Our apartment on Kimberly

Avenue was home. We knew everybody in the neighborhood. Besides, we'd already put up our Christmas tree. "No."

Before I could knock the massive front door was opened by Talbot, a rookie cop. He was a nice guy with a baby face covered in freckles. At Holy Cross's Career Day, Talbot had given a great pep talk about life at the police academy. He'd said new recruits began each day at four in the morning and sweated through exhausting drills and training exercises. This, he happily told us, was followed by hours of mind-numbing classroom instruction. His big finish was if the recruits didn't wash out after four months, they got to carry a gun and arrest bad guys. The part about arresting bad guys sounded like a lot of fun but not enough to get out of bed before dawn.

"Chief Murphy is in your uncle's office," Talbot told us. "O'Rourke is on guard duty. Check in with him."

We went inside and I looked around. The all-white foyer with its huge crystal chandelier was blinding. The black and white marble floor always reminded me of a gigantic marble chessboard and brought on an instant headache. A speck of dust would've stood out in here, but I checked for Pellam anyway. Just because I didn't see him didn't mean anything. For an old guy he could really get around.

"Where's Pellam," I asked.

"In town."

"Thanks." Sonny and I went up the staircase and turned left. The door to Uncle Clive's office was open. A short cop built like a fireplug and with biceps like a gorilla's blocked the door. Nobody was getting by him.

"Seems like a lot of trouble for a break-in," Sonny said.

When I told O'Rourke our names he turned away and

spoke into his radio. After clicking off he tipped his head toward the door. "The crime techs finished last night. Wait for Chief Murphy by your uncle's desk and don't touch anything."

"Sure." Uncle Clive's desk was really a worktable. It and everything else in the room was covered in black fingerprint powder. Nobody was looking so I used my finger to write my name in it. Grinning, I wiped the mess on my jeans. I always wanted to do that.

"Did the cops find anything?" Sonny took his camera out of his backpack.

"Don't know." But I knew what the thief had been after. Two out of twenty-six file cabinets had their drawers pulled out and all their files dumped onto the floor. I didn't need to be psychic to know the files were from the A and W file cabinets. A glance around the neat office told me nothing else was out of place. "The thief wanted the files," I whispered.

"What files?" Sonny's voice echoed in the large room.

"Pipe down!" I hissed. "*The* files."

Sonny stared at me. "Huh?"

Chief Murphy was coming our way, so I hurried on. "Remember the *African Project file and Will file* we hid in the file cabinets when *we* broke in? The ones *I* wanted to take with us, so they would be *safe*. The ones *you* wouldn't put in *your* backpack?"

"Oh yeah!" Sonny got it now. "We should've taken them."

"Duh!" I resisted smacking him upside the head.

"Boys." Chief Murphy joined us and saw my name scrawled in fingerprint dust. "Sage, this is a crime scene."

"Exactly. Sonny and I are here to get a story for the

newspaper." I knew that would irritate him. "What happened?"

"Pellam found the office open when he was making his rounds. Nothing was taken. Clive didn't have a laptop here, only a personal computer."

"Why didn't the thief take it?" Sonny asked.

"He didn't want it, or he ran out of time. Besides, the computer is password protected. Just to be sure we'll get the techs on it." Chief Murphy jerked a thumb toward the file cabinets. "Clive kept his research for his stories in the file cabinets. We think the thief wanted a file, found it, and took off."

So far this wasn't much of a story. I gave Chief Murphy some help. "Do you know who the thief is? Did you get any fingerprints?"

"No and no," Chief Murphy stated flatly. "The thief wore gloves."

"Chief?" Two geeky guys wearing identical navy ski jackets stood in the doorway.

"Quincy. Cho." Chief Murphy waved them over and introduced everybody. "See what you can do with the computer."

Quincy tapped the keyboard. "It's password protected."

"I know," Chief Murphy said deliberately. "That's why you're here. Can you crack it?"

"Probably," Cho said. "We'll take it in."

"Anyone look for the password?" Quincy lifted the desk blotter and ran his hand underneath it. "You'd be surprised how many people write passwords down on sticky notes and leave them lying around." He moved a pen holder with two pens, three pencils and a letter opener. "The guy was neat." Quincy flipped through some pages on an old-fashioned desk calendar. "Nope. Don't see it."

Chief Murphy cut his eyes to me. "Do you know it?"

No clue. Then I caught sight of the sign on the wall, Uncle Clive's only personal touch in here. I studied the words: a newspaperman always tells the truth.

Uncle Clive had told me that a hundred times. It was crazy to think his password would be that simple. But nothing else was popping into my head so it was worth a shot. "Truth."

"Never!" the geeks scoffed and shook their heads in unison.

"Try it," I scoffed back.

Chief Murphy nodded. "Do it."

Quincy typed it in, and the screen lit up like the Fourth of July.

"How about that?" Sonny gave me a fist bump.

I shrugged like it was no big deal.

Chief Murphy motioned to the techs to take the computer. "Call me when you get something."

They nodded. Cho unplugged it and Quincy carted it off.

It was time to get this story rolling. "How'd the thief get in?"

"The mansion was unlocked."

"Lucky for him," I said. Real lucky.

Sonny crouched to take pictures of the files covering the floor. He didn't bother to look at me. "I keep telling you. This is Evansville."

Too easy. I wondered out loud, "How did the thief know Pellam was out? How did he know where Uncle Clive's office was?"

"We don't know."

The macaroni story was sounding livelier by the minute. I pushed. "You must know something."

"Pellam said Clive's office was always locked. There was no sign of forced entry." Chief Murphy let that sink in.

"I bet," Sonny stopped taking pictures, "the thief used lock picks to break in. That's how..."

"...the *thief* must've gotten in," I finished for Sonny, hoping he'd get the hint and keep his big mouth shut.

"Uh-huh." Chief Murphy folded his arms across his chest. "We think that too."

The Chief was pretty smart and was probably betting that's how Sonny and I had gotten in. Owning lock picks wasn't illegal but using them to break into homes or businesses was.

Which was the whole point of having them.

Chief Murphy checked the time. "You've got your pictures. Put all the files in order and back into the cabinets. I don't have time for that. Then you're free to go."

"Oh man," Sonny groaned. "That will take forever."

I gave Chief Murphy a friendly grin. "No problem. We're happy to do it. Right, Sonny?"

"No."

I ignored him. "Are you sticking around, Chief?" Say no.

Chief Murphy's radio went off and he silenced it. "Got roll call in twenty minutes. I'll leave O'Rourke on the door and take everyone else with me."

I gave him a mock salute. "Yes, sir."

His eyes narrowed to slits. "You better not be up to anything."

"Not me." I gave him my best innocent face. "We're here to help. Honest."

"Don't make me regret trusting you." His radio went off again. "Later."

As soon as Chief Murphy was out the door, I grabbed

Sonny's arm. "The Chief will tell O'Rourke to check on us every few minutes." I pointed to the files in front of the W cabinet. "You start over there. We need to hurry."

"Why?"

Criminy. Did Clark Kent have to explain everything to Jimmy? "The thief had to be looking for the African Project or Uncle Clive's Will. That's why the files in the A and W cabinets were dumped out. Since we put the African Project file in the S cabinet under Scam, the thief wouldn't know to look there." I went to the S cabinet and pulled it out. "See?"

"Told you it would be safe."

O'Rourke poked his face in. "How's it coming?"

"Slow." I still had the African Project file in my hands. I blew out a long breath like this was hard work. "These have to be alphabetized."

"Alphabetized!" Sonny yelped. "Why?"

I squeezed my eyes shut and slowly shook my head. "Sonny, Sonny, Sonny. We promised to help."

"You did. I didn't!"

"Get busy," O'Rourke ordered.

"You heard Officer O'Rourke. Get busy."

When O'Rourke went back to his post, I hustled over to Sonny. "The thief wanted Uncle Clive's Will. He looked for it in the W cabinet thinking it would be filed under Will. We left it in the L cabinet, for Last Will and Testament."

"This is getting complicated."

A little. "This time we're taking the files. That's why I told you to bring your big backpack." I stuffed the African Project file into my backpack. "Get the Will file before O'Rourke comes back."

Sonny went to the L file cabinet and pulled open the second drawer. "Got it. Now what?"

Incredible. Sonny had already forgotten what I'd told him. "Put it in your backpack. Then help me get these files alphabetized and back into the drawers."

"Files have words. That's your job." Sonny put the Will file into his backpack.

"We're a team. Benson and Christopher," I reminded him by giving him top billing and then added a little persuasion. "Like Jimmy Olsen and Clark Kent."

"Fine." Sonny sat cross legged on the floor and put his camera beside him. "Now what?"

I should've written this down. I said slowly, "Put the papers back into the files and stack them." Since I wanted to get done in this lifetime, I caved in. "I'll alphabetize them." I started on the A files and then it dawned on me. "Look for anything Uncle Clive wrote in cursive. I want to see if his handwriting matches his signature on his Will."

"Why?" Sonny reached for a stack of files.

"Just a hunch." I'd tell Sonny more when I had proof. Right now, he was having enough trouble putting papers into files. "I saw his signature on an old document. It didn't match the one on his holographic Will."

"Hollow what?"

"That's what Uncle Clive's last Will is called because he wrote it himself." Sonny looked puzzled so I tried again. "He printed all the legal stuff, you know like who got what, in capital letters. At the end of the Will, he signed his name."

Sonny stuffed a fistful of papers into a file and tossed it on top of a pile. It slid off. "So?"

So maybe nothing. "His signature on the old document was easy to read. His signature on the Will wasn't." I opened a file with spreadsheets. Each page showed a list of items like computers and desks with a price next to it. I read the tab on the file. It said accounting and the date was almost twenty years ago. "It's strange his signature would change so much. I'm just curious, that's all." I put the file in a stack. Then I remembered Faith's twentieth anniversary project for the newspaper. It might be interesting to do a story about how much it cost to remodel the newspaper. I put the file in my backpack.

"You think too much," Sonny muttered. "Hurry up. We need to send Faith our story."

We worked in silence for a while. About halfway through I got to my feet and stretched. "Did you find anything Uncle Clive wrote in cursive?"

"Nope. Just a bunch of emails and old newspaper clippings." Sonny was still sitting cross legged on the floor and surrounded by files. "Try his calendar."

I wanted to scream. Next time I was definitely working solo. Instead, I said as patiently as I could, "The techs took Uncle Clive's computer, remember?"

"Not the calendar on his computer. The calendar on his worktable."

"Yes!" I should've thanked Sonny. Instead, I scampered over and snatched up the calendar. It was the kind no one used any more, was the size of a paperback novel and lay open on the table. Each page was for a different day. Not surprising, it was open to the date Uncle Clive got arrested. It's hard to socialize when you're in jail.

I went through the few weeks before his arrest and saw notes written about lunch appointments, deadlines, and things to remember. The notes were all written in the same messy scribble. Just like his signature on his last Will. I started to rip off a few pages but remembered this was a crime scene. Chief Murphy would freak if I took anything.

That cracked me up, so I took the calendar. I'd worry about Chief Murphy later. Time to go. "Ready?"

Sonny's head was bent over a picture. "You gotta see this."

I put the calendar in my backpack and came over. "What?"

"This lady looks like your mom and the guy with her looks like your dad. Don't know who the old dude is." Sonny turned the picture over. "It says Arieli Antonetti. White Sands Casino, Las Vegas."

"Let me see." I saw a smiling Tess standing between Marty and another guy, probably Antonetti. The picture was really old, and Tess and Marty were really young. Behind them a cocktail waitress balanced a tray of drinks and desperate people sat at blackjack tables clutching cards like their lives depended on them. One fat, bald guy looked like he was arguing with the pit boss. Two security guys wearing serious faces and probably gun holsters under their sports coats stood at the ready. Whoever the bald guy was, he wasn't welcome. The picture showed all the glamor of a low budget casino.

"Who's Arieli Antonetti?"

"No idea." I studied the picture. Antonetti had slicked-back white hair and an uneven scar running from his right cheekbone to his chin. He had black beady eyes, and his mouth was one hard line. My guess, Antonetti was either a crime boss or a loan shark.

Sonny already had his cell phone out and was typing.

"Stop!" I grabbed his cell phone out of his hands.

"Hey!"

O'Rourke stuck his head in. "Everything all right in here?"

"Sonny was getting the alphabet mixed up." I reached for a file and waved it at Sonny. "X comes after W."

O'Rourke gave us a hurry up gesture with his hand. "I've got to get back to the station."

"Okay." I waited for O'Rourke to go outside. "This is a burner phone, remember? If you use a website to look anything up, it can get traced back to you. We'll do a computer search later."

"Sorry." Pink flashed over Sonny's face, and he bit his lower lip. "Forgot."

"No worries." Getting mad at Sonny was like getting mad at a puppy. Neither one would ever understand why.

Facts and questions exploded in my head. White Sands Casino was in Las Vegas. Tess and Marty had lived in Las Vegas. Tess said Marty had gotten in with a bad crowd. Antonetti looked the part. Did Uncle Clive do a story on the White Sands Casino? Sonny found this picture with the W files. I looked for a White Sands Casino file but didn't find one. Did the thief take it? Then another thought hit me. Uncle Clive had known Tess.

"We need to get back to the newspaper," I said.

"What about these files? You said we had to alphabetize them."

"No time for that." I was already sticking loose papers into any old file. "Help me get these files back into the cabinets. If Chief Murphy says anything, we'll say O'Rourke wanted to get back to the station." And I want to get back to the newspaper and do a computer search on Antonetti.

Sonny hopped to his feet and got to work. The W files went pretty quickly. "Now what?"

"Help me with the A files. Open the drawers and I'll hand them to you."

We filled three drawers and were starting on the fourth. By this time, I'd given up being neat. I was on my knees and gathering a bunch of files when I got my first paper cut. It really stung and I stuck my finger in my mouth.

"Are you bleeding?"

I shook my head, no. Keeping my finger in my mouth I started to hand Sonny a file. Then I saw it.

Partially hidden under the file was a red and green pompom. My heart tumbled in my chest. In an instant I remembered Tess waving goodbye to me after the press conference. I remembered the red and green pompoms on her gloves. The room was whirling around me, and I was having a hard time breathing.

"What's the matter?"

I held up the pompom for Sonny to see. "Tess was here." I wobbled to my feet and shoved the pompom into my pocket.

Tess was the thief.

CHAPTER TWENTY-SIX

"Wait up," Sonny called.

I shook my head, raced out of the mansion, and ran over to my bike.

"Hold on."

"No." I jammed my bike helmet onto my head. "I don't want to wait. I don't want to talk about it." A ragged breath escaped. I didn't want to believe it was true.

"You should hear Tess out. Maybe there's a reasonable explanation behind all this."

"Go back to your daytime TV, Dr. Sonny. There's no reasonable explanation. Tess broke into the mansion. She broke into Uncle Clive's office. She and Marty were friends with some really bad guy."

"Marty and Tess lived in Las Vegas. They were friends with lots of people."

"Here's what really stings." My temper was hot, and my fists were clenched. "Uncle Clive knew her, and he never said one word. Not one word."

"Okay." Sonny straightened his glasses and looked away. "That one's a little harder to explain."

"Everything she told me was a lie. She didn't miss me. She didn't look for me." I shrugged into my backpack and pulled on my gloves. "It was all one big con."

"Give her a chance."

I gave Sonny a stony glare. "No."

"Ask her at lunch tomorrow. If you don't like what she says, then okay." Sonny waited.

"No."

"I get it. You're mad."

Mad didn't cover it. I felt betrayed. I wanted to yell, to scream. I wanted to punch something. I would've cried if I could.

"You're an investigative journalist," he pressed. "Shouldn't you be interested in both sides of a story?"

No! Yes. "Maybe."

Sonny tried again. "She's still your mom."

That was low. "Get on your bike. I want to get back to the newspaper. I want to get to work. I...." I let the rest of it hang in the air. "Just do it, okay?"

"Okay."

As soon as I climbed onto my bike my cell phone started vibrating in my pocket. It was Cisco. No hello, hi, or how's it going. Just a one-line text. *Truth lies in the lies.*

What was that supposed to mean? I glanced around half expecting to see him lurking behind a tree, wearing camouflage gear, branches on his head and black out paint on his face. There was no one.

The guy was definitely strange and in his own world. What got me was how he always seemed to know what was happening in mine.

I dropped my cell phone into my pocket. It was a good thing I hadn't called him off the Tess search. I had questions for him, but they'd have to wait. Sonny was already halfway down the driveway, and I peddled hard to catch up. When we reached *The Evansville News*, we parked our bikes at the rack and hefted our backpacks. As soon as we walked through the front door Faith hustled over.

"About time you two showed up." She fell into step beside us. "We'll run the mansion story as a simple break-in, but the good news is since it was at the mansion and Clive owned the newspaper and he was bound to have made a lot of enemies in his career as a successful newspaper publisher and now he's *dead* we should be able to get some mileage out of it."

"You shouldn't put the who, what, where, when, why and how into one sentence," I said just to annoy her. "Only amateurs do that."

"Yup but I'm still the boss." She grinned, showing off her perfect white teeth. "I can do what I want."

Faith was in a good mood and that annoyed me. I kept walking and she followed us into the newsroom. When we dropped our backpacks onto the desk, they made loud *thunks*.

She eyed the bulky backpacks. "What's in there?"

"My camera equipment," Sonny stuttered and tossed his coat on top of our backpacks. "A lot of camera equipment."

Faith waited.

There was no getting rid of her, so I sort of told the truth. "When we were putting the files away, I saw a file on accounting. I thought we could use it for a story."

"Boring." Faith put both hands on her hips and her right foot started tapping the floor. "Give me something."

"The file is almost twenty years old. Uncle Clive made a list of everything he bought to remodel the newspaper and how much it cost. It would make a good twentieth anniversary story."

"Hmm." Faith's head tick-tocked as she weighed the possibility, but her spiky hair stayed in place. "Not bad." She checked her cell phone. "I've got a meeting. Bring me what you've got in thirty minutes."

Which was nothing. "Sure."

"Sonny, you're working with Whiny today. He'll show you how to do a photo layout. Leave your backpack and follow me."

Sonny gave me a half wave and worried look.

"Have fun." I waved back.

When I was sure they were gone I texted Cisco. *Is Tess Langley my mother?*

His reply was quick. *Yes.*

I thought about that before sending the next text. *Is the woman here Tess Langley?*

There was a two second delay before my screen flashed. *Are you stupid? Read my texts.*

That was rude but at least I had one answer.

I logged in and did a search on Tess Langley. Only Facebook came up. That was odd. No one could hide in this high-tech world. I tried Tess Christopher. Nothing.

Antonetti was next. It wasn't hard to get info on White Sands Casino. On its face it looked to be legit. I did a deeper search. Las Vegas news articles were more interesting. People who tangled with Antonetti ended up dead. So far Antonetti had led a charmed life and was like Teflon. Nothing bad stuck to him. Only the people who worked for him went to jail—never him. It was no question the casino was a front for all the bad stuff he was into. The real question was why wasn't he in prison?

The answer was simple: In Las Vegas cash was king. A

guy with a casino could afford to hire a clean-up crew to keep him squeaky clean.

I did a search for pictures of Antonetti, but the guy was camera shy. In fact, the only picture of him anywhere was in my hot little hands. The newspapers called him a recluse. I looked that one up. Recluse meant a person who avoided other people. If anyone knew what Antonetti looked like, he wasn't talking.

Being a smart bad guy Antonetti had discovered the way to a long life was to be invisible.

So how did the picture of him, Tess and Marty end up in Uncle Clive's office? Since Uncle Clive knew Tess and Marty, maybe he'd been at the casino. Maybe he'd been the one who'd taken the picture. If so, did he keep it for a souvenir? No. Uncle Clive wasn't the sentimental type. Was it for a newspaper story? Again, no. Uncle Clive wrote only local stories.

My guess was if Uncle Clive had written a story and run a picture with Arieli Antonetti, Uncle Clive would've wound up dead. And way before now.

So why keep the picture? I was missing a major piece of this puzzle.

It was too late to ask Marty and Uncle Clive any questions. They were both dead. Tess was the only one left with the answers.

Did I really want to know? Yes.

I made up my mind. I'd meet her for lunch tomorrow and ask her flat out. After all, I was an investigative journalist.

Noise from the newsroom reminded me I had a story to do for Faith. I opened the accounting file and started with the first page.

I was better with words than I was with math. Skipping

to the last page I found the total in neat black and white type: $4,367,042.67.

Holy moly joly. That was a lot of dough.

My cell phone vibrated. Hoping it was Cisco I jumped on it, but the caller ID said Unknown. "Hello."

"Where are you?"

It was Faith. She was chewing bubble gum and I wondered what today's flavor was. "How'd you get my number?"

"Sonny." She popped a bubble. "I asked him when I was showing him the art department. The kid was so blown away by all our toys he answered without thinking." She laughed. "I'm glad he wants to be a photojournalist and not an investigative journalist. That kid can't lie to save his life."

No kidding. "What do you want?"

"Your story. Bring it with you." She hung up.

When I reached her office, Faith was alone. She motioned me in. "Do you like working at the newspaper?"

"It's what I've always wanted." She'd caught me off guard and I felt heat rush up my neck. At least I didn't say something dopey like it was my dream.

"Me, too." Faith put both elbows on her desk. "What other job pays you to snoop through people's lives? There's nothing like juicy gossip." Now she leaned back in her chair and studied me. "Clive always said the truth was better than gossip."

Not quite. "Uncle Clive said, 'A newspaperman always tells the truth.'"

"Truth," Faith argued, "can get in the way of a good story."

Not true. "He said the truth was the truth."

She changed the subject. "Why do you want to be an investigative journalist?"

This was beginning to sound like a job interview. Since I already owned the newspaper, I had nothing to lose. "A librarian gave me a book about investigative journalists. They went to places I'd only read about and solved cases no one else could." This was getting too touchy feely. Sonny must be rubbing off on me. I could feel my face getting redder by the second.

"That's a hard job. You don't see people at their best and you get doors slammed in your face a lot. Stick with human interest stories. Nobody shoots at you. Nobody hates you."

"I want to make a difference." Where did that come from? But it was true. Sonny was definitely rubbing off on me. I changed the subject. "Why are you being nice to me?"

Faith laughed. "I like having someone under forty to talk to once in a while, even if it's you."

"You have Whiny."

Faith made a face. "Brothers don't count." She held out her hand. "Give me what you've got."

I did. Faith went to the last page and choked on her gum. "That was a lot of money back then. Hey, it's a lot of money today. We could play up the money angle and tell our readers how much $4,367,042.67 would be in today's money. There's a rule for that." She tipped back in her chair and stared at the ceiling. "Take $4,367,042.67, invest it at 6% and multiply it by, in our case, twenty years." She shook her head. "Can't do it. I suck at math, but I know it's a lot. You figure it out."

I almost said I was lousy at math too but stopped in time. I didn't want her to think we were bonding. "Okay."

Faith reached for a pen and crossed off several items on the list. "Some of this has been replaced with the latest equipment. We spend a small fortune every year on technology. You gotta sell a lot of papers to make ends meet."

Maybe that's why Uncle Clive majored in business administration and finance. Smart guy.

"Here are a few tips for your story." Faith tossed the file my way. "Go to Barry in Personnel. Ask him for names of people who worked for Evans and are still here today. Interview them. You want to get a take on how the paper improved." She clicked her pen a few times. "See Erin in Circulation. Ask for names of subscribers who've been with us since Evans. Interview them. Get their take on what they like, don't like since Clive took over."

"Okay."

She chewed on her gum and popped a bubble. "For the real skinny see Hattie in our lunchroom. That woman's a gossip hound. She knows all."

"We have a lunchroom?"

"Didn't I tell you?" Faith cocked an eyebrow. "It's on the fourth floor. Clive put it in. It's open 24/7. Serves breakfast, lunch, and dinner. Junk food and snacks are available all the time." She pointed her pen at me. "It's free. Help yourself. Sonny too."

If Sonny found out there was free food, *The Evansville News* would have to rewrite their business plan in order to survive. "Okay."

Faith was staring bug-eyed at me. "Why are you still here? Go!"

Our fun time was over. I was hungry so I decided to start with Hattie and took the stairs to the fourth floor. By the time I reached the lunchroom I was out of breath.

The lunchroom was quiet. Three reporters sat at a table near the window, drinking coffee and munching on chips. The big round-faced clock on the wall said 3:25. It was too late for lunch but not too late to get a snack and a story from Hattie.

The lunchroom reminded me of the one at Holy Cross; only the smells coming from the kitchen were a lot better. I grabbed a lunch tray and got in line behind a woman with a cell phone wedged between her ear and her shoulder. A leather messenger bag was draped over her other shoulder, and she was fumbling to put an iPad into her purse.

"If I get one more call from Pritchard, you'll lose your reason for living. Do you hear me," she snarled into her cell phone and then disconnected. She looked over her shoulder and scowled. "You weren't supposed to hear that."

"What?" I gave her a blank look.

"Nice try kid. "I'm Anna Zimmerman," she held up her cell phone, "and that was my son Jake. Last day of school before winter break and he's in the principal's office. Again. What an idiot. I'm hoping the army will take him."

I didn't know what to say so I didn't.

"You're Sage Christopher, our new owner. Word travels fast." She looked me up and down. "You want to be an investigative journalist. Clive talked about you. Said you were smart. Why?"

"Why what?"

Now she frowned. "Keep up kid. Why do you want to be an investigative journalist?"

For the second time today, I found myself giving the same answer. This time it was easier. "I want to write stories that tell the truth."

"Mm-hmm. Good luck with that one. Nice meeting you." She turned to the woman behind the counter. "Hattie, I'll have the chicken tenders and French fries."

I watched Hattie load up a plate with golden chicken and fries. She had a face as round as the lunchroom clock and hips as wide as a park bench. She handed the plate to Anna. Anna moved down the line and took two chocolate chip cookies.

"Hi. I'm Sage Christopher."

"Of course you are, honey." Hattie's eyes were kind, and her voice was warm. "I'd know you anywhere. I knew your daddy." She left it there. "What can I get you?"

"Um." I didn't want to spoil my dinner, but I'd missed lunch.

"I have just the thing." Hattie slid a large slice of pepperoni pizza onto a plate and waited until I put it on the tray. "Anything else?"

This was my chance. "I'm writing a story about the changes Uncle Clive made to the newspaper. What can you tell me?"

"Oh honey." She chose a chocolate chip cookie, put it on a small plate and then handed it over. "Your uncle was the best. He gave me a chance when no one else would." She wiped her big hands on her apron and her eyes grew misty. "My Samuel was really sick. After he died the bills kept rolling in. I'd never worked and had five little kids to support. The bank wanted to foreclose on my house. I had no idea what to do."

I was afraid Hattie might start crying, so I asked, "What happened?"

"Mr. Christopher came right to my house. He knew my Samuel. Mr. Christopher said *The Evansville News* was getting a lunchroom and asked if I'd run the kitchen. I told him I didn't know anything about running a kitchen at some fancy newspaper."

The kitchen behind Hattie boasted a gleaming copper cappuccino/espresso/latte machine, a soft serve ice cream machine, refrigerators, freezers, microwaves, double ovens, a

12-burner stove, and other shiny appliances. Fancy must mean expensive. I'd look it up in the file. "Then what?"

"Mr. Christopher laughed in my face and said, 'Hattie, if you can raise five kids, you can run a kitchen.'" She waved a hand around her. "That was then, and this is now." One tear ran down her plump cheek. "I'll never forget him. Never forget what he did for me and my kids." She wiped the tear away. "I'll miss him forever."

"Thank you." I picked up my tray and found a table.

The pizza was good, but Gram's chocolate chip cookies were better. While I ate, I searched the accounting file. The lunchroom was listed on page five. When I saw the cost, I stopped eating. Who knew pots and pans could cost so much?

On my way out I saw a junk food basket next to the drop off for trays. Being a good friend, I got two Snickers, two Baby Ruths and two bags of M&M peanuts for Sonny and me. I started on my M&M peanuts first. A better friend might've waited but I was still hungry.

I munched while I walked and thought. The lunchroom was a good idea. No wonder Uncle Clive had been popular. When I reached the newsroom Sonny was already there. I tossed him the candy and he immediately tore off the Snickers wrapper.

"This place is so cool." Big bite of Snickers. "They got like everything." His eyes were bright, and he chewed in double-time. The sugar rush was kicking in. "This is better than Journalism Club. I can't believe I'm here."

"We're a team. Benson and Christopher."

Another big chomp and the Snickers was history. Sonny considered the Baby Ruth and went for it. "Faith says we have the weekend off. But she wants the first draft of your accounting story by tomorrow night or you're dead meat.

Can you?" Half the Baby Ruth was gone, and Sonny was talking at warp sugar speed. "We're having lunch with your mom tomorrow. Don't forget. She's counting on us."

"No sweat." I'd be there and I was counting on getting the truth.

CHAPTER TWENTY-SEVEN

"Uh." I stopped in the doorway to our living room. "What is that?"

"It's the Grinch." Gram patted his bony shoulder. The 4-foot high, green strange looking guy was decked out in a red and white suit next to our Christmas tree. "I love him! He's so Christmassy."

I knew the Grinch. I didn't know why he was in our living room or how I'd missed him in our garage. I liked Christmassy but most people would've gone with a wreath or a plate of Christmas cookies. "Amazing."

The giggles were back. "I know!" Gram pressed a button. The Grinch wiggled his fat butt and belted out, "You're a mean one, Mr. Grinch."

The fire in the fireplace crackled bright and our living room was toasty, but it had nothing to do with Gram's rosy cheeks. The half glass of sherry on the end table gave her away. Pops wasn't home yet, and she'd had a few nips.

"There's more." Gram stood aside. A ragamuffin looking mutt sat at the Grinch's feet with a cardboard sign clenched between its teeth. The sign read, "Maybe Christmas, the Grinch thought, doesn't come from a store."

The dog was cute in its way, but the Grinch wasn't too bright. Everyone knew Christmas came from a store. Otherwise, there'd be no presents. That reminded me I needed to get Gram and Pops a gift.

Gram introduced us. "Max is the Grinch's dog."

"Right." I knew that.

"Frances." The front door banged shut behind Pops. A minute later he came in juggling a large shopping bag and a gigantic white box tied with a gold bow. "Sorry I'm late. I had to stop by Mr. Ashton's law office."

I went on guard. "Why?"

"Good news. Mr. Ashton got Slimy's case against you dismissed." Pops gave the box to Gram and set the shopping bag on the floor. "That's over."

"Thanks." It was great news, but the white box had my attention. Something inside the box was banging against all four sides. A lot. I had to ask. "What's in there?"

Gram and Pops exchanged looks before Gram handed the box to me. "Merry Christmas," they sang.

More banging from the box. "You got me a bomb?"

"Open it!" they chorused.

A low hiss was followed by nonstop scratching. I lifted the lid and looked into the face of a very ticked off Merlin.

Meow.

Merlin leaped out of the box and landed softly on all fours. He strutted over to the Christmas tree and sniffed a crystal ornament. When Merlin caught sight of Max his back arched like a black croquet hoop. *Hiss.*

"I, I," I stumbled over the words. "Wow. I've always wanted a cat." Now I'd have to get Gram and Pops a really nice Christmas gift. But what? It would be hard to top a cat.

"Violet called after your meeting with Mr. Ashton. She said you and Merlin hit it off. Violet thinks he's about three years old." Pops looked to Gram. "We thought, hoped you'd want him."

"Besides it's Christmas and Merlin needed a home." Gram smiled hopefully at me. "No one should be alone at Christmas."

Violet had said the same thing. She was right. "Wait until I tell Sonny," was all I could say.

"Frances, let's eat in here while we decorate." Pops didn't give the Grinch and his furry pal a second look. He went over to the fireplace and spread his hands out to warm them. "I told Sage we'd make s'mores."

"Absolutely. Let me get Merlin settled first. He needs to know this is his home." Gram pulled Merlin's bed out of the shopping bag and placed it under the tree. "Here you go."

Merlin gave the bed a passing glance before hopping onto the fireplace hearth and stretching out onto his side. He shot out a front leg, unfurled a pink tongue and began grooming his paw. Merlin was home.

"I'll help you in the kitchen." Pops winked at me. "Are you up for some serious decorating?"

A jolly feeling bubbled inside me. I couldn't imagine cramming anymore Christmas into our living room, but it was fine by me.

Pops left to help Gram. Merlin was working on his other paw, so I went to sit by him. Now that I had a cat, I wasn't sure what to do with one. I started by giving the top of his head a little scratch.

Merlin instantly stopped his grooming, gripped the edge of the hearth with both front paws and went perfectly still. He looked ready to bolt.

"Okay. No head scratching. Got it." I ran my hand down his back the way I'd seen Violet do.

Merlin stared up at me.

I checked the doorway before slipping my cell phone from my pocket. "Wait until you meet Sonny. He's my best friend." I took Merlin's picture and sent it to Sonny with a quick text. Then I gave Merlin's back another rub. "You'll like him."

Merlin flicked his whiskers. They were long and surprisingly white.

"I'm sorry about Mr. Vickers." The old man must've been Merlin's best friend. I'd read some pets never get over losing their owners. "That's hard. I'm new here, too." I let out a sigh. "I hope you'll be happy here."

Merlin put his chin on my thigh.

"Gram makes the best breakfasts. She even makes her own whipped cream." This time I stroked Merlin's shoulders.

Merlin's motor began soft and low in his throat and grew louder. *Purr.*

I stroked some more. He *purred* some more. We were off to a good start.

Pops brought in a tray piled high with submarine sandwiches and jutted his chin toward the coffee table. "Can you put the books on the end table?"

"Sure." To get up I had to move Merlin's chin aside. He objected. *Yeow.*

Gram came in and set a tray with three mugs of steaming apple cider next to the sandwiches. "I love hot apple cider. It's so festive." The smell of cinnamon and apples filled the air, making our living room smell like hot apple pie.

When Gram handed me a mug, I stared. There was a stick in it.

"Do you like hot apple cider?" Gram asked.

Don't know. "Yes." What's with the stick?

"Wonderful. The cinnamon stick gives it an extra touch." Gram used the cinnamon stick to stir the cider in her mug and took a sip. "Mmm. Heavenly."

I gave the cinnamon stick a few twirls in the cider before trying it. Hot apple cider steam went up my nose. Not bad.

While we ate and decorated, I told Gram and Pops about my day at the newspaper. It didn't take long to fill our living room with Christmas. Merlin did his part by sniffing or rubbing against the decorations and knocking a few off the tree.

When we emptied the last box, Merlin jumped inside and hunkered down. Then his ears slowly came up followed by two green eyes. He kept the rest of himself safely hidden in the box. That struck me as funny, and I laughed.

Meowww. Merlin dropped out of sight. He didn't have a sense of humor.

"We need to get Merlin a Christmas stocking," Gram said, "and things to play with."

I'd heard pet owners did that, but I didn't think Gram wanted mice running around in our apartment. Still Gram was right. Merlin shouldn't be left out of the fun. "Sounds good."

"Time for s'mores," Pops declared.

"I'll get them." Gram smiled happily at the living room before heading to the kitchen.

"This is a wonderful Christmas," Pops said. "We're glad you're here."

"Me too." My first real Christmas.

Gram carried in a tray with graham cracker squares, a bag of marshmallows, skewers, and jumbo Hershey chocolate bars. She handed the skewers and marshmallows to Pops. "You're in charge of these."

Pops put two marshmallows on each skewer and handed me one. Gram broke the chocolate bar into squares and put a square on top of each graham cracker.

What was all the fuss about? S'mores didn't look very yummy. They looked more like earthquake rations.

Pops motioned me to the fireplace. "The fire's hot so this won't take long." Pops held the skewer close to the flame and the marshmallows went quickly from white to golden brown. "Try it."

I did and sugary smells filled the air. Merlin gave up on the box and came over. He sat in front of the fire and scooted his rump under himself to watch. Within seconds my marshmallows were blistering and ready to drop off the skewer.

"Sage, let me." Gram took the skewer and placed the marshmallow goo on top of a cracker with a chocolate square. She covered the whole thing with another graham cracker and pulled the skewer free. "Enjoy."

Merlin rubbed against my leg, reversed direction, and rubbed again. *Meow. Meow.*

"Uh-huh. Cats can't have chocolate." Even I knew that. I wiped the edge of the cracker with my finger and blew on the melted marshmallow. When it was cool, I put my finger close to Merlin's mouth. He sniffed, his whiskers twitched and then his rough tongue licked the marshmallow from my fingers. It tickled.

"Now you try it," Pops suggested.

I took a bite and chocolate and marshmallow oozed out. I licked the edges fast, swallowed and nearly swooned.

Pops laughed. "That's why they're called s'mores. You have to have some more."

Gram was already building another round.

I broke off a chunk of graham cracker and placed it in front of Merlin. He sniffed, drew back his head and then batted the piece with his front paw. In a flash of black fur Merlin was off and playing a fast game of feline soccer across the hardwood floor.

"Forget the toys," I told Gram. "Buy him graham crackers."

We ate until we were stuffed.

"What are you doing tomorrow?" Gram started gathering up the plates.

Uh-oh. On Saturdays Gram made a special lunch for Sonny and me but we were meeting Tess at the hotel for lunch. I shouldn't have kept Tess a secret this long but now I had no choice. I needed to keep quiet a little longer. Get some answers first. I went with the first idea that popped into my head. "Sonny wants to go Christmas shopping."

"Sonny!" They exclaimed at once and exchanged looks.

Okay so it wasn't my best idea, but it was sort of true. He'd promised to help me pick out a present for them. Just not tomorrow. Besides, keeping secrets at Christmas time wasn't lying. I think.

"That doesn't sound like him," Pops said slowly. "Are you sure?"

I wanted to kick myself for not straight out lying. I was so much better at it than telling the truth. "He may not *buy* anything tomorrow. He's excited about working at the newspaper. When he gets paid *then* he can buy something." I smiled. "You know."

They didn't.

"You can pick up a stocking for Merlin," Gram suggested. "Try the gift shop on the corner of Mulberry. I saw some really cute ones in the window."

"Okay." A yawn came out of nowhere. Bed was calling my name and I still needed to go through Uncle Clive's calendar tonight. I started to pick up the mugs, but Gram waved me off.

"You've had a busy day."

"Thanks." I tucked Merlin under my arm and picked up his bed. Merlin snuggled against me and rubbed his whiskers along my cheek. I couldn't believe he was really mine and I let out a sigh. Gram and Pops were looking at me. I knew I should say something, so I went with the truth. "This is the best Christmas."

Gram smiled. "We're glad."

"Good night," Pops said.

When I got to my room, I dropped Merlin's bed on the floor at the end of my bed. "You can sleep here." I pulled the comforter down, fluffed my pillows then slid my cell phone under them.

Merlin took that as an invitation, hopping onto my bed and curling into a ball on top of my pillows. He immediately dropped into sleep.

I changed into my pajamas, got Uncle Clive's calendar, but I couldn't get into bed without waking Merlin up. I was really tired, but it didn't seem right to disturb him. The poor cat had lost his owner and he was in a new home. I tried sliding under the blanket but only half of me made it.

Merlin was making snuffling sounds. I kept one foot on the floor and wiggled my butt hoping he'd scoot over. He didn't budge.

I wiggled a little more and managed to get more of the

blanket around me. Scrunching down I put my head on the edge of the pillows. I opened the calendar and tried to read but got a crick in my neck. "Can you move over?"

Merlin's snores grew louder.

Sitting up I slowly pulled out the bottom pillow from underneath the top pillow. Merlin shook himself awake, growled, and smacked at the pillow with his paws.

"This is nuts. We gotta share." I picked him up, put him alongside me and rubbed his back. Merlin pinned his emerald eyes on me and flicked one ear.

Then I got busy. Starting from the date of Uncle Clive's arrest, I worked my way backward through December. He'd made scribbly notes about things to be done at the newspaper. Nothing interesting. I thought about his signature on the marriage license application. It had been so neat. He must've been really happy about getting the newspaper for free. Too bad he'd also gotten Olivia.

On a hunch I skimmed through the days until the end of December. There were a few notes here and there. Again, nothing interesting.

I started to close the calendar but stopped when I saw the page for the day Uncle Clive died. He'd written Antonetti.

Somehow, I'd missed it the first time around.

I wracked my brain for why Uncle Clive would have a meeting with Antonetti and why in Evansville. The newspapers said no one had seen him in years.

Something was off.

My cell phone vibrated. A text from Cisco. *Antonetti + Marty + Slimy +Clive + you = one common denominator.*

I stared at the message. Marty used to say that if things didn't add up, look for the common denominator. Really weird that Cisco would say the same thing. And now.

I scrubbed my hands over my face and studied Cisco's text. What could the five of us have in common?

Then, just like that, everything clicked into place. And, just like that, I knew where the two million bucks from the African Project had gone.

I slipped out of bed and turned off the light. Being careful not to wake Merlin, I shoved the calendar under my pillows, wiggled back in and closed my eyes.

The Case of the Missing Fortune finally added up. Sleep came over me and I drifted off.

CHAPTER TWENTY-EIGHT

"Why did we have to get here so early," Sonny grumbled. "Your mom said noon."

Last time Tess had beaten me to the library. This time I'd been determined to get here first. I hitched my computer bag onto my shoulder and took a quick look around. "I've never been inside the Evansville Hotel before. It's a busy place."

"Sage! Sonny!" Tess called from an overstuffed chair next to the fire. She got up and threaded her way through a family of five. "Hi."

I couldn't believe it. She'd done it again. "Hi Tess."

"You're early," Sonny blurted out.

"Sorry. I guess I've been a teacher too long." Tess led the way to the restaurant and gave the hostess her name.

"Welcome. I'm Emily. We have a window table for you." Emily was about twenty and cute enough to get away with wearing a really ugly Christmas sweater, red striped leggings, Ugg boots, and an elf hat covered in glitter. She picked up three menus and gave us a bubbly, "Right this way!"

We followed along.

"Remember," Sonny grabbed my arm and whispered, "be nice. Give her a chance to explain."

"Okay, okay."

"I'm glad you came," Tess said when we sat down.

"Thanks." I managed a smile and hung my computer bag on the back of my chair.

She put her large purse beside her chair. "Are you hungry?"

Sonny's favorite words. "You bet. How much can I get?"

"All you want." Tess looked at me. "What about you?"

"A little." I'd checked out the menu online, but I pretended to look it over. "Gram made pancakes and a bunch of other stuff for breakfast."

Tess tried again. "Your grandmother sounds wonderful. I'd like to meet her."

Not going to happen. "Okay."

A waiter appeared. "Welcome to the Evansville Hotel. I'm Todd and I'll be serving you today. What can I get for you?"

Sonny went first. "I'd like a double cheeseburger with bacon, onion rings—make that French fries—no make that onion rings and French fries and an extra thick chocolate milkshake with whipped cream."

Todd's job was to take the order, not lecture about the evils of cholesterol. He tapped it into his iPad.

"For you?"

I wasn't hungry but eating would buy me time. And I needed to pump Tess for information. "A BLT on wheat toast and a vanilla milkshake."

He nodded. "Miss?"

"The Summit Salad with strawberries and walnuts, dressing on the side, and iced tea, please."

Another nod. "Coming right up."

Outside our window three kids raced by on their way to the park, followed by a barking Golden Retriever. A second later a Chihuahua scampered behind them, his head held high and pink tongue hanging out.

"Sage has a black cat named Merlin," Sonny announced.

I gaped at him. What brought that on?

Tess was busily unfolding her napkin. "I know." Her eyes darted my way before putting it on her lap. "I mean, I could tell you have a cat."

"How?" I'd had Merlin less than twenty-four hours.

"Cat people always know other cat people. It's a vibe." She laughed and her dimples showed. "I have a cat named Beethoven," she told Sonny.

"You both have black cats," Sonny chimed in. "That's so funny."

No, it wasn't. I wanted to smack Sonny into next week. Tess didn't say her cat was black. Now she'd know we checked her out on Facebook. I kicked him under the table instead. He yelped and I talked over him. "Merlin is great."

Tess pretended not to notice Sonny clutching his ankle. "Evansville is a nice town. Everyone is so friendly."

I wasn't an investigative journalist for nothing. I got right to it and put the red and green pompom on the table. "I found this in Uncle Clive's office at the mansion. It's from your glove."

Surprise flickered across Tess's face but was quickly replaced by a bright smile. The dimples were back. "Thank you!" She picked up the pompom like it was a long-lost treasure and put it in her purse. "I wondered what happened to it."

That's it? No, "how did I get it?"

I wasn't letting her off the hook this easily. "Uncle Clive's office was broken into. The thief went through the file cabinets, looking for something." I let that sink in.

Tess stared at me, not blinking. At that moment she reminded me of Merlin. Only she had blue eyes not green. And I trusted him.

"I found the pompom under a file. You're the thief."

"Oh." Tess's voice dropped and her eyes filled with tears. Long moments went by. "When we met outside the library," her lower lip trembled. "I wasn't honest with you. Clive and I kept in touch. He knew I was struggling, and he sent me money."

"Wait." I held up my hand. I'd been right. "You knew Uncle Clive?"

"Sure. Clive visited Marty and me a few times. He always brought his lawyer friend Sylvester."

Slimy had known Tess too and that made me mad. "So, you never hired a private investigator to find me. That was a lie." Another con. "Why did you really come here?"

"I *did* hire a private investigator," Tess insisted, "and he told me you'd been sent to Evansville." She sniffed and reached into her purse for a tissue. "I couldn't believe my good luck. I called Clive and he told me all about you. He was so proud of you." She patted her eyes. "He was thrilled to know you'd be following in his footsteps."

"Dude. That's why he left you the newspaper." Sonny nodded. "Makes total sense."

Maybe. I needed to get Tess back on track. "Why did you break into Uncle Clive's office?"

She rubbed long fingers over a worry line on her forehead and looked away. "Clive had a picture of me, Marty and Antonetti. Marty worked for Antonetti. His casino is really a front for illegal gambling and things you don't want to know about. The cops would do anything to get him."

Sonny elbowed me. "Hey, you were right."

Not now Sonny. "Why is the picture so important?"

"Antonetti hasn't been seen in years. No one knows what he looks like. He communicates by email only. Antonetti knew Clive had the photo and wanted it back. Clive refused. I don't know why."

There had to be more. "What about you?"

"Antonetti was blackmailing me. He said he'd get me fired unless I got the picture for him. Antonetti said he'd tell my school about my past, my depression. He'd tell them about Marty and say I was as bad as he was. Even gone, Marty still haunts me. I'll never escape the past or him."

I knew the feeling.

"I love my job." Her lower lip trembled again. "I didn't want to help Antonetti, but I had no choice." She said softly, "I need my job. I know that's no excuse for what I did but it's true."

Sonny agreed. "We'll help you. Sage has the picture."

"Really?" Shock flashed in Tess's eyes. "Please give it to me."

It was just like Marty to get mixed up with a guy like Antonetti. It was just like Marty to make a mess for someone else to clean up. "Why didn't you take the picture?"

Tess's thin shoulders slumped. "I couldn't find it. When I heard a car in the driveway, I thought it might be the police. I ran."

"It was Pellam. He's the butler," Sonny told her. "You're lucky you didn't get caught. He would've called the cops."

Tess put a hand over her mouth, squeezed her eyes shut and shuddered. "I was never so scared in my life."

"You gotta give her the picture," Sonny insisted. "She's your mom."

That did it. I took the picture out of my computer bag and handed it over.

"Thank you," Tess murmured, and her eyes filled again.

I watched Tess put it in her purse. "How will you get the picture to Antonetti?"

"He'll email instructions."

Todd was back with our lunch. He looked from Tess's teary eyes to me and then to Sonny but kept quiet. Only discreet waiters got good tips. "Salad, Miss?"

Sonny sat up and cocked his nose in the air like a hound. "Food! Oh boy."

Todd smiled and set Sonny's lunch in front of him. "For you." Todd put my plate in front of me. Drinks followed. "Anything else?"

"No thank you." Tess put a straw into her iced tea.

I picked up my BLT and bit in. I had to admit it was good.

Tess moved the romaine around with her fork before settling on a strawberry. "We have strawberries year-round in California. They're my favorite."

Mine, too. I had no idea if strawberries grew in Connecticut, but it didn't seem likely. They needed a lot of sun. I'd been here almost a month and it'd been freezing every day. The only strawberry thing that didn't need sun was ice cream.

"I was going to wait for later," Tess reached into her purse for a gift bag and an envelope, "but this seems to be the right time. I bought you both a present." She gave the gift bag to Sonny and handed me the envelope. "Merry Christmas."

"For me?" I took the envelope but didn't open it. "Thanks Tess."

Sonny tore into his gift. "Oh man. It's a vintage Superman comic book." The comic book was in a plastic cover. He opened it to the first page. "Wow. Thanks!"

"Open your gift." Tess gave me a shy smile.

I did and an airline ticket fell out. "What's this?"

Tess brushed a strand of hair behind one ear. "We're both on winter break. Please come to California for a few days. It's only about seventy degrees but that's warm enough to surf. I could teach you. Or we could go to Disneyland or Universal Studios. Anywhere you want."

"Can't." I put the ticket back in its envelope and set it on the table. I have grandparents. I have a job at the newspaper. I have a Christmas tree. I have to see snow fall for the first time. "I have a cat."

She gave me a hopeful smile and laid a hand on the envelope. "The ticket is open ended. You could visit this summer. You'd like it in California. I live at the beach."

"Sage wants to live at the beach." Sonny chomped on an onion ring. "He wants to get a boat."

I wanted to strangle Sonny. For some reason when he got around Tess he couldn't shut up.

"Think about it." Tess slid the envelope back to me.

"Okay." I shrugged and put it in my computer case.

"Can we get dessert?" Sonny interrupted. "I'm still hungry."

My cell phone vibrated, and I pulled it out of my pocket. "Sorry." I looked at Tess. "It's Faith. We're working on a story for the newspaper. I'll text her back. It'll just take a second." I started typing.

"She texts you on a Saturday?" Tess cocked an eyebrow.

"Faith is our boss at the newspaper. Actually, Sage is,"

Sonny babbled on, "but he can't be the boss yet because he's not old enough. He just owns the newspaper. We're working on a twentieth anniversary story. For the newspaper. It's about Uncle Clive. I'm doing the pictures."

I put my cell phone away. "Sorry."

Todd magically appeared with dessert menus. "Did you save room for dessert?"

"You bet." Sonny searched the list. "Oh man. Can't decide. Fudge sundae or cheesecake or red velvet cake. All three would be good. Maybe apple pie. Gotta have ice cream. And whipped cream. And that little cherry on top too. And nuts."

My cell phone vibrated again. "Sorry." I read the text quickly and got up. "Go ahead. I have to get something to Faith." I pushed in my chair and slung my computer case over my shoulder. "Thanks for lunch Tess."

"Sage!" Tess started to get up.

I was already heading out the door.

CHAPTER TWENTY-NINE

I found a park bench away from the noise of the hotel. I had a lot of work to do and not much time to do it. When I pulled out my computer, the envelope with the airline ticket came with it. California would have to wait. I had bigger things on my mind. Sliding the envelope into my jeans pocket, I got to work.

An hour later I'd written my first story for *The Evansville News.* I pressed Send and sat back. Faith would probably rip the story to shreds but I felt pretty good about it.

There was only one thing left to do. I dug the envelope out of my pocket and walked back to the hotel. At the front desk the associate on duty looked as old as the hotel but she was doing her best to check people in. I got in line and waited my turn.

"Welcome to the Evansville Hotel. May I help you?" The name Agatha was boldly written in gold gel on her Christmas tree pin. She glanced around to see if I was with anyone.

"Hi. I'm Sage Christopher." I put the envelope on the

counter. "Could you call Tess Langley's room? I need to give her this."

Agatha moved to her computer and tapped a few keys. Her forehead wrinkled and she tapped a few more. Keeping her eyes on the screen she shook her head. "I'm sorry. We don't have anyone by that name."

"You mean she checked out?"

Agatha was nice but firm. Behind me people were getting impatient. "No, dear. We do not and have never had a Miss Langley here."

"Thanks." I took back the envelope and shoved it into my pocket. Tess had conned me again.

Outside a damp chill hung in the air as heavy as my mood. Above me dark clouds were rolling in and I tried to think. Questions flitted in and out of my head but not one answer. Turning up the collar on my jacket I let them go and started walking toward downtown. I'd promised Gram I'd get Merlin a Christmas stocking.

"Keep moving and don't make a sound."

Something hard jammed into my back. I'd never felt a gun before, but I was pretty sure this was it. "Mom?"

Tess barked out a laugh. "Now you call me Mom. All this time it's been Tess. Too late, kid. What tipped you off?"

"Uh."

"You heard me. What?" No laugh this time.

"Uh, two things." I tried turning around but she jabbed me again in the back.

"You said you knew I had a cat."

"Oh yeah." Her snicker was low and throaty. "Stupid mistake." Gone was the sweet convincing tone she'd used before. Now it was hard and rough. "What else?"

"What do you mean?"

"Keep up, kid. You said two things. What else?"

As long as we were talking, she wasn't going to shoot me. I hoped.

"You cried a lot."

"I practiced that!" She snorted in disgust. "Thought it was a nice touch."

"I never cry."

"Oh yeah? I can make that happen. Shut your trap and keep walking."

"Okay." I dipped my hands into my jeans pocket, fumbling for my cell phone.

"Unh-unh. Keep your hands where I can see them."

"Where are we going?" I thought about screaming but for once no one was around. Amazing.

"See the gray van?"

"That's an Amazon van."

"No, it's the genius van. Because that's what I am—a genius. People are so gung-ho about prime delivery they don't think twice when they see one." She beeped the van open. "Makes a great cover. Get in. I won't tell you twice."

I was stalling. Someone had to come by. "Do you even have a cat?"

"Me? I hate cats. But I did my homework and found out you liked them and always wanted one. Then," she gave me a little shove inside, "I just happened to overhear some gabby old woman named Violet who works for your lawyer. She was in Weinstein's grocery store, telling everyone how you'd gotten a cat." She motioned with her gun to a seat. "Park it. We're going to have a little chat."

"But," I stammered, playing for time, "you're my mom. You're on Facebook. I saw pictures. You were in them."

"Get serious. I'm nobody's mom." She rolled her eyes. "Anybody can make a profile on Facebook. A twelve-year-old can photoshop pictures and make it look like the real thing."

"So, you don't live at the beach?" I put my computer case on the floor by my feet.

She laughed in my face. "With this red hair? Forget sunblock. I'd need a force field, or I'd fry." She turned serious. "Like I said, I did my homework. You were always yapping about how you hated the cold. You wanted to go to Florida. Get a boat. Blah, blah, blah. For my cover I invented a beach house in California, and you fell for it."

She was right. "Why is the picture so important?"

"Ah, where to begin?" Tess sat across from me and put the gun in her lap. She kept her finger on the trigger.

Every good investigative journalist loves a story with a wow finish. I unbuttoned my coat and settled back but kept my eyes on the gun. I didn't want me being shot dead to be the wow finish.

"If the police got the picture," Tess began, "that would be very bad for me. Let's just say the man in the picture went missing—permanently."

Yikes. "You mean the guy arguing with the pit boss?"

"Nah." Tess laughed long and hard. "Everybody argues with the pit boss."

"Who?" Now that we were sharing, Tess laughed a lot. But she wasn't telling me everything.

"The other guy."

She and Marty were in the picture. Antonetti was in the picture. "Marty's dead. There is no other guy." Now I was really lost.

Tess pulled the picture out of her purse and held it up. Using the barrel of the gun, she touched the face of the man with the scar. She gave me an unblinking stare and then waved the picture back and forth like a metronome. "Tick, tock."

"You're Antonetti," I said slowly. "Scar Face is the missing guy."

"Yup." She sighed heavily. "Congressman Bruno was friends with Clive and Slimy."

She was right. Slimy even had a picture of Clive and Congressman Bruno on his wall. Everybody had been younger then. That's why I hadn't recognized Congressman Bruno in this photo.

"Bruno was a nice guy, but he double-crossed me on a land deal." She clucked her tongue. "Shouldn't have done that. I regard money very seriously."

Me too but not enough to kill for it.

"The cops have been looking for Bruno," she let the picture flutter to the floor and giggled, "but they won't find him."

That's why Uncle Clive kept the picture. He knew the truth. "If the cops found the picture, they'd recognize Bruno. The picture was taken in your casino. They'd figure out you're Antonetti and go after you."

"You're catching on."

This couldn't be the end of the story. "Why come here? Why pretend to be my mom?"

"You talk too much, you know that?"

I knew I wanted to stay alive. I laughed like we were old friends. "C'mon tell me. I can keep a secret."

Tess waved the gun in the air. "I won't bore you with the long story. Here's the short one. Then we gotta get outta here."

A long story meant I'd live longer. "I like long stories."

"Knock it off." She raised the gun in warning. "Clive

wanted to update the newspaper, but he needed cash. He and Slimy ripped off two million bucks from an architect named Coffey who was supposed to build homes in South Africa."

I interrupted. "Did Coffey die of Black Water Fever in South Africa?"

"Coffey died all right." Tess used her free hand to make a slicing gesture across her throat. "But it wasn't because he was sick. He was a loose end."

I shuddered. It's not always fun to be right. "Then what?"

"The two million wasn't enough, so Clive and Slimy came up with a dumb idea. They'd go to Las Vegas and play blackjack to get the rest."

Uh-oh.

"They lost *big* time."

"How big?" I always won at blackjack. It wasn't that hard.

"About half a million."

"Whoa!" No wonder Uncle Clive wanted Olivia's money. After looking at the accounting file I'd figured out Uncle Clive had sunk the two million from the African Project into the newspaper. Too bad he hadn't gotten the rest from Olivia.

"Clive was desperate. Back then Marty was working for me and convinced Clive to ask me for a loan. Clive used the mansion for security." She pointed the gun at me. "Hate to break it to you, kid. The mansion's mine, not yours."

I tried to look sad. Losing the mansion was bad but Gram and Pops would get over it. I still had the newspaper and everything else.

"We made a deal. When Clive paid me, he'd get the mansion back. Instead, Clive kept dumping money into the newspaper. I checked and it's worth a fortune. Oh, he'd pay me a little," her eyes narrowed into slits, "but he never paid off the loan. I wanted my money. I put the squeeze on him. Told him to pay up or else."

"Where do I fit in?"

"Poor Clive. Got trouble raining down on him from all over. He tries killing his wife for her money, but he can't even get that right. You rat him out and he lands in jail. He knew he'd get convicted of murder, so...." She let that trail off.

Now that I knew the truth, I was surprised Uncle Clive hadn't committed suicide earlier. Talk about rotten luck.

"The kicker was when Clive wrote a new Will. Instead of leaving everything to his slimeball friend Slimy, he left everything to you."

Thanks Uncle Clive.

"I told Slimy to get me my money or else." She gritted her teeth. "He told me he had a plan. He was suing you for three million. Forget that. The lawsuit would take years. I wasn't waiting another minute."

The pieces of the puzzle were coming together. Once that happened, I'd be out of time. "You went to see Slimy so you could persuade him to help you."

"No way. I went to kill him."

"You," I said slowly, "were Slimy's eleven o'clock appointment."

"The fool let me in. He always was a sucker for a bottle of Scotch. I made it look like suicide." She smiled, showing dimples. "Clive's suicide gave me the idea. Anyway, Slimy was a loose end. He had to go. He knew too much." She smiled again but this time no dimples. "Turns out my plan was better than his."

I got it now. "You pretended to be my mother. You were nice so I would like you and want to live with you. All that talk about living at the beach and having a cat. You invited Sonny to lunch today, so he'd see you give me an airline ticket."

"Exactly. When you don't go home tonight the police will talk to Sonny. Everyone will think you changed your mind and went to California with your dear, long-lost mommy."

"Then you'd have me and my money."

"Wake up." The laugh was back. "You're a loose end."

Faith had said I was a loose end. I was really beginning to hate those words.

"I only want your money. I checked the court records. Mr. Ashton is a fast worker. He transferred Clive's property to you right away, but he didn't include a list of the property."

Antonetti + Marty + Slimy +Clive + you = one common denominator. Cisco had been right. The common denominator was money. In the end it always comes down to the money. Always.

"I'm thinking you'll have a tragic surfing accident." Tess pursed her lips. "Sometimes bodies are never found." She hitched both shoulders and let them fall. "By then all your money will be my money."

That wasn't very motherly. I went back to stalling. "Why did you break into the mansion? Was it to get the old Will?"

"The old Will would tell me what Clive owned and where to find it. It would save me the trouble of hunting for it."

That had been my idea too. I felt a twinge of guilt but let it go. "Why didn't you take the Will?"

"I couldn't find it." Her voice was testy. "Clive must've hidden it. I got the picture and got out of there. Then *you* showed up today with *another* copy." She scowled and muttered, "Clive was always so distrustful. Anyway," she smiled, "time's up."

So soon? Didn't seem fair.

She used her free hand to toss me some bungee cords. "Tie your hands and feet. Be quick."

I was.

I threw the cords in her face and went for the gun. Both our hands were on it, but her finger was still on the trigger. She got off four shots. One shot whizzed by my ear and ricocheted off the ceiling. Another took out the windshield. Two more hit the seats and stuffing flew out.

"You brat," Tess gasped and slammed the gun butt against my temple.

I saw stars but hit her in the face with my computer case. Her nose gushed blood and her hands flew up. The gun dropped onto the floor. In an instant I scooped it up.

"Gimme that," she growled.

"No."

"I said gimme that." Tess lunged for me and tripped on my computer case.

Jumping aside I watched her skid face first on the floor of the van, leaving behind a trail of blood. If the van was a rental, she was not getting her deposit back.

The back door to the van was yanked open.

"Sage!" Chief Murphy climbed in and took the gun away from me. "Are you hurt?"

I was a little dazed but alive. "She is."

Tess rolled over onto her side and covered her bloody face with both hands. "You little wretch! You set me up. You conned me."

"Yeah." Now you know how it feels.

Faith poked her head in. "Way to go! Leaving your cell

phone on like that." She held up her cell phone. "I got it all. This is going to make one great story. Forget Pulitzer. We're going for a book. At least movie of the week. Hey, I bet we can sell it to Hollywood!"

Chief Murphy slapped handcuffs on Tess's wrists and got her into a sitting position. He nodded to us. "Both of you outside. Wait in the cruiser."

We climbed out of the van and Chief Murphy began reading Tess her Miranda rights.

"Good thing you emailed your story to me," Faith said. "If she'd killed you, we wouldn't have it."

"Or me." I raised a hand to my throbbing face.

"Well yeah," Faith agreed. "Thanks for sending me the picture with Congressman Bruno and Tess--uh, I mean Antonetti. We'll give it to the cops. They may never find his body, but they'll know what happened to him."

That was something. "Thanks for calling Chief Murphy. I was getting worried he wouldn't believe you and wouldn't come. He doesn't like you much."

"True but I think I'm wearing him down." Faith popped a bubble. Today's choice was lime. "Anyway, we're a team. Don't forget it."

Were we bonding? Weird but something inside told me it was all right. "Did Chief Murphy call Gram and Pops?"

"They're meeting us at the station. It's going to be a long night. The Chief has a lot of questions. Mostly how you figured everything out." Her voice softened. "It took guts to take down your mom."

"She's not my mom."

Faith moved on. "You were right yesterday. You know about wanting to report the truth. That's why Clive left you the paper."

I wasn't so sure about that. "It doesn't make sense. He

didn't love me. He didn't even know me." I threw my hands up into the air. "I ruined his life."

"Clive ruined his own life."

That sounded like something Sonny would say. Maybe they watched the same TV shows. "I guess."

"Clive knew you would write the truth about this story," Faith insisted, "no matter what. You two are alike in so many ways."

Newspapermen, yes. Murderers, no. Still, knowing Uncle Clive had trusted me gave me a good feeling.

"Think of this as payback. Clive's way to get even with Antonetti. Because of you Antonetti is getting arrested for Congressman Bruno's and Slimy's murders. Because of you she's going away for a long time." Faith started laughing.

"What's so funny?"

"You have a knack for getting people arrested." She laughed again. "Pretty amazing, Boss."

The day I'd be Boss was a long way off, but I'd get there. "Thanks."

My cell phone vibrated in my pocket. I pulled it out and read the two-word text from Cisco. *Good job.* I didn't bother looking around. I knew I wouldn't see him.

"Who was that?" Faith asked.

I shrugged. "Just a guy."

Lights winked on in nearby houses and the smell of their wood burning fireplaces drifted over to us. A group of carolers stopped in front of the Evansville Hotel and launched into a peppy "Rudolph the Red Nosed Reindeer." Soon people came out to listen.

Evansville was a pretty sight.

"We need to get in the cruiser," Faith reminded me.

"Yeah." I buttoned my coat and pulled on my gloves. I needed to ask Chief Murphy for my computer. Hopefully it wasn't totaled. Clobbering a hitwoman probably wasn't covered under warranty.

"Look." Faith tugged on my sleeve and pointed upward. "Now it's really Christmas."

Big fat, white fluffy snowflakes as soft as cotton were falling from the late afternoon sky. Finally, my first real Christmas. I had a family. I had a cat. I had a Christmas tree. And now my Christmas wish had come true: I was seeing snow fall for the first time.

The Grinch had been right. Christmas didn't come from a store.

Because Christmas wasn't a thing.

Christmas was home. And for the first time in my life, I had one.

The End

TRADITIONAL S'MORES

Ingredients:

8 large marshmallows

1 4.4 ounce milk chocolate bar, broken into 8 pieces

8 whole graham crackers, broken into squares

Directions:

1. Put a marshmallow on a skewer and set a stovetop burner or outdoor grill to low heat. Very carefully turn the marshmallow over the heat for 1 to 2 minutes until the marshmallow slightly puffs and begins to turn brown, or to your desired doneness. Repeat with remaining marshmallows.

2. Place each piece of chocolate onto one graham cracker square. When the marshmallows are toasted, carefully remove from the skewers and place on top of the chocolate. Place the second graham cracker square on top of the

marshmallow and squish down to melt the
marshmallow into the chocolate.

Enjoy!

PEANUT BUTTER COOKIE S'MORES
Follow the above recipe and directions but substitute
peanut butter cookies for the graham crackers.

HOT APPLE CIDER
Ingredients:
6 cups apple cider
¼ cup real maple syrup
2 cinnamon sticks
6 whole cloves
6 whole allspice berries
1 orange peel, cut into strips
1 lemon peel, cut into strips

Directions:

1. Pour apple cider and maple syrup into a large
   stainless-steel saucepan.
2. Place cinnamon sticks, cloves, all-spice berries,
   orange peel, and lemon peel in the center of a
   square of washed cheesecloth; fold up the sides
   of the cheesecloth to enclose the bundle, then
   tie it up with a length of kitchen string. Drop
   the spice bundle into the cider mixture.
3. Place the saucepan over moderate heat and
   cook until the cider is very hot but not boiling,
   about 5 to 10 minutes.

4. Remove the cider from the heat. Discard the spice bundle.
5. Ladle cider into big mugs or cups, adding a fresh cinnamon stick to each serving if desired.

ACKNOWLEDGMENTS

Society may value perfection in people, but readers do not. Every protagonist has a flaw or an Achilles heel for a reason. If the main character were perfect, he'd be boring. And absolutely irritating.

Sage has had a hard life and for most of it he's taken care of himself. It's easy for readers to see why he's motivated by money and why it represents security. But the *Never Believe* series isn't about Sage's hard life. It's about the choices he makes. Sage doesn't always make the best ones (who does) but he comes to realize it's never too late to be the person you want to be.

Many thanks to my best friend Robyn Matias for her constant support and never telling me once that I should stick to my day job.

Many thanks to my incredibly talented writers and illustrators' group: Teri Vitters, Priscilla Burris, and Gina Capaldi. Their work leaves me speechless.

Many thanks to Retired Detective Lieutenant Kelly Carpenter, Brea Police Department, for patiently answering my endless questions about police procedure.

Many thanks to Deborah Halverson and her invaluable editing comments.

Many thanks to Jonathan and Jynafer Yanez, Archimedes Books, for guiding me through the boggling process of getting my book published.

I couldn't have done this without you.

ABOUT THE AUTHOR
KATHLEEN TROY, JD; PHD

Kathleen Troy is a published author, children's book publisher, movie producer, writing and law professor at Cypress College, and former Director of Education and Development for the Archdiocese of Los Angeles. Kathleen is an active member of Sisters in Crime and Society of Children's Book Writers and Illustrators and has won several awards for middle grade and young adult books. Dog training is Kathleen's passion, and she has achieved recognition, most notably for training service dogs for hospice work.

Kathleen welcomes hearing from you. Please get in touch with her at www.kathleentroy.com.

STAY INFORMED

I'd love to stay in touch! You can email me at kathleen@ kathleentroy.com

For updates about new releases, as well as exclusive promotions, visit my website and sign up for the VIP mailing list. Head there now to receive a free story

www.kathleentroy.com

Enjoying the series? Help others discover the *Never Believe Series* by sharing with a friend.

www.ingramcontent.com/pod-product-compliance
Lightning Source LLC
Chambersburg PA
CBHW022022310726
48972CB00006B/1760